"YOUR MAJESTY!" SHE CRIED.

His hand was on her cheek, caressing it lightly. His arms, tight around her, were vise-like in their strength. She dared not scream and, in a moment, could not, as his lips closed on her mouth. He lifted her easily in his arms and bore her to the bed.

"The . . . the Queen's bed!" she gasped.

Her head was whirling. His fingers were on the laces of her bodice. In a moment, she saw her gown billowing to the floor. She cast a quick glance at the door. She could reach it in a moment and be away from him, running down the hall. But even as she made the first hasty move, she knew it was impossible. It was too late . . .

j

A JOVE BOOK

Printed in the United States of America

First Jove edition published September 1979

10 9 8 7 6 5 4 3 2 1

Jove Books are published by Jove Publications, Inc., 200 Madison Avenue, New York, NY 10016

THE
GOLDEN
GALATEA

Prologue

Wrapped in her warmest woolen cloak, Lady Blanche Carlisle stood on the deck of the small packet bearing her toward the dawn-illumined coast of France. Her hood, none too securely fastened by her mother, had fallen back, and her blond curls, caught by the strong September breeze, swirled about her little face. She made no attempt to brush them away, she was too intent in gazing at the nearing shore.

"Golden fleece," thought the man beside her, a smile quirking the corners of his thin mouth, a corresponding glint lighting his somber eyes. "If Jason had his Argonauts about him, perhaps he would set sail again in search of this same gold." Impulsively, he caught some strands of her silky hair and wound them around his fingers, loving the touch of them. Playfully, he tugged at her curls and she looked back at him. It was an oddly provocative glance for a little girl who was only a few months past her sixth birthday, he mused. A moment later, he had dismissed this particular fancy as unworthy of him. He released her hair and she, shaking her head like a young pony freed from its reins, resumed her contemplation of the far horizon.

It was a marvel she was not tired. She had been standing there for most of the three hours it had taken them to cross the channel, though at first she had been looking at the receding coast of England, distinguishable in the dark by a few flickering lights. He wondered if she were aware that she might not see her country again for many a long year. Of course, she must be, he decided. Her mother would not have scrupled to upset her with the news. At the thought of the woman, his lip curled with contempt. He remembered the first night he had seen her, what a spectacle she had made of herself. Of course, he had come bearing news of her husband's death, but he had given similar messages to other wives and they had not broken out into loud wails. The child, on the other hand, could match the bravest of them with her calm. She had resisted his efforts to cuddle and kiss her. It had been the mother who had clung to him, burying her head on his chest while her wails had turned into the dry hacking sobs of the hysteric.

Petted, beautiful Audrey Carlisle lacked the inner strength to deal with sudden widowhood and the ensuing flight from Carlisle Castle, so soon to be commandeered by the all-victorious Puritan Army. She, he thought, had been born to play the great lady in an ordered household by day and the wanton in her husband's bed by night, all sighs and moans of ecstasy. There was not much mystery to Audrey. Her very name seemed to indicate her flighty nature.

It was odd that she should have borne so reticent and reserved a child. One, who when told of her imminent peril, had taken a deep breath then actually joined him in comforting her mother. Of course, at six she might not have realized her danger. Certainly, she was far too young to be fully aware of the implications of her father's death at that last decisive battle of Preston, which had ended with the Royalists in flight and the king captured. He frowned. Once again, he was kneeling on the blood-soaked ground, the stench of sweat and gunpowder heavy on the August air. Beside him, lying where the child's father had fallen, was Charles Carlisle, Viscount Clarewood, named for the king in whose cause he was dying.

The lad, he was little more than twenty-five, had looked into his face out of wide glazing eyes, the color and shape of which his daughter had inherited. "My lord, Audrey and—Blanche to—to France—m'father."

"To France, Charles, to your father," the older man had repeated loudly, reassuringly, hoping that he was heard and understood by the dying man. He also hoped the boy would not linger much longer, for soon agony would supplant the dulling shock of the ball in his chest. Though he was a veteran of many campaigns, and was used to death in all its guises, he was fond enough of Charles, the son of his old friend Tony Carlisle, to wish him a speedy transition between this world and the next. A moment later, his wish had been granted, and he was later able to tell Audrey Carlisle that her husband had died bravely and with a word for her at the last.

He had a moment of regret that the lad had gone before his wife had borne him a son, but perhaps that was just as well, considering that his lands were forfeit to the crown—or what would pass for a crown under Cromwell, damn his bloody soul to hell!

On the night of their escape, a younger child would have been an encumbrance. Blanche had not been. Her ability to follow orders and to do exactly as she had been told was amazing. Perhaps she owed that to the discipline she had received from her nurses. No, all the discipline in England could not have given her the sort of courage she had demonstrated. She must have inherited it from Charles Carlisle, that poor young gallant, who ought to have been standing there, protecting his family.

A sudden heave of the vessel nearly toppled him, and certainly it ended his melancholy reflections. He hastily glanced at the little girl and was relieved to find her still upright, clutching the ropes.

"You're quite a sailor, my lass," he commented, patting her shoulder and finding it very damp. "Lord, your cloak's well-nigh soaked through. Hadn't you better go below before you catch an ague?"

"Please no," she replied quickly. "There's no air below and mama's feeling queasy."

He smiled at her, "You're a game one, child, no question about that, the way you've weathered this voyage and our rough ride to the coast. I shall tell your grandfather. He'll be very proud of you."

Her eyes widened and she fixed them intently on his face. Wistfully, she said, "I do not remember grandfather, though mama says I have seen him. Is he much like papa?"

Not wishing to disappoint her and yet not wanting to give her false hope, he said carefully, "I think you'll find a likeness." He decided upon a conciliatory lie. "Your father spoke much of you to me, little Blanche. He was forever praising you."

"Was he?" Her voice had an upward lilt, and the smile accompanying her words was like the emerging sun. It imparted an entirely new dimension to her face and he, looking on it, found himself in a prophetic mood. She would be, he knew, a beautiful woman, one of those legendary creatures for whom Argosies are dispatched. Instead of Jason, he thought of Helen, Helen of Troy, and was glad of the falsehood that had brought him the glimpse. He promised himself that he would not lose sight of Blanche. Even though he would not, could not, cease to intrigue for the cause of Charles I or, he mused a trifle grimly, that of his son, the soldier would still return to France from time to time. He knew he would always be welcomed by her grandfather. Tony Carlisle had been a comrade-in-arms until a disgust with his king's lack of foresight had caused him to resign his command and eventually retire to a château in Chinon, province of Touraine.

He himself had not approved of the decision at the time, having the Englishman's natural distrust of the French. However, Tony Carlisle had no such prejudices. Diamant, his château, was an inherited property.

One of Carlisle's ancestors had been an Angouleme, which meant that Blanche had the same blood which had flowed in the veins of the fabled Isabella of Angouleme, the voluptuous and flagrantly unfaithful wife of King John. Though it had to be considerably distilled through some four centuries of coupling, the idea of the relationship pleased him. Without a downward glance, he summoned a swift image of the child to mind—her wide, well-spaced eyes, just slightly tilted, her straight little nose, her mouth, beautifully shaped and full, a pink bud which would ripen into a red rose. A full mouth indicated a passionate nature, though such a tendency in Blanche would probably be held in check by her reserve. All the better, in common with some woods, she would be slow to kindle but once coming to full blaze, the flame would be hot and burn brightly.

He had a moment of longing to feel the warmth of that particular fire, then, he sighed. Given his analogy of wood, she was yet a green twig, her time of ripening some eight years in the future. In eight years, he would be fifty-six, a poor match for fourteen. He felt his cheeks burn. His imagination was indeed taking him far afield. He might be some dissipated Turk intent on procuring one of the five-year-old slaves that thronged the brothels of Constantinople, and to even think of this lovely little maiden in such context was perilously close to blasphemy. Furthermore, it was unlike him. He, General, Lord Marchmont, had never coveted virgins. Let those who wished for heirs to carry on the family name settle for these nubile lasses. He preferred some seasoning and, more important, a dash of spice such as no simpering damsel could provide. His brother, the earl of Glenmore, had married one of these rich, insipid girls, who in three years had produced two sons, which said much for her fecundity but little for her character which was, in his estimation, pure cow.

"My lord," into his musing came the petulant voice

of Audrey Carlisle; yet, considering the untoward direction his thoughts had taken, he was not sorry for the interruption. As he swiveled to face her, Blanche ran forward to her mother.

"Mama, are you better then?" she asked eagerly.

"I am not in danger of fainting again, but I am vilely unwell," she answered, and fixing her resentful eyes on him, she asked, "Shall we be docking soon?"

He waved an arm at the narrowing expanse of waters between ship and shore, "As you see, my Lady Carlisle, quite soon, depending on the winds." He gave her a conciliatory smile, thinking with a certain grudging pity that she did look ill. Her tawny hair hung in loose, dark strands over her pallid, green-tinged face, and her expressive green gold eyes, her best feature, were dull and vacant.

"Quite soon's not soon enough for me," she said irritably. "I vow, once I've set foot on land, I'll never cross water again!" She sighed, "Nor shall I have the chance with those rogues in residence at the castle and our lands forfeit and C-Charlie—" she looked down quickly, her lip trembling.

It behooved him to offer her solace, but her complaints had set ill in his ears. The contrast between child and mother was even more pronounced. With an effort, he forced himself to be comforting and kindly, the staunch friend on whom she could rely. Yet, before he could say anything, Blanche seized her mother's hand and pressed it to her cheek.

"Do not weep, mama," she begged. "sure papa must be happy in heaven."

"Happy?" Audrey echoed. "Listen to the child. Oh, to be innocent again. To be innocent and not to crave—" a deep flush rose from throat to cheeks, and turning from them both she stared fixedly into waters, now sparkling under the rising sun.

He found he could pity her now. She was still very young, sixteen when she had married, seventeen when Blanche was born, an heiress who had wed for love and had probably received a goodly share of it from her ardent, lusty young husband. The future would look particularly dim to her, being bereft of lover and fortune too, settling with her child in a strange house with a man she hardly knew and who would certainly not indulge the whims of a fretful widow.

Tony, bless him, was much like himself when it came to women. He preferred light, pretty creatures with a gift for clever repartee and a talent for imaginative lovemaking. One of these women would undoubtedly be in residence at Diamant, a situation which would not diminish Audrey Carlisle's unexpressed but extremely obvious frustrations. Once more, he found himself looking ahead and wondering. . . .

"Oooooh," Blanche murmured, "look!" She pointed to the sky.

He did not obey her command. Instead, he stared into her face. For once, her reserve had dropped and she was childishly gleeful, waving her arms up and down. "The white bird—the big white bird, see, he's flying toward the sun. See mama!"

Audrey looked up and sighed, "Why are you so excited?" she asked in a dull, depressed voice. "It's no different from any other bird."

"Oh, but he is, mama," the child insisted. "He's so much higher than any I have ever seen before." Blanche continued to wave her hands up and down, even more energetically. "Oh, how I should like to follow him—up, up, up!"

There was a look of such ecstacy in her eyes that he felt alone and excluded from her joy. Putting his hands on her little shoulders, he gently pressed her waving arms down to her sides, pinioning them in his embrace. Kneeling beside her, he said, "Would you like to hear a fairy story, Blanche?"

He had her instant attention. "Oh yes, I love fairy stories, I often read them, and one day I shall write them too. Dame Alys has predicted it."

"Dame Alys was her nurse," Audrey told him. "The

silly servants at the castle were forever saying that she had the sight."

He had been momentarily taken aback. "Write them, eh?" he said finally. "That's a very large ambition for a little girl, almost as large as flying, I should think. Women were not meant to write, my child."

She was surprised. "But papa said I might. He said there was nothing I could not do if I wanted it enough, and I do want to write. I've written poems already and I keep a daily journal."

"Indeed?" he smiled indulgently. "Well, if it pleases you, I should think there was little harm in it. Still, I think you might find my story most appropriate. It's about Icarus, who flew on wings of wax but learned to his sorrow that you must not stray too close to the sun, my sweet Blanche."

Chapter One

The sky was brightly blue. Fields of golden flowers stretched on either side of the horseman making his way up the rocky, pitted road. Beneath his high leather boots, he felt the heaving of Pegasus's mud-stained flanks. There was foam on the stallion's neck and green spittle dripping from his jaws. He had been ridden overlong and should have been stabled in Chinon, but his master was in no mood to wait, not even for a change of horses. His destination had been in his mind and now, at last, it was in his immediate vision—the nearing towers of Diamant and somewhere in that massive structure, little Blanche Carlisle, his intended bride.

Soon he would be seeing her and more important would be concluding the negotiations begun the previous year, after Cromwell's forces slew his brother and family, and he became the earl of Glenmore. Though his estates had been annexed by the Protectorate, he believed the condition to be temporary. In common with many Royalists, he spied for the monarchy, and, in the course of secret forays into London and into the surrounding countryside, he had learned that many people were sorely shocked by the execution of King Charles and were still loyal to his son, already proclaimed king in Scotland. Furthermore, the Protectorate was beset with problems, and Cromwell could control his parliament no better than the king he had murdered. Thus, since he was sure he could look forward to the restoration of the monarchy and with it, all his properties, the matter of an heir was suddenly of prime importance. He needed a wife, and who better than the child whom he had come to love so dearly.

Though he was, perhaps, a poor bridegroom for a girl so young, she would grow older, and meanwhile he would be patient. Actually, despite the age difference, she was very lucky. It was a good match for her; unlike many of the exiled cavaliers, he had kept his monies from the grasping Puritans. Recently, he had purchased a home in Paris, a lovely place, located on the Ile Saint-Louis. She should love that. She was fond of water. How she had enjoyed it when he had taken her sailing on the Loire, two years ago. He had acquired the property after the arrival of Tony's letter signifying unqualified approval of the proposed match and concluding:

> For I do love the little wench and anticipate the day when she will take her place as the chatelaine of Glenmore, a position worthy of her beauty, her intelligence, and her grace. Her mother wishes me to tell you that she is of my mind.

Remembering those words, Glenmore smiled a trifle sourly, knowing that Audrey's acquiescence or the lack of it had had little bearing on her father-in-law's decision. He was not one to pay heed to the wishes of his mistresses, and that was precisely what she had become less than six months after her arrival at the château. Possibly, he reasoned, she had hoped that the father would eventually supplant the son as her husband, but Tony had been quick to show her he had no such alliance in mind. Doubtlessly, it had been a bitter lesson for her to learn, but she had managed to adapt herself to her new life with some grace. She was a woman who could not exist in a lonely bed. Not even the threat of social ostracism had kept her from accepting Tony's invitation, and actually, her living arrangements were not generally known to society. Ostensibly, she was the inconsolable widow of Charles Carlisle, and if she looked very blooming in her habitual weeds, she was, after all, still under thirty. Dismissing the thought of Audrey, he mused on Blanche, whom he had last seen two long years ago—on the eve of her tenth birthday.

He had brought her a bauble, he remembered, a diamond on a thin gold chain, and she had thanked him gravely, her self-possession having increased considerably as she grew older. There were times, when looking at her, he was reminded of the old tale of a princess, sleeping until awakened by a lover's kiss. There was a dreaming quality about little Blanche that filled him with excitement, especially when he thought of her waking to his kiss in his own vast bed.

At ten, there had been the promise of an early blooming. Her bosom, he had noted, was round under her bodice and in the ensuing years, must have become even fuller. He frowned, remembering that he had promised Tony that the betrothal would not take place until her fourteenth birthday. He suspected Tony of being unwilling to part with his pretty grandchild but, while he understood him, his impatience was mounting. He was lonely without a woman about, and lately he had been without a mistress, for though he scarce dared admit it, even to himself, he was not as potent as he had been even two years earlier, and if there were to be a legitimate heir he needed to hoard his strength.

Flicking his whip over the flanks of his panting horse, he galloped toward the gates of Diamant, then slowed to a walk. It was impossible for a connoisseur of beauty to approach the château without marveling at its exquisite outlines. It was built of a stone which looked yellow in some lights, golden in others. Today was one of its golden days, and its slate roof sparkled as though it had been fashioned of silver. A series of fanciful towers, some square, others domed, and still others peaked, were flanked by a long stone balcony. The whole rose over a moat covered with lily pads and stocked with fat red carp. In the rear of the building stretched acres of patterned gardens adorned by statuary, some of which aroused his envy—the beautiful little *Venus* by Del Verrocchio and the Sansovino *Apollo,* one of the master's lesser works to be sure, but still something of a miracle. He found most of the other statues in the collection uninspired, mere space fillers. The long promenade, bordered on either side by clipped cypresses, pleased him, as did the ornamental fountain with its plunging sea horses and in its basin, a half-submerged mermaid, whose lovingly carved features and slim beautiful torso made one long for a glimpse of the artist's model. Soon he would be strolling down those gravel paths with little Blanche. He put spurs to his horse.

Diamant was guarded by a high wall bisected with a pair of tall wrought-iron gates. Just beyond them was the gatehouse, and the keeper, who knew him, hastened to let him in. A burly man with muscles bulging under his smock and appraising, watchful eyes, he bowed low, touching his forelock and grinning. "Monseigneur," he said respectfully, his smile revealing a set of brownish broken teeth, some of them possibly sacrificed to his position, for there were always vagrants about.

"Michel," he acknowledged, pressing a coin into the man's big calloused palm. Riding across the bridge, he was heading for the courtyard when he heard a shriek of childish laughter.

From a point some yards away, two children came running, a little girl, pursued by a tall, thin boy. Both were covered with dust, their faces smudged with mud. Their garments were coated with it and their feet as well. From the looks of them, they must have been wading in the moat, he thought distastefully. He wondered that Michel had let them through the gates. He did not like the idea of Blanche associated with such ragamuffins. They might even be Gypsies, but as they approached, he saw that they were quite fair, probably the children of the servants and, as such, ought to have been working in the kitchen or the stables. He was about to ride on inside when he heard the boy cry out and he halted, amazed.

"Give it to me, give it to me," he was demanding in cultured English.

"Shan't," his little companion said, retreating and laughing at him teasingly. "I found it. It's mine."

"I showed you where to look," he exclaimed. "You wouldn't have found it, if it hadn't been for me." Lunging at her, he grabbed her sleeve.

"Watch out!" she shrieked. "It will break."

He pulled her to him by the captured sleeve, "Open your hand," he ordered sternly.

Sticking her hand behind her back, she said defiantly, "I shan't."

"I'll make you," he threatened, securing her other arm.

"You shan't," she repeated, trying to pull away and in the action losing her balance and falling down. She gave a little cry as her hand opened and a small egg cracked against the stones, its yolk leaking into the crevices between them.

"Ooooh," her face crumpled. "Look it's broken and it's all your fault."

"Oh, I say," her companion knelt at her side. "I am sorry, I didn't mean it to break."

"You did, you did so," she accused, a catch in her voice, "You did it on purpose, Rupert, and I shan't ever forgive you."

"I didn't, I swear it," he said earnestly. "Don't cry, please don't." Taking her hand, he held it comfortingly between both of his. "Come, I'll show you where we can find some more eggs."

"I don't want any more eggs," she told him. "I should have put this one under my pillow and it would have hatched into a beautiful bird and I should have written a story about it—how the bird was really a prince in disguise and—" she paused, staring at him indignantly. "You're laughing at me. Why?"

"You couldn't have hatched it, silly," he stated loftily. "Only its mother could do that. You see—" He looked up and for the first time became aware of the man, sitting motionless on his horse, observing them. The little girl, following his glance, rose quickly, a welcoming smile on her grimy face.

"Oh, you've come to see grandfather again," she exclaimed, moving toward him. Before he could answer her, she had run a caressing hand over the horse's neck. "Oh!" she exclaimed. "It's so wet—he's sadly lathered, poor thing."

"I've ridden a long way this day," Glenmore acknowledged in a tight voice. With an effort, he smiled, "You remember me, I see."

She looked surprised, "It's not like that I should forget *you,*" she said. "You're Lord Marchmont." With all the grace of a princess, she indicated the boy at her side. "And this is my friend Rupert Godwin, lately arrived from Germany."

"Germany?" he inquired. "From the court?"

"From the court, my lord," the boy answered. "The court of His Majesty, Charles II, King by Grace of God." He had spoken with pride and a touch of defiance, as if he had anticipated a challenge.

"By grace of God, indeed," Glenmore echoed. He looked at the girl and with another effort managed to say jovially, "Well, well, my child, you've been having a fine time, I can see."

Her eyes glinted with pleasure, "Oh, yes, Rupert has showed me where the waterfowls nest." Confidingly she added, "And I found an egg."

"And broke it, it would seem." Glenmore's hooded gray eyes rested coldly on Rupert's face. "Your play's rather rough, isn't it, young man."

"No," it was Blanche who answered. "He was only teasing. He's always teasing me." The glance she shot at Rupert was tender. Drawing near him, she continued, "It was his by rights. He showed me the nest."

"But it was you who found the egg, Blanche," the boy said quickly.

"As you should have in another second," she responded.

"Come, I hope you'll not fall into another argument," Glenmore forced a laugh and pulled his horse back so quickly that it snorted loudly and tossed its head. "I must have this beast stabled and rubbed down."

"Yes, you ought," Blanche agreed. "It seems sadly tired."

"There are many fresh horses to be had in the village, my lord," Rupert said judicially.

"I am aware of that, young Master Godwin," Glenmore responded coldly, "But I was eager to reach Diamant. If you'll excuse me," his gaze lingered on Blanche, "I must go and pay my respects to your grandfather and your mother."

He wheeled his horse away. He was astonished and disturbed by his emotions. The hand clutching his whip was trembling with the effort it had cost him to keep it at his side when, incredibly, he had longed to lash it across Rupert Godwin's face.

The sweetness in Blanche's voice and the softness in her eyes when she had addressed that wretched boy had infuriated him. Equally maddening had been the way Godwin had looked at her. It hinted at a camaraderie which could in time develop into something far more serious.

Who was this Rupert Godwin, he wondered indignantly, and what's the folly that had let them come together? Certainly, he was exercising a disturbing influence on her. She had possessed the serene beauty of a Van Dyke portrait when he had last seen her. Now, she looked like a peasant brat. That had to be the boy's doing. When had he arrived? How long had he been in residence? Too long, too damned long! Riding into the courtyard, he dismounted quickly, throwing down some coins for the hostlers and then striding toward the door. He wished that the porter had not opened it so readily. It would have given him some pleasure to have lifted and slammed down its heavy knocker. Instead, he had only the momentary satisfaction of seeing a stable cat slink within distance of his toe; with a savage thrust of his spurred boot, he hurled the creature into the air. Its outraged and agonized yowl followed him into the house.

"Who was that old man?" Rupert demanded, gazing after Glenmore.

"It was he who brought us from England," Blanche explained. "He was papa's friend and was with him when he died."

"I didn't like him nor he me," Rupert said positively.

She looked at him in surprise, "Why shouldn't he like you?"

The boy frowned, "I don't know, but I'm sure he didn't. There was cold steel in his glance. He was hard put to speak politely."

"Oh, I'm sure you're mistaken," she assured him. "He's very kind. When he was here last, he gave me a diamond on a chain, a fine stone of the first water, mama said."

"He's fond of you," Rupert nodded. "That was very plain. In fact—" he broke off, his frown deepening.

"In fact—what?" she pursued.

Rupert shook his head and ran his hand through his thick bronze curls as though he were pushing some disturbing idea away. "I didn't like him. I didn't like the way he looked at you, either." Seizing her hand, he added, "Come, I'll show you where there's a fine badger hole. Wouldn't you like to see that?"

"Oh, I should," she agreed happily, entwining her fingers through his. "Do you think we might see the badger, too?"

"There's a chance we might."

"Oh, how lovely, I should like that above all things, Rupert," she exclaimed, laughing with delight.

"But they are only children, my lord."

Audrey Carlisle sat at her ease on an immense, golden bed, a color flattering to her tawny ringlets. She had exchanged her mourning dress for a gown of a sea green silk. Several heavy, gold chains were wound around her neck, and among the rings on her fingers was a new one, a fine emerald in a diamond-studded setting. He was surprised at that. Tony was rarely so generous.

She had been reading when the servant ushered him into her chamber, and the book still lay open on her lap. As she talked, she ran her hand up and down the book's polished leather cover, a gesture suggesting that she was not quite as calm as her tone and manner indicated. "Blanche is an innocent, and the boy's still at the rough-and-tumble stage. He's not fourteen, yet."

Glenmore said brusquely, "At thirteen, I had already seen action in the field and away from it. There was a young serving girl in my father's castle—"

"A serving girl?" Audrey echoed. "Would you be comparing my daughter to a—"

"No, Lady Carlisle, I would not," he assured her hastily. "I am sure that she's as innocent as you maintain. One needs only to look at her to be aware of that, but she's fond of him. I discerned that too, by looking at her." He brought his clenched fist down on his knee.

Her eyes rested on his hand which unclenched under her scrutiny. "I think you mistake them both," she shrugged. "He's the first lad of her rank she's seen. Naturally, they'd be friends."

"Where's he from?" Glenmore rasped. "What's his family? I don't know the name."

"His estate's in Yorkshire. His father's the Marquis of Yule, but his lands were confiscated by Cromwell, and he's impoverished like the rest of us." She sighed and in spite of his inner turmoil, Glenmore had some difficulty in suppressing a smile. He wondered how many louis d'or had been lavished on her brocade slippers. He said, "Why's he here?"

"His father brought him. There's a Jesuit seminary not far from here where his younger brother Owen will study and, in time, take orders. On occasion, Rupert rides out to visit him. They are very close."

"Does that mean that the boy will stay with you indefinitely?" queried Glenmore.

"No, not indefinitely, my lord. Six months more at the very most."

"Six months!" He glared at her. "I don't like it."

She was silent a moment, then she said softly, "You've no cause to be jealous, my lord. It's all arranged, isn't it?"

There was something in her glance that gave him pause, a lurking anger? No, anger was too large a word for what he thought he read. Resentment perhaps, was the better description, but why? Perhaps it was because she had not been consulted about the plans for her daughter's future, or was it possible she did not approve? However, her approval was not important.

"I am not jealous," he said coldly. "Actually, I have the girl's own happiness in mind. I'd not want her to be a grieving Juliet when she plights her troth to me. Another six months spent with that young cub and who knows what damage might be done."

She shrugged, "Who knows, indeed? But you must speak to her grandfather, my lord. Of course, it might be embarrassing to send the lad back to Germany as if, perhaps, he were in disgrace."

"I'll not demand that, Lady Carlisle," he smiled. "I've a mind to marry her now."

Audrey suddenly clutched her book, her fingers whitening from the pressure. This time there was no mistaking the anger in her eyes. "That's rather soon, my lord. No matter what you may think of her feelings for young Rupert, she's yet very much of a child. Green fruit needs ripening if it's to satisfy the palate of a connoisseur."

"You need not concern yourself on that count, Lady Carlisle," he replied. "She'll have my name but no more until I deem her ready."

"And when might that be?" she demanded.

"Fourteen," he replied.

"Have I your word on that?" she asked in a low voice.

He surveyed her with surprise. Nothing he knew about Audrey Carlisle had led him to suspect her of maternal anxiety. He had always deemed her far too self-involved to spare much concern for her daughter or anyone else existing beyond her own narrow orbit. Yet, meeting her eyes, he found in them the anxiety which had also been apparent in her speech. He said conciliatingly, "You have my word on it, Lady Carlisle."

"No, *no, NO*!" Each negative was louder and less controlled than the last, uttered in a tone alternating between treble and bass in a husky voice, which, in common with its owner, hovered on the brink of manhood. "My brother and you—You and my brother. You, oh, Blanche, oh, no, no, no!" Thrusting an arm against his eyes, Rupert burst into tears.

Blanche too had been shocked out of her natural reserve. She had been weeping on and off since her grandfather and her mother had told her she was to live in Paris with her old friend, the Earl of Glenmore.

"They'll address you as Madame la Comtesse," her mother had said with a mock curtsey and a little smile. Blanche had noticed, however, that her eyes remained grave.

"Comtesse, Mama, why?" she had asked wonderingly, and she had learned to her amazement that a man, older than her grandfather, had done her the dubious honor of asking for her hand in marriage. Her amazement had quickly turned to horror on learning that his request had been honored and that she had been promised to him for the past year. "But—but he's old," she had wailed. "He's an old, old man!"

"Not so old, neither!" her grandfather had contradicted testily. "He can give me but a year or two."

"He's very wealthy, child," Audrey had added quickly. "You'll not want, no matter what dynasties may rise or fall." Her mother, at least, had spoken persuasively. There had been no persuasion in her grandfather's manner. To all her tearful objections, his answer remained the same.

"It has been decided. I've given my word. Glenmore is a fine man, my old comrade-in-arms. His ancestors, like our own, came to England with William of Normandy. Believe me, my dear, we know what's best for you."

There had been some further discussion about gowns and jewels for the betrothal ceremony, due to take place within a fortnight, and then, they had excused her.

She had run to find Rupert, and at the far end of the gardens, by a wide, round pool, flanked with stone benches, she had told him.

He swallowed his tears, swallowed again, then sniffed them back, wiping his reddened eyes. "A—a man must not cry," he muttered, then he flushed and glared at her. "But he's ancient."

"Yes," she agreed hopelessly.

"He shan't have you," Rupert cried hotly. "I'll prevent it!"

Hope flickered faintly in her eyes. "Might you?" she whispered. "How?"

He was conscious of an expanding and a heightening, too, as if in that very instant he had gained both years and inches. When he spoke, the husky immaturity that clouded his tones, surprised him. He thought he must sound as he now felt, a man. "I shall take you away from them," he said staunchly. "We shall go this very night, Blanche."

"Oh," she breathed, clutching his arm. "Oh, Rupert, I should like that above all things." A moment's glance into the clear waters of the pool brought her an image of the two of them, and an odd fancy flitted through her mind. She wished that the reflections in the pool were real, for then no one would be able to separate them from the water, and they might dwell forever in its depths. The idea faded, vanquished by reality. Drawing a long, quavering breath, she said dubiously, "Yet, how can you?"

"We'll meet at midnight, when they're all sleeping. I'll saddle my horse myself, and we'll ride far, far away from here," he said positively, as if he already knew which direction they would take.

Tony was sleeping heavily as he usually did after making love, and usually Audrey would have been sleeping too, exhausted by his demands. On this evening, however, she lay wakeful, thinking of Charles, remembering the hardness of his young body under her wandering fingers. There had been no superfluous rolls of flesh; his skin had been hard and resilient. The feel of it, the smell of it. At the memory, there was an aching in her eyes that boded tears. Blinking them back, she wished she could dispense with her memories as easily, but they would not remain dormant and she knew why—Blanche, little Blanche, so soon to be married to the earl. Not even the knowledge that she would be wealthy and eventually able to enjoy the solace of younger lovers helped to assuage the guilt she felt over her complicity in the matter. Tony could not understand her scruples. He had pointed out that marriage between couples of such disparate years was common enough, but still she did not think it fair that twelve and fifty-four should be joined.

Supposing Glenmore would not wait? Supposing his eagerness to possess the child triumphed over his common sense? She shuddered away from the thought of Blanche's misery. Yet, as an experienced man of the world, perhaps . . . she tensed, hearing the floorboards creek beyond her door. Footsteps? One of the servants? No, it was too late for that. Reaching for her robe, she eased herself from the bed, and, flinging it about her, moved silently to the hall door. Opening it a crack, she was grateful for the moonlight pouring through a great eye of a window in the hall, for it illumined the small form of her daughter, as she started down the stairs.

"Well, Master Godwin?" Audrey stood in the main hall of the château, holding a candle. Its wavering light fell on the startled and anguished faces of the boy and girl. Dressed for the road and carrying small bundles of clothing, they stood hand in hand, Blanche tearful and Rupert defiant, as Audrey continued caustically, "Is this your thanks for our hospitality?"

Rupert quivered, "I am sorry for it," he said in low, shamed tones, "but she—but we—"

"My dears," Audrey sighed, dropping her air of offended dignity, "where would you go?" How might you exist?"

"I could work," the boy offered eagerly. "In the stables—at an inn—"

"Perhaps you could," she agreed. "But Blanche, how would she fare?"

"I'd work, too," the little girl looked at Rupert lovingly, "I'd milk cows and—"

"Folly!" her mother interrupted. "You, neither of you have any inkling of what it's like out there—" she waved a hand at the door. "You do not know what can happen within yards of our gates. The world is a cruel place for the young. You'd starve. Believe me, I speak the truth. But enough! Go back to your chamber, Rupert, and you, Blanche, you come with me."

"You can't take her!" Rupert actually grabbed

Audrey's arm. "I shan't let you give her to that old man!"

She wrenched herself from his grasp, "Must I rouse the servants," she muttered between her teeth. "Must I have you confined? What would your father say to that, Rupert?"

He hung his head, staring hopelessly at the floor, "Your pardon, Lady Carlisle," he whispered.

"Oh, my poor boy," Audrey sighed again. "It's a pity you're not younger or older. Believe me, I am sorry for both of you, but it cannot be helped."

He raised his head, but he did not look at her. Instead, he faced the sobbing Blanche. "My dearest," he said gravely, quite as if he were already a man, "do not cry. One day we shall be together again and then—no one shall separate us, that I promise you, on my life." Gently, he drew her into his arms and kissed her."

"Oh, Rupert, Rupert," she clung to him desperately, "I—I should like that above all things."

Standing in the prow of the barge, floating down the Seine, Glenmore was thinking of Isabella d'Angouleme. Odd, how often her name had arisen in his mind during the last week; he had even ridden to the Abbey of Fontrevault to view the Angevin crypt where she was interred. In the graceful effigy that adorned her tomb, he had found a slight resemblance to little Blanche. Had it been even more marked when she, too, was twelve, her age when she was wrested from her promised suitor Hugh de Lusignan to become the bride of King John? He flushed, envying the monarch. He had not waited for his young bride to mature. He had taken her that first night and never left the bedchamber for a week, if the chronicles could be believed. Yet, he must abide by his promise even though Blanche was his possession, bound to him by marriage, observed in all due solemnity in the chapel of Diamant.

He frowned, remembering how pale she had been, clad in a rich gown of azure silk, trimmed with fine lace and stitched with seed pearls; she had stood beside him, staring straight ahead. There had been a moment when he had feared she might not murmur her responses, but after a slight hesitation, she had dutifully answered the priest. Her reluctance had distressed him. Equally upsetting had been her failure to look at him. Instead, she gazed at the paintings on the wall or at her family. Tony and her mother, he had noticed with some annoyance, had both seemed far less happy than the occasion warranted.

However, they had provided a lavish wedding feast. The noblemen who lived in the vicinity, as well as dignitaries from the town were all assembled to toast the newly married pair. There had been acrobats and dancers and even a trained bear, but Blanche had witnessed none of it. Shortly after she had taken her seat beside him at the table, she had been taken ill. Too much excitement had been her mother's diagnosis, and Tony had concurred. They had sent for her nurse, a silly, brainless creature, who had cried and clucked over her, treating her as if she were still in the nursery and actually carrying her from the room.

True to his promise, he had made no effort to visit his little bride that night. Instead, he had retired to his chamber. Thinking about it now, he laughed. It had been a very strange wedding night, but he was content. At least, he need no longer concern himself with his youthful rival, Master Rupert Godwin. He had no place in the life of Lady Marchmont, the countess of Glenmore.

"Ah, look at that great bridge!"

He turned quickly for it was a child who had spoken eagerly, excitedly. Had his wife finally awakened to the splendors of the great city that lay on either bank? He grimaced. It was not Blanche who had spoken, it was Josette, the little peasant, recently recruited as her personal maid. She was a dark-haired, dark-eyed, merry little girl, who had loved every moment of the long journey from Chinon. Now, sitting in the stern of the boat, she was chattering happily with one of the sailors. He wished she would pass some of her excitement onto Blanche.

He looked down at her, standing a few paces away, near her mother, and was reminded of that first time they had been on the water together, the channel, six years earlier. It was in memory of that crossing that he had chosen to bring her up the river rather than across the bridge to the island. They were nearing his dock and for the first time since he had bought it, he was happy to be returning to his home, for no longer would its vast halls and huge chambers be filled with the sound of silence. He shivered slightly as he recalled his early days in the mansion. He had been very lonely, but all that would soon be changed. Moving to Blanche, he caressed her shoulder gently, only to see her draw away.

"Shall we be docking soon, my lord?" Audrey asked quickly. "I think Blanche is tired. I know I am."

"In a few moments," he said shortly, wondering if he would ever regain his old rapport with Blanche.

Looking into his rueful eyes, Audrey was almost sorry for him. In the past, Blanche had been fond of the man she now called husband, but since the wedding she had not given him so much as a smile. Yet, her demeanor toward everyone was much the same. She was sober and quiet, speaking only when it was absolutely necessary. Indeed, there was something almost tragic about the change in her, Audrey thought, and then she tried to laugh. A child of twelve could hardly know the true meaning of tragedy.

She pursed her lips. It was a great pity that Rupert Godwin had come to Diamant. At the time, she had thought he would be a companion for her lonely little girl. Who would have believed that the two children could have become so passionately attached to each other and so quickly? Yet, passionate or not, childish memories were short, and she could only hope that the diversion of Blanche's new surroundings would help her to forget him.

Blanche, staring down into the river, was not seeing the turbulent Seine, she was looking into another body of water, mirror still and with a reflection of Rupert's face in it. She saw it so clearly, his high cheekbones, his strong, cleft chin, his straight nose, his golden eyes, his waving bronze hair. He was smiling at her and she smiled back, adoringly.

Noting her expression, Audrey was considerably relieved. The child was in a better humor. The mother turned her attention to the house that rose above the dock and found its windowed facade magnificent. "Oh," she breathed to Blanche, "it's fit for a queen."

She made similar remarks as they were being shown through the mansion, but by the time they had wandered through huge rooms, had marveled at painted ceilings adorned with sculptured nymphs and satyrs holding up immense gold-leaf garlands, had admired floors of patterned marble and pillars of lapis lazuli, had been briefly enchanted by the trompe-l'oeil gardens painted on the walls of the music room, and had seen the vast stretch of real gardens, she had exhausted her supply of compliments. It was not a house, it was a palace, and its grandeur was overpowering.

Standing in the banqueting hall with its frescoes depicting the bounties of the four seasons and its ceilings decorated at intervals by statues of the twelve months, each holding a fruit, flower, or vegetable, Audrey felt depressed. Did the earl expect Blanche to preside over the fifty to one hundred people who would sit down at the long, polished table? It was soon, too soon for her to be in so formal an atmosphere. Much as she had decried the relationship, it would have been far better for her daughter to go looking for badger holes with Rupert than to be mistress of this mighty establishment.

Her depression increased as they went up a curving staircase to the second floor and through two large drawing rooms. She barely acknowledged the beauty of the mirrored ballroom which adjoined them. She was tired of the lavish decorations, but there were more to come in the bedrooms. These faced the gardens and ran to no less than sixteen vast rooms, the bride having her own four chambers at the end of the hall. Much to Audrey's relief, these did not adjoin Glenmore's suite.

On entering Blanche's bedchamber, she managed to say with forced enthusiasm, "I vow, I am envious. Look, my dear, is it not beautiful?"

"Ooooh," gasped Josette, who was accompanying them.

Blanche did not answer her mother. She looked at the huge, airy room with its view of the distant city, its lovely furniture, and its canopied bed hung with pale, pink silk, with the same indifference she had shown throughout the entire tour of the house.

By this time, Glenmore's chagrin was almost palpable and again Audrey felt it necessary to create a diversion. She found it in the ceiling, which was painted to represent a sunlit sky. It was decorated with the signs of the zodiac and centered by the statue of a winged man. She pointed at him, "That does not look like an Eros." she said.

"No," Glenmore answered, turning to Blanche, "he is called *Icarus.*"

"Icarus," Audrey repeated. "The boy who flew too near the sun?"

"Yes," he replied, his eyes still lingering on his wife. "Do you recall that tale, my love? I told it to you once."

She nodded, staring at the statue. "His wings melted and he fell into the water. Later, I wrote a poem about him, wherein he was saved." She actually smiled up at the statue. "I like him. He's very beautiful."

With some surprise, he realized that it was the first direct answer she had given him in days and also the first remark she had made since entering the house. He should have been pleased that she remembered his story, but there was something in her entranced gaze that excluded him. He frowned at the sculpture, wishing that he might think of some excuse to have it wrested from the wall and thrown into the water.

Before leaving Diamant, Glenmore had promised to provide Blanche with a lady-in-waiting, who would be a teacher too. He knew the very person for the position, he had told Audrey and Tony. A Scotswoman of impeccable lineage, her name was Esther de Coligny, the widow of a French officer. "She is unmistakably a lady," he had stated. "In my opinion, she is ideally suited to instruct Blanche both in her studies and in the management of a noble household. She herself is a distant connection of the Hamiltons."

Much to his secret annoyance, Audrey had insisted on interviewing the woman before she was installed. Almost as though she feared, he had thought indignantly, that he might have appointed one of his mistresses to oversee his bride. Yet, since he was quite aware of just how much a concession had been granted him regarding his marriage, he acceded to Audrey's request.

Madame de Coligny came to the house the day following their arrival in Paris and was interviewed in the library. She was a tall, slender woman dressed so plainly that Audrey suspected her of Puritan leanings. Fortunately, this proved to be a fallacy.

"To my mind, Lady Carlisle," she said bluntly, "those wicked king murderers should have their round heads lifted from their shoulders by the same axe that severed the neck of our martyred King Charles, may heaven grant him peace." Immediately after she had expressed that bloodthirsty sentiment, she clapped her hand to her mouth, looking extremely self-conscious, "Gracious, I hope I've not shocked you, my child?"

"No," Blanche shook her head.

"Good," Madame de Coligny said, adding abruptly. "I see you've ink on your fingers. Have you been writing?"

"She writes very well," Audrey said. "I think she's quite gifted."

"Indeed," Madame de Coligny looked interested. "What do you like to write, child?"

Blanche did not answer immediately. She stared at Madame de Coligny for a long moment before saying hesitantly, "I write poems and stories—and I've also written a play."

Madame de Coligny clapped her hands, "Very good. That's what I like to hear, especially about the play. Do you know that it was a woman who brought back drama to the world?"

"A woman—whom?" Blanche demanded shyly.

"A nun named Hroswitha, she spent her life in a Benedictine abbey and it was through reading Terence in Latin that she began to write her own plays and thus revived a lost art."

"Oh," Blanche's eyes gleamed. "I should like to hear all about her."

"And so you shall," Audrey said. "That is if Madame de Coligny will consent to instruct you."

"Will you, madame?" Blanche asked with an eagerness that brought tears to Audrey's eyes. She had never expected to hear that note in her daughter's voice again.

"Please, you must, Madame de Coligny," she breathed.

"I shall on one condition." Madame de Coligny addressed Blanche.

"What is that, madame?" she inquired softly.

"That you are serious about this writing. I am of the opinion that gifts should be used, not put away in drawers or chests should some other fancy such as needlework or beading strike you. If you are serious, I shall be glad to work with you and teach you as much as I know."

"I am very serious," Blanche said gravely.

"Good," she smiled. "Then, I shall be delighted to stay."

"Oh," Blanche clasped her hands. "I am so pleased, Madame de Colingy."

"And so am I," she answered. "I am in need of this position, being widowed and poor, but I would rather scrub the stones of Paris than be quartered with someone I do not respect. I think we shall deal very well together, my child—er, my Lady Glenmore, as I should have been calling you from the beginning." She paused and then added, "I might tell you that I'm not at all comfortable with all these fancy titles. I should like to be called by my name, which is Esther and might you be merely Blanche?"

"Please," Blanche said. "I'd like that very much." She looked down suddenly, "I—I do not want to be called my Lady Glenmore."

Esther de Coligny's eyes softened, "Well, as to that, my dear, there will be times when you must bear with it, but not between the two of us."

It was agreed that Madame de Coligny would move into the mansion that evening, and as she walked with her through the corridor, Audrey said, "I am content to leave my daughter in your care."

She received a sharp, shrewd look, "I wish she were *entirely* in my care, my lady. She's a charming child and very sensitive. She must be treated gently."

Her meaning seemed only too clear, and it worried Audrey enough to tax Glenmore with his promise later that same day. She received an impatient, "But you've my word, dear Lady Carlisle. Believe me, I am not a man who'd force his attentions on a frightened child."

She would have been more pleased by his answer had he not already forced his ring upon her daughter's finger.

All too quickly, Audrey's fortnight in Paris was at an end and she was bound back to Chinon. In all her twelve years as a mother, she had never felt the deep unhappiness she experienced as she bade farewell to

Blanche. "I shall miss you, my own, my lamb," she said, covering the child's face with kisses. "But come December, we'll be reunited, never fear. Meanwhile, I am glad I leave you with Esther." She looked at the woman appealingly. "You've all my confidence, madame." she murmured, not daring to speak with greater frankness, for Glenmore was waiting to hand her into her coach.

"I wish you a safe journey, Lady Carlisle," he said courteously.

"I thank you, my lord," she answered, managing a small smile. and trying not to recoil from the touch of his hand as he helped her up the steps to the coach door. It was so cold, she thought, a cold, dry old hand, which one day would caress her daughter's smooth young body. Settling down in her seat, she shuddered, and Marie, the maid she had just hired, looked at her with some concern.

"Madame is chilly?" she asked solicitously.

"No," she said sharply and leaned out of the window to blow another kiss at Blanche. Yet, she was cold, cold with fear, for as she looked into the enigmatic face of the man she must call her son-in-law she noticed harsh lines about his mouth. Odd that she had not seen them before. It was a cruel mouth, and his gray eyes were so cold. She longed to order her coachman to stop urging his horses forward, longed to go back to Blanche, but she dared not. He would think her mad and what would Tony say?

A wave of anger and resentment swept over her as she thought of the bargain made between the two men. Though she, by necessity, had accustomed herself to the idea, she had not approved the marriage. Why had she not forbidden it? As a mother, she certainly had that right. No, it was not true, she had only those rights her husband's father chose to give her. If he had remained only Charlie's father, it might have been a different tale, but she could not have borne to live like a nun for six long years, and had, accordingly surrendered to his importuning. No, if she were to be truthful as one must be, at least with one's own self, the surrender had come before the invitation, and she could not regret it, not entirely. With a certain self-contempt she knew that her fortnight of continence was weighing upon her and that she wished the six horses pulling her toward Diamant were each equipped with wings.

"Yet—" she whispered to herself, "she's so very little." Her thoughts were back on Blanche and with them came her tears. She leaned back in the corner of her coach, unwilling and even ashamed to show her maid her anguish and her fear.

Audrey's tears were still on Blanche's cheek. The child felt their wetness and wiped them away with some surprise. She had never seen her gay young mother so upset, nor had she, in all her years, remembered being so often in her company. Together they had explored her new home; together they had ridden through the streets of Paris; and there had been an unexpected, informal visit with the dowager queen of England, Henrietta Marie, who was always eager to see English émigrés. The queen was a sad lady, who dressed in deepest mourning, spoke English with a thick French accent, and constantly wept. Though whether her tears were for the cruel death of her husband or for her eldest son's adamant refusal to be baptized a Catholic was not immediately clear, since she mentioned both wrongs practically simultaneously.

Blanche had also seen the young King Louis XIV, though only at a distance. It had seemed to her that he looked unhappy, too. "La, child," her mother had laughed, "he's not unhappy. He was crowned in Rheims last month and all his enemies are defeated. Would that our poor king had fared so well."

Blanche had not known what Audrey had meant, but later Esther explained about the Fronde and the defeat of the prince of Condi, who had, like Cromwell, hoped to overthrow the throne. It was amazing how well the girl liked Esther. She had liked her from the start, which was amazing she had heard her mother tell Glenmore. "She likes so few people," Audrey had confided, adding a little anxiously, "You realize that she's always been quiet and undemonstrative."

Blanche could have told them that she liked and even loved people who were kind to her, and that until this last fortnight she had never been sure that her mother had even noticed her, save when she had appeared, candle in hand, to part her from Rupert Godwin. Thinking about him, the tears she could not shed when she had bade farewell to her mother welled up in her eyes. She would not forgive Audrey for her interference that night, nor would she forgive the old man, who had taken her for his wife. She had written in her journal, *"I do not love him. I shall never love him, never, never, never. I love only Rupert and shall love him all my life."*

"Well, little Blanche," she felt his hand on her curls, "I pray you'll not be lonely."

She suffered his touch, though she longed to pull away, and there was no warmth in her voice as she answered, "No, my lord, I shall not be lonely. I have Esther with me."

There was a thread of anger in his voice as he replied, "You've a husband, too." He tried to cover his resentment with a conciliating smile. "I may be a trying companion now, but I trust that in time we'll deal well together. I am—very fond of you, my dear, and believe me, I know what's best for you. You'll want for nothing as long as I am here."

She remained silent, not knowing how to answer him. It was Esther, who said gently, "You must understand, my lord, that she's confused. So much has happened in so short a time."

Rage blazed forth from his eyes, "You need not explain her to me, Esther. I know her through and through." Turning on his heel, he strode across the courtyard.

"What did you say, my dear?" Esther looked down at Blanche.

"Nothing." she murmured.

Esther, who had heard her barely articulated, "No, you don't," winced. To her mind, that protest had been as hurtful as a cry of anguish. Kneeling, she drew the little girl into her embrace. "Oh, my darling, I wish you might have gone with your mama," she whispered.

It was with surprise and some pain that she heard Blanche answer, "But Esther, I much prefer to be with you."

It was late and the candle beside Glenmore's bed had burned low. He had been reading, but he scarcely knew the matter of what he had read. The words had been turned meaningless by his intrusive thoughts, which were all of his wife, sleeping at the other end of the corridor. It was her first night without her mother. Audrey had given orders that Josette sleep in her room, but these he had countermanded, sending the girl up to the third floor where the other servants slept. He remembered her sulky and suspicious look. He had a mind to strike it from her face and send her back to Diamant. However, since Isabella seemed fond of her—*Isabella?* Startled, he wondered why he had used that name instead of Blanche?

Was he growing senile and forgetful as his father had been before the end? But that was nonsense. His father had been past seventy when his mind had wandered. He was still comparatively young. His body was muscular and its youthful fires were not yet banked. Isabella—Isabella of Angouleme had been but twelve when she had known her husband John, known him as Eve had known Adam.

Rising from his bed, he paced back and forth across

the room. "Two years," he muttered. He had given his word to wait two years, but he had waited six already, no, not six, it had not been decided six years ago. But it had. He knew that too. In his mind, it had been decided when he had first touched that soft, silky hair that had been blowing about her face. He could still feel its silken touch. Yet, he had given his word. . . . But might she not be lonely in her rooms with none beside her? He had given his word, but could he not see her sleeping and never touch her? There would be no harm to watch her while she slept, no harm at all.

Blanche had gone to sleep looking at the winged boy who had plunged from the sky into the water and who now lived under the waves. Immediately she had closed her eyes, he called to her. She was joining him, and they were together in the depths of the pool at Diamant. Strangely, they were not even wet, as one might think they would be under water. She remarked on it:

"How strange it is, Rupert?"

"No, it is not strange, my Blanche. I'll show you where the waterfowl nests. Come with me."

"But you mustn't break it," she protested. "Look, its all over the stones, my lovely bird." She looked at him indignantly. "Why are you laughing? You mustn't laugh!"

"We shall find a badger hole and live in the fields. You'd like that, wouldn't you?" he said gently.

"Oh, I should, I should. Let's go. Quickly, quickly."

There was a brightness in the pool; a brightness and a warmth close to her cheek, a warmth that burned.

"Oh . . ." she murmured.

"Child, I did not mean to burn you with the wax. Did it hurt?"

She opened drowsy eyes and looked into a man's face, half-illumined, half in shadow from a candle flame. "But where is he?" she cried.

"He?" the candle flames were in his eyes.

"He fell into the water—the winged boy."

"You've been dreaming, child."

"No—I—I saw him—Rupert."

His eyes narrowed. He set the candle down with a hard little bang. "I tell you, you're dreaming. There's no Rupert about. He's gone, gone forever!"

She was wide awake. "Oh, I couldn't have been dreaming," she moaned. "I saw him—I saw him in the water."

"Water?" he laughed harshly. "There's no water and no one in your room save myself." Seizing her by the shoulders, he shook her roughly. "You must stop dreaming about him. You are my wife now. Mine!" He shook her a second time, and she cried out, trying to pull away from him.

He released her and sat down on the edge of the bed. "Come, come, do not be afraid," he said more gently. "I came but to bid you a good-night, your first alone beneath my roof, our roof, my child. All I possess is yours, my Blanche, which can mean little to you now, but one day—" he ran his fingers through her curls. "Silk," he whispered. "Softer than the finest silk—" he touched her face and stroked her neck, then gathering her in his arms, he began to kiss her, soft little kisses ranging over her face and throat, while she lay as stiffly as a statue, as an effigy on a tomb. He stopped and drew back, biting his lip. "I've frightened you, I see." he said bitterly. "I love you. I have loved you half your life." He stared into her frozen face. "I'll not take you now, though it is my right. You are my wife. Good Christ, you set me on fire. You do not know your powers!" He moved nearer to her again. She was breathing shallowly now and her eyes were squeezed together as if she were in pain. "Not yet, not yet," he muttered. "It's too early, damn you! I'll leave you to your sleeping."

By the time he had gained the hall, he was trembling all over, yet he was glad of his restraint. It was not the time to take her. She was too young, and her head was still full of that young cub. He would hold to his bargain and wait. However, he would have the workmen in tomorrow and have them destroy the winged statue.

Chapter Two

Crowds! Myriads of people milling about on the narrow streets and overflowing onto the shop-lined Pont Neuf, more throngs on the stairs leading to the riverbank, more yet on the banks—walking, fishing, washing clothes or their own filth-caked bodies, wrestling or fornicating, urinating, squatting, puking in or near the water. The river teemed with tiny boats, perilously close to each other, yet going in a thousand different directions, skittering out of the way like flocks of frightened fish as the larger barges of the nobility bore down upon them.

Glenmore, astride Sheba, his skittish black mare, was hard put to find a passage through the streets on this September afternoon of 1656. He had grown weary of counting the times he had been forced to pull Sheba to a halt, his way blocked by a wagon or a coach, by a fight, a duel, a whining beggar, or a tumbler, juggler, puppet show, card-reader or astrologer, each with his audience of dolts, who stood about like so many simpletons, not having either the will or the courtesy to clear the way, unless prodded by his spurs or whip.

A grubby child of eight or nine grabbed at his boot, small, filthy hand outstretched for alms, smile provocative, gesture obscene, screaming imprecations when he kicked her away. He glared about him angrily. No matter how often he returned to Paris, he was always infuriated by its crowds, its squalor, and its noise, not that it was much different from London or any other great metropolis, but the French themselves were different, amazingly elegant on the one hand, incredibly crude on the other, and in the streets the latter predominated. Glancing toward the makeshift riverside hovels that rose up like so many rain-spawned mushrooms, he wished a fire would raze the lot of them. Certainly, the city would be the better for it and the way would be cleared for him to make his way home.

He was tired, more than tired, bone-weary. He had been on horseback the better part of five days, riding along the wretched roads from Calais. Before that, there had been a choppy channel crossing, and before that, all the tiresome precautions attendant on his meeting with the group of Royalist insurgents that called themselves The Sealed Knot. Undeterred by their aborted uprising of the previous year, they were still eager to undermine the Protectorate and bring Charles II to the throne. His meetings with them and with other equally determined factions had kept him out of France for six long months.

He grimaced. It had been a difficult time, harder for him than all his other missions in the past two years, for his thoughts had continually strayed to Blanche. She was now four months past her fourteenth birthday, and his pact was at an end. He had waited so long, far longer than he had thought he could. Indeed, if he had not been away so often, he doubted if he could have abided by his promise. In a sense, however, it was as well that he had. She was less wary of him now, and if they had never quite achieved their old camaraderie, at least she no longer treated as a stranger. Her manner toward him was, he thought wryly, much like that of a ward or a niece. Yet, perhaps when he bedded her, that might change. He would be very patient, very gentle. She might respond to gentleness, to petting and stroking until, almost without her knowing it, she would be aroused. After all, she was her mother's daughter, and there must be some seed of passion in her nature. He would only have to nurture it—to bring it into flower.

He spurred his horse forward and as the animal quickened its pace, he heard a plaintive cry. Looking down, he saw that a ragged child had evidently been struck by one of Sheba's flailing hoofs and was now bleeding and strained tight against the bosom of a weeping peasant woman. Tossing her a coin, he said roughly, "Out of my way, you," and rode on oblivious to her stricken howls.

It was close on half an hour before he turned in at his own courtyard. Then, framed in a doorway, he saw a woman's form. For a moment, he ceased to breathe—was she awaiting him? Then, as the woman came forward, he expelled his breath in a disappointed sigh, to be followed by a frown. His mother-in-law was looking up at him with a very strange expression in her eyes.

It had been an impulse that had brought Audrey to Paris. It had been seven months since she had last seen her daughter, four since she had heard from her. It was disquieting since she had been accustomed to hearing from her regularly, lovely little letters describing sights she had seen in the city and at the Louvre or the Palais Royale. She had been much with the widowed Henriette Marie, who had taken a fancy to her. She had described the queen's court delightfully, furnishing charming vignettes of her ladies and the little princess. And now—this silence. Had Glenmore violated his pact, she wondered; or was she ill? Finally, she had confided her fears to Tony and had received his permission to investigate.

By the time she had reached her destination, her fears had increased; nor were they alleviated when she met Esther in the hall, for on seeing the mother Esther had shrieked, "But—it's impossible, my message could not have reached you so quickly—I sent it only two days since."

"Your message?" With vision of plague or some other virulent disorder, she asked, "Is my daughter ill or—or—"

"No, not ill," Esther had replied. "She—I should have written before, but I thought it would be a passing thing. I never expected that she—that he—"

"He!" Audrey pounced upon the word. "Her husband—did he hurt her or—"

"No, the earl's not even here. It was the queen or rather—Oh, Lady Carlisle, please let us go into the library. I've much to tell you and we'd best sit down."

She had been discomfited but relieved as well, for obviously Blanche was not sick or dead. Yet, certainly something was the matter for she had never seen calm Esther so disturbed. When at last they were closeted in the library, she had asked, "I think you mentioned the queen."

Esther nodded, "As you know, she's fond of her—Oh, we've had such a time! I've had servants posted at all the gates—both night and day—for fear she'd steal past them into the streets and they none the wiser until she'd gone, and the good Lord knows what would happen to her then. Oh, it passes all understanding."

Audrey said tartly, "And what you're saying passes my understanding, too. Are you talking about Blanche or—"

"Yes, yes, Blanche." she nodded.

"She wants to run away?" Audrey asked. "To—Rupert. He's not in Paris, is he? No, he couldn't be. I've heard from his father. He's in Cologne."

"No, no word of him has passed her lips. Nor do I say, she'd run away. She'd only move forth among the rabble to wash the feet of beggars and to seek, if possible, the lepers, if any are to be found in this vicinity."

"What?" Audrey cried. "Are you telling me—she's turned saint?"

"I am saying that she has been sadly influenced. The

queen, as you know, is deeply religious, and it was she who introduced Blanche to a new confessor—a young man named Father Etienne. Since that time, she speaks of nothing but cloisters and prayers. She has neglected her writing and her other studies, and she spends most of her waking moments in chapel or being instructed by Father Etienne or with the queen, who naturally encourages her in this madness."

"Cloisters—" Audrey frowned. "You mean she thinks of being a nun?"

Esther nodded, "Yes."

Audrey looked at her incredulously, "But it passes all comprehension." she said finally.

"No, it doesn't," Esther contradicted crisply. "Young Father Etienne is most persuasive."

"Young?" Audrey said. "How young?"

"In his early twenties, I should say, and consumed by faith. He has influenced many to take their religion more seriously—the ladies, I should say."

"Ah," Audrey nodded. "I begin to see—but I shouldn't think that Blanche—she was never unduly religious."

"She's of an age," Esther sighed. "When I was fourteen, I was minded to run away and bear arms like my brothers."

"And I wanted—" Audrey flushed. "Well, never mind that—where will I find Blanche? At her prayers?"

"Yes. It's where she generally spends her days. I fear you'll find her sadly changed. It's almost impossible to coax her to eat. At the most, she'll take but a crust of bread and a little milk."

"Why did you not send for me sooner?" Audrey demanded. "Well, no matter. I'll talk some sense into her."

The boast had been vain, and while it was as well that Glenmore had returned, Audrey cravenly wished that she were still at Diamant, for how was she to explain the sackcloth and the hair shirt and worse yet, the fasting that had turned the girl into a hollow-eyed little wraith, speaking of a life of service to the poor. In her ears still rang the words of Queen Henriette Marie. "We think she has the making of a saint, Lady Carlisle. Never have we witnessed such devotion in an age nearly devoid of faith. I have hopes that one day she might have her own order."

Glenmore listened to Audrey's tale with a mixture of incredulity and anger. "But," he exploded after she had repeated the queen's words, "does Her Majesty forget that Blanche is my wife?"

"Her Majesty is of the opinion that in the face of a vocation so strong, mere marriage vows must be put aside. It is God's will, she told me." Audrey kept her eyes carefully trained on the cobblestones so that he might not read the mockery in them.

"Indeed," he exclaimed. "And what do you believe, Lady Carlisle?"

She shrugged. "In my opinion, my lord, it's a passing fancy, but I believe too that it must be treated with respect."

"Respect?" he repeated sharply. "I am to encourage her to join a cloister, then?"

"Hardly, I only suggest that you do not ridicule it. If you jeer or laugh at it, you'll only drive her to defend it, and it will be the harder to root out. I've not agreed with her. I've only listened. It were well that you did the same."

He gave her a brief nod, "I thank you for your advice, Lady Carlisle," he said curtly. Without another word, without stopping to change his muddy, sweat-stained garments, he hurried to the chapel.

Though Glenmore was far from a religious man, his innate love of beauty had caused him to make the chapel one of the jewels of his house. It was a small, circular room, and its ceiling was painted with a representation of the Virgin and Child, surrounded by cherubim, and backed by rosy clouds in an azure sky. The altar was sculpted in lilies and roses, and the huge cross surmounting it bore an ivory Christ with an ebony crown of thorns. Flanking the altar were two great Byzantine lamps, and high on the back wall was a rose window. As he entered, he found its multicolored light filtering onto Blanche's bowed golden head.

As Audrey had warned him, Blanche was in brown sacking with a heavy rope knotted around a waist which had grown noticeably more slender. Her feet were bare, and, even in that dim light, he could see that the fingers that were telling the beads of her rosary were almost transparent.

She was not alone. Beside her knelt a Franciscan monk. His head was tonsured, but the hair that curled away from the bald circle was richly bronze, and at Glenmore's entrance, the father turned up a face wasted by fasting but yet startlingly handsome. Looking into his stern, dedicated eyes, Glenmore experienced a shock and wondered why Audrey had failed to mention that Father Etienne looked very like Rupert Godwin. All at once, the reasons behind Blanche's conversion were only too clear.

His hand clenched and he thrust it behind his back to keep himself from smashing it against the priest's jaw. It was necessary, most necessary, for him to keep his temper. Not only did Father Etienne enjoy the friendship of Henriette Marie, it was only too evident that the child worshipped him. Brutality would only negate all the progress he had made in reestablishing their friendship. He said calmly, "Father Etienne, I am Glenmore."

There was a flicker of surprise in the priest's eyes, but he was on his feet in an instant. "Ah, my lord, I have long waited the opportunity to speak with you."

"And I would speak with you," Glenmore answered, bestowing a brief smile on Blanche, whom he found looking at him anxiously. "I trust you are well, my dear." he said.

"I am well—and in the arms of Christ," she answered in a low voice.

Glenmore's eyes narrowed but he merely answered, "So may we all be."

Moments later, standing in the hall beyond the chapel, he was still fighting to control his anger as he confronted the young priest. However, he managed to say quite calmly, "I find my wife much changed."

The young man nodded solemnly, "Yes, she has changed. She has accepted Christ."

"I was of the opinion that my wife was already of the Christian faith." Glenmore said.

"True. We are all baptized Christians," Father Etienne agreed, "but the gift of knowing him is not always granted immediately. We are obliged to seek him in order to see the true light, and once that beacon is glimpsed, then we have found Christ and he has found us and our lives are altered accordingly. You will see, I think, that your wife is not as she was when you left her."

Glenmore felt a constriction in his throat and a tightening in his chest which he properly identified as rage. However, he managed to retain his calm as he replied, "I can see she has undergone an alteration of spirit. She also looks very thin. Was it at your suggestion that she embarked upon this strenuous fast?"

Father Etienne shook his head. "No, she wanted to fast and as the saints of old, to partake only of the Holy Sacrament. However, in the interests of her health, I have insisted that she have a portion of bread and milk each day."

"I see," Glenmore nodded.

"Your young wife has provided an example to us all. In a few short months, she has given herself wholly to Christ. Though this will no doubt come as a shock to you, as her husband, I feel it my duty to tell you that she has already progressed to a higher spiritual level—one that has removed her from earthly alliances. In common with such young women as Saint Agnes, the Blessed Virgin Martyr, and Saint Marie Magdalene dei Pazzi, who died in our own century, she has dedicated her virginity to Christ and is determined to join the newly founded order of the Sisters of Charity."

"The order established by Monsieur Vincent at the hospital of Saint Lazare?" Glenmore asked.

"You are well informed, my lord. Yes, I have taken her to watch Monsieur Vincent at work among the poor, and she is most eager to join the community. It is not often that one so young is visited by the Divine Grace, but when it happens, it must be respected and honored, as I pray you will agree." Though the priest's gaze was stern, there was a pleading note in his voice that surprised Glenmore. "Of course, this matter must yet have your approval, my lord."

"Must it indeed?" Glenmore's efforts to quell his sarcasm were not entirely successful.

"We have prayed, she and I. Also the good sisters and Monsieur Vincent have added their prayers to ours. We have prayed that you will allow her to relinquish her earthly possessions, as she most earnestly desires, and to follow Christ in the service of the poor."

Through clenched teeth, Glenmore said, "She's young indeed to travel so long and so arduous a path, Father Etienne."

"Your wife is no longer a child, my lord. In these last months, she has become a woman in faith and I ask you, I beg you, to recognize the Lord's will."

"It would seem that I have not much choice." Glenmore said.

The young priest's eyes glowed. "Does that mean you do agree, my lord?"

Glenmore spoke slowly, choosing his words carefully, "I am only returned just now from a long and a most tiring journey. The matter calls for careful consideration on my part. Might I sleep on my decision?"

The priest said, "But of course, my lord, and while

you sleep—we shall pray." Raising his hand in blessing, he intoned, *"Pax vobiscum,* my son."

Fury such as he had seldom experienced possessed him. Standing near his bed, he raised his whip and struck again and again, shredding its silken coverlet, but seeing beneath the leather thong, a writhing phantom, its shadowy features stamped with the likeness of Father Etienne. Finally, aware of the futility of his actions, he tore the coverlet off and flung it on the floor, to join the fragments of a porcelain platter and the scattered pages of a book he had ripped in half. In each fragment he saw some separate part of the priest's young body, the priest who, with his talks of saints and charity, had filled young Blanche with a holy zeal which would turn the very thought of her deflowering into a sacrilege.

Then, would he see her go radiant-eyed into the service of Vincent, to spend her life caring for the abandoned brats, the diseased poor, the rotting whores of Paris? That would be a worse sacrilege. Yet, what could he do against the shining shield of her new devotion? He could wait, as her mother had advised, but waiting would accomplish nothing. She needed to be freed from the pernicious influence of the young priest. He could not believe that her devotion was genuine. Whether she knew it or not, she was in love with her confessor's Rupert-Godwin face. As for Father Etienne, a derisive smile curled his lips, he was like all priests, shrouding his venal nature in the habiliments of religion! They were the same—from the humblest curate to the pope himself!

He could not remember when he had lost his faith, perhaps the last grains had disappeared when Charles I was beheaded. He was not sure. He only knew that he believed in nothing, and that his very lack of belief would sustain him in the only course of action open to him. With that in mind, he took a small flask from a chest in his dressing room and went in search of Audrey.

Fingering the flask, Audrey looked at Glenmore in horror, "No," she protested. "You mustn't think of it."

"Damnation," he exploded, "you speak as if I meant to poison her."

"But—but to excite her and make her weak against her will with this stuff? Have you thought what it might do to a mind that's firmly fixed on heaven? It—it could send her into madness. The change you want must be wrought with time and care. Slowly, my lord."

Glenmore ground his teeth. "On the contrary, Lady Carlisle, it must be done quickly or not at all! If you don't want her cloistered for all her natural life—"

"I've told you," she interrupted, "that I think she will recover her senses in time."

"And I tell you that the queen and Father Etienne will not give her a chance to recover them. When she does come to her senses, as I think she must, it will be too late for recanting."

He spoke earnestly and, she believed, out of more than his thwarted passion. Furthermore, she was inclined to agree with him. Blanche had fallen prey to a pair of fanatics. She shuddered. She did not want her daughter, a beautiful child with all her life before her, to live the sterile existence of a nun, particularly one who must wash the sores of paupers. The thought revolted her. Yet, in a sense, the alternative was almost equally frightening, for in doing as Glenmore suggested, she would share the blame with him. Unlike the earl, she had not lost her faith, and the idea of divine retribution and its attendant fires was not one she liked to contemplate. Still, she had more than half made up her mind when she asked, "The potion will not harm her?"

"Not at all," he assured her. "It's mainly alcohol, and its often served at wedding feasts to ease the tremors of the bride and to stimulate her senses too. I'll give you a vial of it, and you'll put it in her milk. It's colorless and almost tasteless, though perhaps it would be wise to sweeten it with sugar."

"She'll take no sugar, my lord. Bread and milk's all she'll have. It's a wonder she's not weak as any newborn kitten." She gave him a long look. "I pray you'll be considerate."

"I'll be most considerate, my lady. Have I not already proved that I can exercise restraint?"

She nodded and sighed, "Very well. Fetch me the vial."

Blanche was feeling very giddy. Audrey, sitting by her bed an hour after she had drunk the doctored milk, looked at her with an anxiety that was not entirely feigned, "I fear you're a little feverish child." she said.

"My head," Blanche rubbed it, "it seems so heavy—or so light. I d-don't know which. And why does everything move, mama?"

"Move, child? What do you mean?" Audrey asked.

"It goes around and around—" Blanche complained.

All manner of regrets had invaded Audrey's mind, but making an effort to ignore them, she said accusingly, "You've had precious little to eat these last few days, my dear."

"But I've felt so well, mama," Blanche exclaimed. "So well and so happy." Her eyes grew radiant and her thin cheeks were flushed, "Benedicam Dominum in omni tempore; semper laus in ore meo, Gloria."*

"That's all very well, my Blanche, but you must consider your health. One cannot go without food forever. No wonder, you feel dizzy."

"That is not the reason, mama," Blanche said earnestly. "I am not yet strong enough in Christ. Father Etienne says that when I have joined the good sisters of Saint Lazare, my strength will increase a thousandfold."

* I will bless the Lord at all times; his praise shall be ever in my mouth.

It was the thought of Father Etienne that had vanquished Audrey's scruples, and at her daughter's reference to him, the woman felt them diminish even further, sanctimonious little beast! She brushed Blanche's fair curls back, "Try and sleep, my darling," she said gently.

Blanche moved restlessly on her great bed. "Soon I shall no longer be resting here, mama. I'll have a pallet of straw as did Christ in his manger, and then I'll not be dizzy any more."

"I—I'll bid you good night, my love." Audrey kissed her daughter's brow and went out swiftly.

Glenmore was waiting just beyond the door, a candle in his hand. "How is she?" he demanded urgently.

"She complains of dizziness, my lord," Audrey frowned. "She seems very weak and, as you know, she's had little to eat in these past weeks. I wonder—" she fell silent. There was no use in addressing the empty air. As she left, she heard the key turn in the lock of Blanche's door.

There was an acrid taste in Blanche's mouth, and her head still felt curiously light, as if it were floating free above her neck. She giggled at the notion, but quickly stifled her laugh, remembering that God did not like levity. Then, hearing footsteps, she looked up to see Glenmore, clad in a magnificent brocade robe, coming toward her, carrying a candle.

"Your mother tells me you're not well, my dearest," he said solicitously.

She started to shake her head, but since that made matters inside it considerably worse, she stopped. "I do feel odd," she admitted reluctantly.

"You've not been eating enough, my dear," he said, setting the candle down on the table. "Why have they not drawn the curtains round your bed?"

"I do not like them," she told him. "I like to see the moonlight and the rising sun."

"Do you?" he smiled. "I, too. I wish there were more of a moon this night, but it's sadly shrunken." He sat down on the edge of the bed. "And so, my sweet, I am told you'd leave me?"

"I have been called," she said. "God has sent for me."

"I see. You do not think it unusual for God to have claimed you, when you are yet my wife?"

She raised trusting eyes to him. "Father Etienne has told me that earthly ties have no meaning when Christ calls us."

"I see," he ran his hand over her head, brushing her hair back from her face. "And are you prepared to leave all comforts behind you and embrace poverty?"

"Oh, yes," she nodded. "Father Etienne says I've no choice but to obey God's commands. He told me that you would understand that."

"Did he?" He played with a lock of her long hair. "When I left for England, you told me that you planned to be a great writer. I've brought you back some plays by Shakespeare and by Ben Jonson."

"Oh, have you!" she said eagerly, then her face changed and she shook her head, "but I may not read them." She stifled a tiny sigh, and then added, "but I will still write. I may even write plays."

"That does not seem likely, if you're to be a nun."

"Hroswitha was a nun. Esther has told me about her. She wrote many plays to the greater glory of Christ, which is what I mean to do."

"How may you write plays when you are bathing the feet of lepers?" he inquired, slipping his hand to her neck, gently caressing it.

She moved restively, "Please—" she protested.

"Please—what, child?" Edging closer to her, he began to stroke her cheek and then her shoulder.

"Please—" she said again.

He pushed the covers down to her waist. Under her plain cotton shift, he saw the swell of her breasts. They were beautifully rounded, as he had thought they must be. He cupped them in his hands. " 'Thy two breasts are like two young roes that are twins, which feed among the lilies,' " he whispered. "That is from the Bible, my Blanche. Also from the Bible is this: 'Behold, thou art fair, my love, behold thou art fair; thou hast dove's eyes.' " Bending down, he pressed his lips on each cheek just below her eyes and felt her quiver.

Moving back from her, he blew out the candle and shrugging off his robe, slid beneath the covers, wrapping his arms around her flinching little body.

"No, no, no," she whispered, trying to free herself from his tightening embrace. "You must not lie with me. I—I've made a vow."

"A vow?" he pushed up her shift and began to caress her breasts.

She wanted to push him away, but she did not seem to have the strength, not even when he wrenched her shift over her head, leaving her naked. His fingers were on her nipples, circling them gently, and then she felt his mouth against them. She managed to push him away, but a moment later his lips were on her throat. She felt so strange, warm and cold. His hands were everywhere, stroking her thighs, reaching around to her buttocks, and whenever she touched him, she felt his bare skin beneath her hands. She was frightened, terribly frightened. Her head was whirling, and there were odd sensations coursing through her body.

"Go away, my lord, leave me," she begged, only to have her protests silenced by his tongue, thrusting deep into her mouth. She coughed and gagged, trying to pull away, but it was impossible, she had to endure it. Finally, it was withdrawn and she felt it tracing the delicate convolutions of her ear. The feeling was not totally unpleasant, but she did not want him so close to her. She made another effort to wriggle out of his embrace, but instead found herself beneath him. Fiercely, he pushed her legs apart. There was a quivering between her thighs as if something alive were seeking entrance, something that thrust and thrust against her, bringing with it a hurt that caused her to cry out, "Please, do not, do not—" she sobbed, piteously.

He did not heed her. He was breathing harder, gasping as if he were running a race. His body was rising and falling against her's, until at last there was a mighty thrust bringing with it a tearing agony so sharp that she screamed loudly and then, locked tightly against her husband, she felt the throbbing thing embedded deep within her. The darkness turned to blackness and for a while, she knew nothing more.

They had told him Blanche was ill, "from fasting and privation," her mother had said caustically, eyeing him with some anger. It was close on a month since he had seen her. It had been a hard time for him, a period of scourging and fasting, of hair shirts and knotted chains around his waist mortifying his flesh. There had been sleepless nights, but these had been less disturbing than those nights which had brought him from his pallet to his knees to pray away the devil-sent dreams that tormented him, as he had never been tormented in all his twenty-two years.

He did not understand himself. No, that was not true. He understood the nature of his agony all too well. When he had been summoned to the house to hear Glenmore's long-postponed decision, he almost wished he could send another priest in his place, but that was impossible. The child would be hurt, and besides, he wanted to see her. He had to see her.

As he followed a lackey down the hall, he passed Lady Carlisle and pausing to greet her, read shock in her eyes and flushed, wishing he had been able to draw up his cowl and hide his haggard features from her all-too-knowing gaze. He resented her for asking, "Have you been ill, Father Etienne?"

"No, Lady Carlisle," he answered almost roughly. "I

am quite well. I trust and pray the child's out of danger?"

"I should say she is, father, but you will soon see her for yourself."

He had no right to ask the question, but he could not restrain himself. "Has the earl reached a decision, then?" he blurted.

"You'll soon learn of it, father," she told him, indicating the door the servant had just opened for him. Dropping a deep curtsy, she rose and went on her way.

He was in an immense library filled with paintings and, he flushed and looked away quickly, undraped statues of pagan goddesses from Greece and Rome, standing in niches set between high shelves of books. A glance at the ceiling brought him a sight of more pagan dieties lolling in the high grasses backed by a distant pillared temple. Obviously, Glenmore was a man of Sybaritic tastes, hardly the proper husband for a pious young virgin. He felt his cheeks burn, for directly in front of him was the earl, seated in a thronelike armchair behind a long polished wooden table. It was covered with papers, some of them dispatches from the looks of them. There were also quills, parchments, sealing wax, and sand, the mark of a busy man. Near the table was an immense globe of the world mounted on an ebony stand. Another map filled half the wall behind him, and next to it a window faced the river.

The sunlight pouring through the glass was not kind to the earl. He looked his age, but much of the grimness Father Etienne had marked on their first meeting had vanished. In its place was a contentment that softened his harsh features. The priest noted too that his eyes glowed with an almost youthful fire. As he assessed these changes, the priest was aware of a coldness in his own heart, a coldness he barely comprehended.

"My Lord Glenmore, God be with you."

"And with you, Father Etienne," Glenmore smiled. "I pray you—have that chair." As the priest sat down,

Glenmore continued, "I expect you are eager for news of my wife?"

"I am told that she is out of danger," he replied.

"Yes, I would believe her out of danger, father, but you, I think, are more interested in her soul than in her body, and would know her decision. Isn't that true?"

"I should like to know *your* decision, yes," the priest emphasized.

"I've made no decision, father. It is for Blanche to give you her answer. I've sent for her and she should be joining us directly." His eyes narrowed and he stared at Father Etienne intently. "But I wonder, have you been quite well? You're not looking as fit as I remember from our previous meeting. A fever, perhaps?"

He winced at this second, less-than-solicitous reference to his nonexistent affliction. "No, I am quite well," he replied.

A draft of cold air hit the back of his neck as the door opened behind him. Turning, he saw Blanche standing on the threshold. His eyes widened in shock and disbelief, while she turned very pale.

"My dear," Glenmore said, "here's Father Etienne come to see you. Have you no words of welcome for him."

She opened her mouth and closed it, looking at the priest, piteously. Finally, she managed to say, "I—I bid you good morning, father."

He did not answer. He could only stare at the girl, who still stood just inside the door. She was resplendent in purple velvet, tricked out with gold ribbons and edged with fine lace. Jewels sparkled in her corsage, pearl drops hung from her ears, and diamonds glittered on her fingers. Yet, it was not her finery that held his attention; it was her eyes which drew him, eyes from which the look of limpid, dreaming innocence had fled, to be replaced by a wisdom which could only have been gained one way. She started toward him and to his horror, he found that even her walk had changed.

A month ago, she had had the awkwardness of a young fawn, now there was something sensuous about her movements. Raising her eyes to his, she said, "I—I did not expect you, father. I have been wondering why you—have not come."

"I—I was told" he began, only to be interrupted by the earl.

"I believe you have a question for my wife." Glenmore rasped.

The priest tensed, clenching his teeth, hating the older man and longing with quite unpriestlike fury, for a sword to run him through. Hesitantly, he said, "Your husband tells me, Lady Marchmont, that the decision concerning your desire to—join the Sisters of Charity, rests with you."

She looked down quickly. Her hands, he noticed, were on the ribbons at her waist, twisting them about, winding and unwinding them around her fingers. Nervously, she said, "I—I've been reminded, father, that—I—I'd taken other vows, vows to my husband in the sight of God, and these must needs take precedence over all else."

He gazed at her restless fingers, indicative of her unquiet mind, and he longed to kiss them, kiss her sad face as well, her face, her lips—horror thrilled through him. These thoughts in common with his dreams had been thrust into his mind by devils! He had to escape from the room. It was becoming airless, suffocating! He said harshly, "I understand. I was mistaken, then, about the depth of your devotion." The moment he had spoken, he longed to recall his words. Certainly, she did not deserve his censure. He read anguish and shame in her glance, and yet another devil urged him toward her. Rising, he faced the earl, "My lord," he said, "if—if I've caused you undue anxiety, I pray you'll please accept my apology. I too should have respected the marriage vows. It—it was only that—"

"Please, father," Glenmore interrupted. "I quite understand and, indeed, I find myself much in your debt.

You've shown me that during the last months, I've sadly neglected my duties toward my wife. I've tried and shall continue trying to remedy my mistake. Now—would you hear Blanche's confession?"

Father Etienne heard the girl's gasp of protest and stepped hastily backwards, "I—I beg your lordship's pardon, but I am unprepared to administer the—the sacrament at this hour. May I have your leave to return upon another day?"

"But of course, father," Glenmore smiled. "We're at your disposal."

The priest quite longed to strike the man full in his mouth, but quelling Satan a third time, he valiantly raised a stiffened hand in blessing, "God be with you, my lord," he said and turning to Blanche, he added, "and with you, too, my—daughter."

Their stricken eyes met briefly, then in a voice from which all nuance had fled, she murmured, "I thank you, father."

Inclining his head, he strode swiftly out of the room. Though the lackeys hastily closed the door behind him, it did not prevent his hearing the earl's low, derisive laughter. He thought too that he heard the sound of weeping and hesitated, longing to go back. But there being nothing he could do, he continued down the hall, trying to tell himself he had been mistaken and knowing he that he had not.

She was weeping. Accusingly, she sobbed, "Why did you make me see him?"

Laughing louder, her husband stepped to her side and caught her in his arms, "Why are you crying, my little angel, when you should be saying good riddance, to that young hypocrite? Lord, Lord, he ought to sling a sword where he now hangs a rosary, for I vow, he's no more priest than I, not with lust and anger glinting in his eyes."

"It's not true," she cried hotly. "He's good,

he's—he—" the words trailed away as he lifted her in his arms.

"Come, I've heard enough about your priest and will have no more of him from you. Your lips were meant for better uses, love." Kissing her hard, he bore her to a long bench beneath the window.

"N-no, p-please," she protested. "Let me be, I pray you, let me be."

He struck her hard across the mouth, "Little bitch," he said harshly, "No doubt you'd rather be mounted by your priest!"

Her cry of pain and horror was stifled as he pressed her head against his chest, then pushing her down on the bench, he flung back her skirts. With a weary sigh, she lay passive while he began to caress her thighs. She had already learned to her cost that any show of resistance only aroused him more.

Chapter Three

Clad in a golden gown worn over a white satin kirtle, richly embroidered with fanciful golden flowers, Madame la Comtesse Glenmore sat at her dressing table, taking surreptitious glances at an unbound manuscript, while her hairdresser, known simply as Monsieur Ganymede, busied himself in combing out her ringlets. He was a small man with a wizened face which was much at variance with the long black locks that flowed over his narrow shoulders, a marvelous advertisement of his skill with the dye pot. He was equally skillful in arranging hair, and generally, he was highly regarded by the ladies of Paris. It was only Madame la Comtesse, who refused to even look at the small mirror on her table to watch how he was progressing. She was far more interested in her papers. She was actually writing a novel! He bit down a rueful smile. It passed all understanding. Novel-writing was for plain old maids like Mademoiselle de Scudéry and others of her set, not for a woman like the Comtesse. She ought to be seen at court more often, gracing one of the king's ballets, and certainly she should take part in the pleasures of the town, the opera, the balls, and the banquets. But this beauty, who could have had all Paris at her feet, not excluding the king himself, chose instead to write books, and when she was not writing, she was reading.

He clicked his tongue. He did not know another lady her equal in looks, not even Olympe de Mancini, most delectable of Cardinal Mazarin's seven lovely nieces. He had heard that madame was a distant connection of the Angoulemes. There was a legend that a member of that family had married a fairy of the woods, a Melusine, who had later changed into a dragon and had flown away. Though one could not really believe so fanciful a tale, it seemed to him that there was a fey, otherworldly quality to the loveliness of Blanche de Glenmore.

Furthermore, she was as cold and aloof, as secretive and mysterious as that fabled ancestress must have been. Unlike his other clients, who were all too ready to confide their innermost-and-often-boring thoughts to him, she spoke very little. There were times when she was totally silent, but these, he had noticed, were generally while her husband was in residence. He frowned. He did not like the earl, and he was sure that she feared him. He could understand that. The man was cruel and ruthless. Ganymede had found him chastizing a servant one day, beating the man as if he had been a dog. He shuddered, remembering how the earl had smiled.

"Monsieur Ganymede"

He started and looked down at his client, "Madame?"

"Please—" she spoke in a gentle, hesitant voice, "you've been combing that one spot for quite five minutes."

"Ah, madame, a thousand, thousand pardons," he exclaimed, his dismay widening his eyes, "my few wits were wandering. Pray forgive me."

"Oh, please, I do." she assured him with a smile. "I'd not have mentioned it, only it's near time for me to leave."

"Yes, yes, I know and madame must not be late to the king's ball." His fingers were busy now. "It's a lovely night, the air is warm but not too warm, and there's a full moon. I am sure that was taken into account when Queen Anne planned it, also the planetary aspects are excellent." He paused and then added thoughtfully, "There are some who say that a full moon has strange effects on certain people. In my village, there was one who howled like a wolf—ah, but never mind that. I know madame will enjoy herself. It will be quite like old times with no expense spared. There." He raised his hands. "If Madame la Comtesse will please to look in this mirror, I think she will find that she is ravishing. I, Ganymede have truly served a goddess!"

Picking up an ornate, gold-backed mirror from the dressing table, he handed it to her, and taking another from a chest at his side, he held it at the back of her head. "You see, madame, how each separate ringlet has a life of its own?"

"I see," she said. "It's well done, Ganymede. You've given me a Medusa head."

"A—Medusa head, madame?" he repeated.

"Of snakes," she elaborated, "each with a life of its own."

"Oh," he grimaced, "what an idea, madame! I believe you do too much reading. Tonight, I hope you'll dance instead."

"If I must," she said, "but I'd much rather be writing. I am close to the end of my novel." Her eyes softened. She looked, he thought, as if she were talking of a lover.

He said, "There'll be time enough for writing when Madame la Comtesse is old and chair bound. You'll not be seventeen again, remember that." He looked at her nervously then, trembling a little at his boldness.

Her eyes were somber. "It's no great thing to be seventeen, Ganymede," she replied. "*I* would—" she paused and shrugged, "but never mind that. You may go."

"Madame is not angry with Ganymede, I hope?"

"Angry?" she gave him a reassuring smile. "With you? Never!"

"Thank you, madame, I bid you a good evening." Bowing, he gathered his combs and brushes together, and packing them neatly into his chest, he bowed himself from the room. He would have been chagrined but not surprised to learn that immediately, the lackeys had closed the tall, cream and golden doors behind him, madame started studying her manuscript again.

Madame's maid, Josette, who had been sitting in a corner, a silent listener to the conversation between her mistress and little Ganymede, raised her eyes to the heavens that lay somewhere above the painted ceiling. She agreed with the hairdresser. Madame spent far too much time at her writing, but how else was she to pass the hours at home since madame's husband frowned on her receiving company when he was away and desired her exclusive companionship when he was in residence? She was of the opinion that madame ought to have a lover, not only for her own well-being, but because it could be so profitable to those who served her. Many a lackey and maidservant had grown rich on tips earned for delivering messages or helping to hide amorous intruders in the advent of a husband's unexpected entrance. She cast a wistful eye around the great chamber. There were so many shadowy nooks and useful crannies.

The immense bed, for instance, with its golden curtains, always drawn back into folds as thick as pillars, a likely place for a hasty seclusion and the old man none the wiser. The windows too, set deep in alcoves and covered by drapery, could easily have been utilized during one of His Lordship's unheralded arrivals, but no matter what hour he appeared in the hall below, he could be sure his countess was alone. She sniffed petulantly. He did not deserve so faithful a consort. Her old dislike for him had grown into a positive loathing over the years. He was a brute, and when she thought about the bruises and the welts she had so often glimpsed on madame's body, she could wish him at the bottom of that channel he crossed so often. Truly, he bore a charmed life, for though his missions were often dangerous he always returned unscathed. She herself could wish that madame were like some of the other ladies mentioned in the servant's hall, those whose visits to apothecary's shops on certain secluded streets, resulted in speedy illnesses and even speedier deaths for husbands they found too cruel or too elderly, and monsieur the earl was both.

A tap at the door roused her from her reveries and brought her to her feet, but before she could open it, Madame de Coligny resplendent in purple brocade, heavily stitched with gold and silver after the Spanish fashion, sailed in, pausing in the center of the room to stare at madame in consternation.

"My dear, you're not ready and the coach below! If we do not hurry, we'll be more than an hour getting through the streets."

Josette bounced forward officiously. "Madame's ready!" she declared. "She needs only her cloak, which I shall fetch."

Blanche blinked up from her pages and smiled at Josette, "Yes, I am quite ready, Esther, but, oh, I wish I didn't need to go. I'm so close to the conclusion—Rupert's about to be released from prison."

"Rupert?—" Esther questioned. "Is that your hero's name?"

Blanche flushed, "Yes. Oh, I can hardly wait to have you read it. I do hope you will like it."

"I must say I am curious about this manuscript. You've kept it such a secret. However, I am sure I shall like it. I always like your writing, my love."

"But this is different," Blanche breathed. "It's so much longer than anything else I've ever tried. If—it is—worthy, perhaps I—could be like Mademoiselle de Scudéry and earn my living by my pen."

"Humph," Esther scowled, "it's always been a mystery to me how that silly woman gained such a large following. Her excessive sentimentality makes me ill. I hope she's not been your inspiration."

"No," Blanche looked down, "I've written of—what I know—I—" she rose as Josette came forward with her cloak but looked at her manuscript regretfully. "Might I not send a message saying I was suddenly stricken?"

"No, you may not," Esther reproved. "It would be most discourteous to His Majesty and to his mother, since it was the queen, herself, who sent you the invitation."

Blanche gave her a slightly exasperated look, but dutifully put her manuscript on the table near her bed. "Perhaps we won't need to stay too long," she said, "I am so very near the end. I—I think I might finish it in another hour."

"We'll see," Esther told her.

After the ladies had quitted the room, Josette sank down at madame's dressing table, and lifting the golden mirror, she held it to her own pert little face, "I wish I were wearing all those fine clothes," she whispered to herself. "I shouldn't want to write, even if I could. I should dance and dance—imagine being invited by the queen!"

Esther, bracing herself against the jolting of the lumbering coach, was thinking much the same thing. Raising her voice so that she might be heard above the curses of the coachman and the running footmen, as well as the clatter of the horses' hooves as they smote the cobblestones, she said, "You should, indeed you must dance, my dear, even if you're not in the mood. Remember, you're there to celebrate the king's forthcoming marriage."

"To my mind that's scant reason for a celebration," Blanche said caustically. "Especially since we all know the decision was forced upon him, and poor little Marie de Mancini, who he really loves, was sent into exile as if she were a criminal."

"It's a pity he could not marry whom he chose, my

dear, but there was the Spanish treaty to be concluded. France had far the best of that."

"Glenmore explained the whole to me," Blanche nodded wearily. "To my mind, treaties should not be negotiated in a marriage bed. I feel sorry for the poor Infanta."

"She might be happy enough," Esther shrugged. "She'll have a handsome husband."

"Who does not love her, does not want her. May God have mercy on him and her, too." Blanche relapsed into a brooding silence.

It was not difficult for Esther to guess her thoughts. Obviously she was comparing the king's marriage to her own. It was a similar situation, even to the lost lover. His name had been Rupert, and though she never spoke of him, she must still love him, for she had named the hero of her book after him. Furthermore, Lady Carlisle had told her that Father Etienne bore a striking resemblance to him. Poor, poor child. In Esther's opinion, hers was the greater tragedy. At least both partners in the royal contract were young, the Infanta thirteen and Louis XIV nearing twenty-two. Though it was not uncommon to thrust a virgin into the bed of a lecher over forty years her senior, it did not make the practice any more tolerable.

Glenmore's constant and excessive demands on his young wife had blighted her youth, and his frequent bouts of unreasoning jealousy had kept her almost as solitary as some Turkish odalisque. It was an unnatural existence for a young girl, but happily, it was an ideal one for a writer, and Blanche was never more content than when she was at her desk in the library or wandering about the bookstalls on the Pont Neuf.

She did not seem to mourn her lack of friends her own age, "They're all so boring," she had told Esther more than once. "I hate it when I am forced to be with them. They talk only of stuffs for gowns or sigh over some lover they've lost or won. I much prefer to be with you."

Esther smiled to herself. She could not be fonder of Blanche, even if she had been her own daughter, which, in truth, was how she regarded her. Still, she was young and needed to be with people her own age. It was a pity she knew no young men. There would be no harm in a friendship or two, nearly every married woman had some cavalier-servant to help her dress, advise her where to put her patches or a new ribbon. It was all quite harmless, just a game. Suddenly, she was reminded of the Vicomte Saint Amaury, whom she had seen at mass the other morning, on several other mornings, actually. There was a man who longed to be a cavalier-servant. She wondered if Blanche had ever noticed him. She rarely looked up from her prayer book, but perhaps that was just as well, especially if the earl were accompanying her, his suspicious were so easily aroused!

It was a terrible situation and she saw no chance of its improving, for much as she hated the earl, she understood him. There had been no child, and of late she had had the impression that his sexual prowess must be waning, for several times she had seen him come slamming out of Blanche's apartments in a rage, to be vented later on the back of some luckless lackey or a horse. Even more significant was his behavior toward his wife. He no longer tried to cajole her. His attitude was one of sullen anger and blame. He was, Esther searched for a simile, like a man who had brought home an alchemist's treasure only to see it turn to dross. However, in this particular instance, he had played the alchemist and won his disappointment fairly.

In her corner, Blanche was looking out on a terrain patchily illumined by link boys carrying lanterns and by a few flickering streetlights. The moon was not only full, it was huge, and as they passed over the bridge that spanned the Seine, she glimpsed its rippled reflection in the inky waters of the river. The sight reminded her fleetingly of another watery vision, herself and Rupert. She wondered where he might be, still with the king, probably. Did that mean he was in Breda now, awaiting word from Parliament? Glenmore, she knew, was there. Would they see each other? It hardly mattered, now. Rupert must have forgotten her years ago. He . . .

Esther touched her on the arm, "My dear," she said, "we've arrived."

Surprised, she looked out of the coach window to find they were at the main gates of the Louvre. A footman was opening the coach door, steps were being placed before her, and she descended, looking up at the great palace in surprise. She had never seen the building so brilliantly lighted. Directly in front of them, the double row of the king's musketeers were wearing new uniforms with shining brass buttons, while vividly colored, curling plumes replaced the bedraggled feathers she was used to seeing. Ducal carriages were rolling directly into the courtyard, but a mere countess did not enjoy this privilege. Holding her silken skirts well above the filthy pavements, she and Esther, accompanied by two young footmen to take them through the throngs, came into an entrance hall, almost as crowded as it had been outside. It was several minutes before they could approach the grand staircase which on this night was a mass of brilliant colors, of brocades, silks, and satins, of diamonds that imprismed the light of the candles in the great crystal chandeliers, of sapphires, rubies, emeralds, and huge, milky pearls.

It seemed to Blanche that everyone was talking at once. The noise was deafening, and the idea of joining the vast assembly was daunting. However, there was no way of avoiding it. Resignedly, she started up the stairs and was agreeably surprised to find the path before her almost clear.

Following her, Esther watched with some amusement as the men and some of the women paused in their upward climb to look at Blanche with undisguised admiration. Of course, most of the women were more envious than admiring. She could not blame them. The French ladies were well enough, some quite beautiful, but there was no denying that they were small and even squatty, while tall, slim Blanche stood out among them like a lily in a mass of marigolds.

She herself had suggested Blanche wear white and gold, but it was the girl who had chosen to restrict her jewelry to a single diamond on a thin gold chain. Though Esther knew Blanche felt uncomfortable in the massive necklaces the earl had bought her, her choice amounted to a stroke of genius since it drew attention to the wearer not the jewels.

Finally they had reached the head of the stairs, and as they started down the corridor toward the ballroom their way was suddenly blocked by a tall, young man. Somewhat to her dismay, Esther recognized the Vicomte Saint Amaury, resplendent in white velvet trimmed with golden lace, which almost matched his shoulder-length locks. He made a low bow to Esther, but kept his eyes on Blanche.

"Ah, Madame Glenmore, I little thought you'd be present tonight, but perhaps I am dreaming. Perhaps, you are only a vision?" He pressed her hand to his lips and then shook his head, "No, you are real!"

Since he had spoken loudly, in an effort to surmount the chatter in the hall, his speech was more a public announcement than a confidence. Much to Blanche's confusion, a number of that public stopped and laughed.

"But she is beautiful! Who is she?" she heard a man near her ask.

"Don't you know, mon cherie?" the woman beside him asked. "The little English . . . whose husband keeps her under lock and key. How did she slip her chain, I wonder?"

"She looks quite frightened," another woman drawled. "I hear he beats her."

"Oh, it's true. She has no spirit left at all."

Blanche was furious. How dared they talk as if she were a poor dab of a thing. She would show them she had spirit aplenty. Turning to the vicomte, she sank down in a graceful curtsy and with a dazzling smile she rose and trilled, "Good evening Monsieur Saint Amaury. Surely you are too extravagant." A trifle defiantly, she took his proferred arm.

He flushed with pleasure. "The truth, my dear comtesse is never—extravagant."

The ballroom of the Louvre was vast and magnificently decorated for the occasion. Great baskets of roses were set on either side of the floor; candles blazed from the walls and in the elaborate, crystal chandeliers. The king was on the floor, leading the first dance. His partner was his cousin Henriette, youngest daughter of Queen Henriette Marie. Blanche who knew her slightly, thought she looked particularly beautiful in a light blue gown that matched her eyes. With her fair coloring, she was a perfect foil for the darkly handsome Louis, dazzling in cloth of gold. He was a marvelously graceful dancer and, in spite of his recent disappointment, she thought he seemed happy enough, until, as he turned in her direction, she glimpsed his cold and stony eyes.

She caught a flash of scarlet against the far wall and recognized Cardinal Mazarin. He was smiling genially, but in common with the king, the exprssion was limited to his mouth alone. Looking into his narrow, watchful eyes, she shivered slightly. She had always thought him sinister.

Quite as if she had read her thoughts, Esther suddenly remarked, "Ah, there's the cardinal. He looks like the cat who ate the canary. Yet, I wonder if he's as complacent as he seems. He did well in Spain, but he might have made a diplomatic error in regards to Charles."

"Charles? Your king?" the vicomte said quickly. "One hears he may regain his throne."

"It looks hopeful," Esther replied. "The earl of Glenmore's in Breda with His Majesty, awaiting word from Parliament."

"What do you think, madame?" he smiled at Blanche.

"I'll believe it when it happens," she replied.

"That's not very optimistic." he commented.

"There've been so many rumors regarding his restoration," she shrugged, "one learns to temper hope with caution."

He raised his eyebrows, "You're very young to be a cynic, madame. But we're not here to settle the affairs of England. The next dance is about to begin—might one hope that you will join it?"

She hesitated. "I ought to pay my respects to the queen," she said, looking towards the balcony where Anne of Austria generally sat to watch the dancing. She was there with her sister-in-law Queen Henrietta Marie.

"You're frowning. What's amiss?" the viscomte demanded.

"Nothing," she murmured. Since the Father Etienne debacle, she had never felt quite comfortable with Her Majesty.

"There are many people waiting," he said. "You'll not be able to approach her."

"Perhaps not," she agreed.

"Come." He guided her down the steps onto the floor. The music of the violins was in her ears and in her feet as well. Smiling, she surrendered to its rhythms.

Esther had been sitting at the side of the ballroom for over an hour, and it was warm and growing warmer, by reason of the crowds and the numerous candles. She made no move to join some of the other ladies who had migrated to the cooler corridors. She preferred to watch the unusual spectacle of Blanche dancing and looking as if she were enjoying herself. She was no longer dancing with the vicomte. As soon as she had stepped upon the floor, she had been surrounded by other eager young men, and at present she was going through the patterns of a saraband with Monsieur, the king's younger brother.

A movement beside Esther caused her to glance in that direction. The vicomte had joined her. Looking at his face, she found it unexpectedly grim. However, on meeting her eyes, he bowed and said politely, "I've not seen you dancing, Madame de Coligny."

She laughed, "Nor will you, Monsieur. My dancing days have been over these twenty years or more."

"Come, I'll not believe that. Would you not care to tread a measure with me?"

"It's gracious of you to offer, but I thank you, no." She was not sure if he had heard her refusal. He was glowering at Monsieur. She suppressed a smile. It was too ridiculous for him to be jealous of Philippe d'Orléans whose interest in women lay no deeper than their gowns, which he too liked to wear. Indeed, there was much that was womanish in his present costume, with its abundance of ribbons, bows, rosettes, and jewels. Certainly there must be some other reason for Saint Amaury's ill humor. Then, she saw the way in which his gaze softened when it fell on Blanche. He might well be half in love with her and, she suspected, it might be a new experience for him.

She shook her head, feeling sorry for him, or should her pity be reserved for Blanche. It was unfair that her vibrant youth must be spent in the company of Glenmore. It was a pity that she could not take the vicomte for her lover, but even if she were so-minded, she would be courting certain death and so would he. She gave him a commiserating glance only to find that the music having ended, he had started across the floor. Others, she recognized the Chevalier de Sainte Croix and the Baron de Bonneville, as well as one or two whose faces were familiar but whose names she had forgotten—were also bound in the direction of Blanche and Monsieur.

With some little satisfaction, she saw that the vicomte had reached the couple first, then the other young men arrived to form a knot around them, hiding Blanche from her gaze. She saw monsieur disengage himself with another graceful bow and then the music for a pavane began, but Blanche and the vicomte did not take their places for it. Instead, somewhat to her dismay, she saw him escorting her from the ballroom.

It had been warm, dreadfully warm, in the overcrowded room, and she felt dizzy. Without the vicomte's supporting arm, she thought she would have fallen. Near the end of a long corridor, he drew her into an alcove to one of the tall windows, and pushing it open, he said, "Take a deep breath."

She obeyed, saying gratefully, "Oh, that's better. I thought I might faint."

"You shouldn't have danced if you were feeling the heat." he said sternly.

"How could I have refused the king's brother?" she demanded.

"Were you thinking it was a royal command, his asking you?" he smiled. "It was merely a courtesy to the most beautiful woman in the room."

She laughed, "You exaggerate, monsieur."

"I assure you that I don't, but I tell you, you needn't have danced with Monsieur. For him, the making of the gesture would have been enough."

"I wish I'd known that," she said ruefully.

"If you were to mingle in society more often, you would, madame. Can one hope that you have finally come forth from your hermitage—and left your books and pens behind you?"

"No," she said seriously, "writing's my greatest pleasure, and reading comes next."

"But sure you should allocate some time for—other pursuits."

"But I do," she answered. "I ride, I walk—"

"And you attend mass," he finished. "But unless madame's husband is in the city, we rarely see her at court or the theater. You lead a very virtuous existence, but perhaps madame does not know that it is no longer counted a virtue for a lady to remain virtuous after marriage?"

She tensed, looking at him warily. The moonlight, pouring through the windows threw his features into shadow, but it was mirrored in his eyes, and even though their expression was unreadable, she felt threatened. She said coolly, "You speak in generalities Monsieur de Saint Amaury. I live by specifics."

He laughed, "Bravo, madame, a good answer and a cautious one, but I cannot believe you mean it."

"I assure you that I do," she replied. Stepping away from the window, she added, "I find myself feeling much refreshed. I must rejoin Esther. She'll wonder where I am."

"Not yet." His arm shot out, pressing against the opposite wall, barring her way. "Please, you must not go, yet."

With a touch of anger, she said, "I may not go while your arm remains in my way. I beg that you will let me pass, Monsieur de Saint Amaury."

"In a moment, but first let me look at you. It's seldom I've had the chance to be so near you. Have you any notion of how beautiful you are? It's the face of a goddess or—an enchantress."

She clicked her tongue impatiently, wondering why she had been foolish enough to let him bring her to this remote part of the palace. For the first time, she realized that the voices of the guests as well as the music from the ballroom were muted. Forcing a laugh, she said, "I've told you that you are prone to exaggeration, vicomte."

"But I do not exaggerate," he contradicted earnestly. "You have a loveliness to dream of—"

"Dream of me, if you choose," she said lightly, "but meanwhile, let me pass." She made another effort to leave, only to find herself imprisoned between both of his arms, one on either side of her, pressing down on her shoulders.

"So beautiful and so untouchable," he murmured, "but with a body that was made for loving."

"If you are prepared to make love to me, vicomte, I pray you will not," she said tartly. "I do not want it."

Laughter edged his tones, "How may you refuse what you've not experienced, my treasure?"

She expelled a short annoyed breath, "I've no desire to experience it, but surely there are many other ladies at this ball who would be only too glad to take my place. I suggest you seek them out."

"I am satisfied with the lovely bird at hand, more than satisfied. I am at your feet, my angel." He moved closer to her and she, shrinking away, felt the chill, restraining wall against her back.

Abandoning all pretense of politeness, she said angrily. "Go! I am not in the least—" her words were lost as, bringing both arms around her, he kissed her so roughly that her lips felt bruised. She struggled to free herself but he was holding her too tightly. She could do nothing but wait until his fervor had passed.

Finally, he released her, murmuring softly, "My dearest—my beautiful, if you knew how much I have longed to—"

His tight grip had relaxed enough for her to move her arms. Quickly she raised both hands and with the added strength of fury, she shoved him back. Caught off guard, he fell heavily against the windows which gave way behind him swinging wide, while he, overbalancing, seemed in immediate danger of falling to his death. With a gasp of sheer horror, she grabbed at his coat, pulling him against her with a force that toppled them both to the floor, clutched tightly in each other's arms.

For a moment, neither could speak, then, much to her chagrin, she burst into tears, "I—I might have k—killed you," she wailed accusingly.

"But you did not," he answered in a shaken voice and released her gently, "Instead, my dear, you saved a life I almost deserved to lose."

"I didn't mean—I'd no intention of—of" she gasped.

"Killing me? No, I am sure you did not. You were only defending the honor I should have respected." He spoke soberly, even somberly. "My dear you must not cry." He smoothed her hair gently back from her forehead and, cupping her chin in a hand that still shook slightly, looked down into her moon-illumined face with a rueful yet tender smile. "Please forgive me. I am so used to the pretense and dissimulation of those women who teasingly forbid those very intimacies they covet, that it becomes very difficult to recognize the truth, even when it is presented so earnestly. Come, my dearest, say you will forgive me."

Choking back her tears, she nodded, "I will. Are—are you sure you're not hurt."

He shook his head, "Only my self-esteem. Why did I fail to understand that you were not like the others? Maybe I did not wish to understand. You seemed so different tonight, so much gayer than usual. I thought—perhaps I hoped that your very coldness had been pretended. I've watched you in mass. Sometimes it has seemed to me that you were aware of my watching and were deliberately enticing me, but now, I think that's not true."

"It's not!" she cried indignantly.

He looked at her thoughtfully, "You are, I believe, afraid of me—of any man. What has made you so frightened? Or must I ask who? You see, my dear, I am beginning to know you." He hesitated, then added tentatively, "I have a favor to ask of you. Will you listen?"

"Yes," she answered in a low voice.

"If we're not to be lovers, mightn't we be friends?" He was looking at her very intently.

"Yes, I—I should like that—" she paused, remembering that she had said something like that to someone years ago. "I should like that above—above all things," she whispered, and she was conscious of a strange yearning toward him. He was still very close to her. If she were to move even an inch, she would be touching him. She longed to touch him because in reaching out to him, she would also be reaching someone else—Rupert, suddenly he was Rupert, too.

"Blanche," he said, and it was Rupert speaking. They were touching, then and she was in his arms, making no effort to free herself, for they were Rupert's arms, as well; and it was Rupert's lips that were kissing her, gentle little kisses on her cheeks, her mouth, her throat, her breasts; and she was responding, locking her arms around his neck, pressing close against him, close enough to feel the beating of his heart. "Blanche, my Blanche," he murmured and then he drew back. "Not here—it must not be here. It is too dangerous. If ever we were discovered—"

"Ohhhh," she looked dazedly into a face that was not Rupert's. She shook her head. "You—you'll think me one of those women, who—who—"

"Hush," his lips brushed her cheek again, so gently. He was not Rupert, but he had been gentle."

"My love, my love," he said huskily. "I could never think of you as anything but an angel. If only we could leave now—"

"No, no, it's not possible," she said quickly.

"I know, but I must see you again. If only I could come to you later tonight—"

"No," she said, perhaps too firmly to this man who was not Rupert. She added quickly, "I—I never know when my husband's coming home and there are people in our employ who are paid to watch me."

"But we must meet," he said. "You know we must."

Confusedly, she nodded. "Yes, we must," she echoed.

He kissed her again. "Tomorrow in mass I'll have thought of a way. You'll be there tomorrow, will you not?"

"Yes, I shall be," she murmured.

"Leave your prayer book on the prie-dieu you use. I'll contrive to slip a note inside. Will you?"

She wanted to say no, she wanted . . . Looking at him, she was no longer sure what she wanted. He had been so gentle and he was gentle now, as he helped her to her feet.

"My beautiful, my precious love, come I'll take you back to the ballroom."

Esther de Coligny had traversed one end of the corridor to the other looking for Blanche and now, standing near the entrance through which she and the vicomte had vanished, she was disturbed. It was not unlike Blanche to remain away from the festivities, but when she disappeared, she generally sought some place where she might dream or read. On this occasion, however, she had been accompanied by a most personable young man. Where had they been going, and why? Various answers to these questions occurred to her, and she liked none of them. Was the young woman borrowing trouble, she wondered? Given Blanche's distrust of . . . She tensed. She had seen them at the far end of the corridor. She moved toward them quickly, saying as she reached them, "My dear, Blanche, I've been looking for you this past half hour and—" she paused in consternation, staring at Blanche's gown which was not only wrinkled but smudged with dust front and back. Another glance showed her that the vicomte's white suit was in even worse condition. "My dears, what have you been doing?" she gasped.

Following her astonished gaze, they both looked down and further surprised her by simultaneously bursting into peals of laughter. The vicomte was the first to recover his poise. "We—had a most unfortunate accident. We—fell."

"Yes," Blanche said hastily, "it was my fault, I—"

"It was no one's fault," he said with a tenderness that Esther found most unsettling. There was something in the way Blanche looked at him that Esther found even more disturbing.

"I can't seem to get it off," Blanche complained. "My brushing only seems to spread the dirt." She rubbed at her skirt.

"Here, let me help you." Esther said. "Lord, Lord," she surveyed the material. "It looks as though you'd fallen into a dust heap."

"And so we must have done," the vicomte agreed. "Imagine, so many hundreds of lackeys employed here and none to wield a proper broom."

"You're right, Blanche," Esther sighed. "Brushing does make it worse. I think we'd best go home."

"I'll see you to your coach," the vicomte said. "I'll have to order mine. I'm afraid these garments are quite ruined."

Esther, looking at them, felt her heart sink. Though there words were merely commonplace, there was a tenderness in their mutual glances that made her most uneasy.

As they came into the lower hall of their house, Esther was pondering the explanation Blanche had offered in the coach. It had sounded logical enough, but it did not quite satisfy her. She believed the story of the near fall, but that she had equated him with her old playmate seemed very odd. She suspected her of dissimulation. It would be ironic indeed if in trying to defend her honor, she had lost her heart. She had it in mind to probe further. As they started up the stairs, she said, "Are you very tired, love, or might we have a little talk?"

"I—am rather tired," she said hesitantly. "My arms ache. I am beginning to ache all over, but I cannot mind that. Oh, think what might have happened if—"

"Come, you mustn't think about it any more," Esther said soothingly. "It was an accident. Certainly, that young man should not have tried to take advantage of you. It might teach him a lesson, though I very much doubt it."

"Come, you are too hard on him," Blanche defended. "He was very contrite and—" she paused suddenly, all the animation draining from her face, leaving it pale and blank. "My lord—" she said between stiff lips.

Startled, Esther looked up to see the earl standing at the head of the stairs. "My Lord Glenmore," she said, trying to sound as delighted as she was surprised. "Welcome home, we are just back from the queen's ball at the Louvre. What a pity you were too late to escort us."

He gave her a brief nod, but his cold glance lingered on Blanche. "Am I to understand that you had some manner of an unfortunate encounter, my dear?"

"It was nothing," she said hastily. "I did not look to see you back so soon, my lord. They told us nothing at the door."

"On my orders, my dear." He paused, waiting until she had joined him on the floor above, then kissing her on the cheek, he continued, "I thought to surprise you and it seems I have. Who was this injudicious young man who tried to take advantage of you, my love?"

"But it was nothing," she laughed. "Nothing at all, I assure you."

"You must let me be the judge of this—nothing," he said, "especially if your honor was involved, for it would be my honor too, and insults must not go unpunished. Come, give me his name and all the particulars. Perhaps I must settle with him before we leave."

"Before we—leave?" she faltered.

"Ah, I see I've betrayed myself and revealed part of my surprise." He glanced at Esther. "Well, so be it, I shall give you both the rest. We leave for England at the end of the week. We must be in Dover to greet His Majesty on his return."

There was a stool near Esther and she sank onto it quickly, as if her legs had suddenly become too weak to support her. "We—we have a king again?" she cried.

"We have a king again," he said triumphantly. "The new parliament received His Majesty's letters from Breda, and it has been unanimously decided that he must be recalled. He'll be landing in Dover on the twenty-fifth of May. From thence he'll travel to London, arriving at Whitehall on the twenty-ninth, his birthday. That's the plan."

"God be praised," Esther was smiling through the tears that had welled into her eyes. "Oh, I can't believe it. Such a long and weary wait! Is it really true?"

"It's really true," the earl said. "I've seen the documents. Come. Let's into the library and toast His Majesty!"

Seated in the shadowy room, Blanche cried excitedly, "The king—the king, long live King Charles." Privately, she was wondering if all the exiles would come home—her mother and her grandfather. She had a Cousin Venetia, who lived in Cologne, she remembered, a fiery-headed child she had seen but once. She dismissed her from her mind and thought of Rupert. She felt her cheeks grow warm. Rupert and the vicomte. There would be no chance to see him at mass again. Was she sorry? She was not sure. And she would be going to England at the end of the week—going to a country she scarcely knew.

In her mind's eye, she saw a tall young man with flowing bronze locks and bright golden eyes, much the shape of those that looked back at her from the mirror, she saw her father, whom she had loved more than anyone else in the whole world. They were in a huge room, not a room, a hall, and high above her hung frayed banners. She could vaguely remember him telling her that one of them had been carried at Crecy and another at Poitiers, "and I'll wear the king's colors at Preston—and we shall hang his banner there." He had pointed to an empty niche. There were fragments of other memories too: the row of beehives in the garden and her nurse, old Dame Alys, visiting each one and whispering to it.

"And why are you doing that, Dame Alys?" she heard herself demand in the piping tones of childhood.

"I am telling the bees, little Blanche, that your father's off to war. You must always tell the bees when there's an event of great importance, such as a wedding or a death, else they'll leave the hive and swarm no more."

"But there's no one to be married and there's none to die," she had said and had seen the old woman blanch.

"Bless the child," she had said softly, "I did mean—any matter that—concerns the family."

But her father had died. Had Dame Alys known beforehand? How could that be?

The sound of weeping was in her ears, and it was Audrey's distraught face that rose before her, and there were the strange, grim-looking men in their dull black suits and close-fitting, steel helmets, who had come to the hall in search of the master they had said, glaring at her mother suspiciously. It was those same men who had occupied the castle. Were they all gone then, and could she go home to that tall, stone building, which she was seeing much more clearly now, even to some of the little thrusting plants that grew in some of the crevices on its twin towers? Her wide eyes fell on her husband's face, and with a little twinge of sorrow, she knew that she would not return to Carlisle.

"You're mighty quiet, my love." he said, a quizzical

look in his eyes. "Is it possible you take no joy in your king's return?"

"On the contrary," she responded. "I take much joy in it. It's only hard for me to believe that it has finally happened. It's only when I pinch myself that I know it's no dream."

"It's no dream, I assure you," he said dryly. "All of us have worked hard for the day, but now our labors are ended—and we shall be well rewarded. At least I hope so. But I've one reward already. Can you guess what it might be, my Blanche?"

"No, I can't."

"It's one I prize above all others," he smiled. "My spying days are at an end, and once we're settled in England, we'll have a proper marriage, you and I. What do you say to that, my love? Are you as happy as myself?"

Meeting his cold, ironic stare, she barely restrained a shiver as she answered, "Yes, my lord. I am content."

"Ah," he smiled derisively, "and what man might ask for more? But I believe I heard you discussing an unfortunate encounter. Might I have the whole of that little tale, my dear?"

"It was nothing," she said hastily, with a quick look at Esther. "Only a man, I do not know his name, made a remark I was not meant to hear, but I heard it. He—he was laughing at me for being—what he called a—a would-be de Scudéry. That was all."

"Was that quite—all?" The earl impaled Esther with his steely glance.

Her heart seemed to be beating unpleasantly near her throat, but she said steadily enough, "Why yes, my lord, it was the merest trifling exchange, and he was quite undone when he learned that he'd been overheard."

"I see." he said. "Well, I am glad that it was nothing worse. I need not sharpen my sword for that." He rose. "I suggest we all retire, for we've much to do in the morning. It's my intention to close this house."

Esther felt a further throb in her throat. "You'll close the house, of course, but might I know what you intend to do as far as my services are concerned?"

"But of course, you must stay with us!" Blanche cried.

"Exactly," Glenmore told her. "That is, of course, my wish as well."

She should have been relieved, but there was something in the earl's manner which repelled and frightened her, and though she was not sure why, she felt personally menaced. It was an effort for her to manage a gratified smile. "Thank you, my lord. I shall be glad to return to my own country. I've missed it sorely."

"So have we all," he nodded, "for though I have been back and forth to England many more times than others of my countrymen in France, it's most disheartening to come as a stranger, an unwelcome stranger at that." He stretched out his hand to Blanche. "Shall we to bed, my love?"

"Yes, my lord." she murmured.

Looking at her frozen face, Esther stifled an unhappy sigh; it was such an untoward ending to what had been an exciting, a happy evening for the girl. She actually wished that she might run before them and bar the way to Blanche's chamber, but instead she could only stand and watch as, grasping his wife's arm, His Lordship ceremoniously escorted her to the second staircase.

He had dismissed Josette and, as was his habit, he was undressing Blanche, his impatient fingers pulling at the fastenings of her cloak, while she, also from habit, stood quietly, making no effort to participate in her disrobing. Yet, she was hard put not to shrink from his touch, hard put not to remember those moments with the vicomte, whom she would never see again. The cape fell to the floor. He began to caress her shoulders and kiss her breasts—then suddenly, he exclaimed, "What's this? What's all this dirt upon your gown?"

She started. She had forgotten all about the dust! "I—fell," she told him nervously.

"You—fell?" he repeated. "How did it happen, and why didn't you mention it before?"

"There was no need to mention it," she said. "I was not hurt."

"Not hurt and the whole of your dress so soiled," he demanded suspiciously. "Where did it take place, this fall?"

"In the Louvre—near the ballroom," she managed an indifferent shrug. "Why—what can it matter where it happened?"

He placed his hands on her shoulders and stared into her eyes, "You know, my dear, I do not believe you."

"Why should I lie?" she countered.

"I do not know, perhaps you'll tell me soon."

"There's nothing to tell!" she exclaimed, then she uttered a little cry of fright as seizing her gown, he tore it in two, and jerking the pieces from her body, he threw them into a corner. "Why—did—did you do that?" she gasped, frightened now. She had never seen him in such a rage.

"I do not like it," he said roughly. "If I were to see you wear it again, it would only serve to remind me of your—fall." Putting both hands around her neck, he continued, "Tell me, my dearest love, about that importunate young man I heard you mention as you and Esther came upstairs. If you do not tell me what I wish to know, I'll see that your friend and ally, Madame de Colingy, remains behind in France."

She looked at him, aghast. "You'd not be so cruel!"

"It's your cruelty'd keep her here. Tell me what happened."

Her heart was beating so heavily it seemed to her that he must hear it or feel its throbbing pulse in her throat. She was terrified, but she could not betray Saint Amaury, not even for Esther's sake. "Nothing," she cried. "N—Nothing h—happened except—except I—slipped and fell."

His fingers tightened about her neck. "You're not a good liar, my love." Suddenly, he took his hands away and grabbing her, threw her on the bed. "I'll not choke the truth from you, it would serve little purpose. There are better ways, but before I employ them, I'll give you one more chance. How did you get those marks on the back of your gown? Where were you lying with your importunate gallant?"

"I wasn't lying with anyone, I fell, I fell, I fell!" she shrieked.

"Did you, my love? I hope you did not hurt yourself too seriously in that fall, for I'd hate to inflict a double punishment."

Looking into his grim face, she read his intent and slipped quickly from the bed, running toward the door. He was after her in a second, and grabbing her, he started to pull her back. Struggling to be free of him, she fell against the table and then cried out because some pages of her manuscript had fluttered to the floor. Forgetting her peril, she started to retrieve them, only to have him thrust her roughly aside.

"What are these—love letters?" he demanded.

"No—it's mine," she said.

"Mine—what is mine? There's no mine in this house save what I choose for you to have."

"It's my writing," she cried.

He picked up the mass of paper, "Ah, yes—your writing."

"Please—give to me," she begged.

Ignoring her, he stared at it, "But how industrious, my love. There must be a hundred pages here. And so closely written, too. It must have taken months, or even years. Why have you not shared it with me?"

"It—it is not finished."

"Not finished?" he inquired softly. "I should say it is."

Looking into his eyes, she read his intent and threw

herself at him. "Give it to me," she cried. "You dare not touch it. Give it to me!"

With a thrust of his elbow, he hurled her away, "I will give it to you, if you'll give me his name."

"He's no one—no one who means anything to me."

He looked down at the manuscript, "But this does, I see. Too much, I fear, far too much I think." He began to tear the papers.

He was tearing her heart; he was tearing her soul apart. "No, please, no," she shrieked, grabbing at them. "No, no, no!"

Pushing her back, he continued to tear the pages into strips and then into tiny pieces, and she, watching with the detachment of despair, was amazed that the work on which she had spent so many, many hours, took only a few minutes to destroy. Finally, he turned to her. "You prize your lover very highly, my own," he smiled.

"I have no lover," she said in a voice from which all expression had fled.

"I do not believe you."

"I do not care what you believe," she answered. "You are nothing to me and never have been. I did not want to marry you. It was forced upon me, and I hated you for that. I've hated you every moment I've had to be with you. I've hated to look at you and to feel your touch on me."

"Doxy, jade!" he yelled, striking her across the mouth.

She hardly felt it. "I did not think I could hate you any more than I have all these years, but now I wish there were a stronger word to use. Hatred alone is not large enough to encompass what I feel." Looking into his furious eyes, she thought she read her death in them, but suddenly he began to laugh, and stripping off his garments, he threw himself upon her, pushing her to the floor. And there, among the fragmented pages of her manuscript, he straddled her.

"My love, my dearest love, I thank you," he cried

triumphantly. "Your hatred's accomplished what love has failed to do—restored my manhood to me."

Wrapped in a light cloak, Blanche stood on the deck of the packet boat that was breasting the choppy waters of the channel. They had left Calais on the nighttide, but deprived of wind, had lain becalmed for several hours. Esther and Glenmore were resting in their cabins, but she had been unable to remain below. Now, holding onto a steadying rope, she breathed in the damp, salt air gratefully, her eyes fixed on the misty distances which looked rosy in the rising sun. A sea wind whipped her hair back from her face. She loved its coolness, loved to watch it swell the sails and set the little pennants to fluttering.

The horror and the depression that had engulfed her since the night of the ball was lifting, being blown out to sea, she thought, and with it, all recollection of St. Amaury, whose embrace had recalled Rupert. She was thankful that Esther had managed to warn him away. She would not have wanted him hurt. Yet, other than that she did not regret him. Inadvertently, it had been his fault that her precious manuscript had been destroyed. Yet, even that sorrow was passing. She felt a surge of new hope, new inspiration. "He did not destroy my mind or my memory," she whispered to herself, and by her side, her right hand curled, as if it were already holding the pen she would soon wield again.

Coming out of the companionway, Glenmore saw his wife standing near the ropes and halted, unwillingly reminded of a September morning, nearly twelve years back, when a little girl had stood beside him, her golden curls wind tossed about her lovely face. He had thought of Jason and the Argonauts off to find the Golden Fleece. He had loved her then, and coveted her. Amazingly, he had won his prize, but, in common with Jason, had brought a Medea to his bed. Fortunately, she was a young one and without a protective shield of sorcery.

He smiled as he recalled the words she had hurled at him. He had wanted to strangle her, but in the end, he had mounted the wench instead, reading in her stricken eyes that his pleasure was the worst punishment of all. He would have to tell the old crone who had sold him the unguents and the potions with which he had been dosing himself that anger was, by far, the better remedy, and he could only hope that its effectiveness would last.

Coming to stand beside Blanche, he grabbed a handful of her flying curls and saw with some satisfaction, the shudder that ran through her slender body. Pulling her back against him and pressing his mouth on her neck, he nipped it so sharply that he tasted blood upon his tongue. "Did I hurt you?" he inquired with mock concern. As she remained silent, he continued, "I know you hate me, little Blanche, but that doesn't displease me. To my mind, your hatred lends you the spice that loving never could."

His words were so much gibberish in her ears. She was thinking of what she would write next, a novel or perhaps an epic poem or even a play. There would be much to inspire her in London, and there would be lovely books to buy. The first moment she had free would find her among the stalls in Creed's Lane, hard by Saint Paul's churchyard. Esther had told her about them and she would take her there. For the first time since she had heard the news of the king's return, she was excited at the prospect of being in England again, and though her husband's hands were hard against her breast, she found she could ignore the pain—for, lo, there on the far horizon rose the chalky cliffs of Dover.

Chapter Four

All the town, all the country, all the world appeared to be crowded into the narrow, sea-front street of Dover or, at least, that was how it seemed to Blanche. Most of the people, herself and Esther included, had been there for hours, awaiting the arrival of the English fleet headed by *The Naseby*, lately rechristened The *Royal Charles*. And now their patience was rewarded, for the ships were finally at anchor, and a barge bearing His Majesty was nearing the dock.

Flags were flying, banners held aloft, and every so often strains of martial music were heard only to be lost in the shouting that arose from the thousands who lined the shore and sood near Blanche upon the canopied quay, a vantage point occupied only by those who had some special influence.

Glenmore was some few feet away from them, standing near General George Monck, a man Blanche knew he could not abide. "He wears a thrice-turned coat," he had told her contemptuously. It was true. He had served Charles I, then Cromwell, but since it was his influence which had brought Charles II home again, the earl could scarce complain. With them was the Mayor of Dover, a small, fat, red-faced man, his forehead wet with perspiration. He was clutching his white staff, symbol of his office, so tighly that his knuckles had turned yellow. Near him stood a perspiring servant holding a red velvet pillow on which reposed an immense Bible covered in gem-studded leather. A subtle reminder, Blanche thought, of Charles's promise that the Anglican faith would be restored. He had been forced to make many promises. Would he keep them all? It hardly mattered now, that's what Glenmore had said, "As long as he keeps his promises to those of us who served him while he was in exile."

Glenmore, she thought contemptuously, had his eye on rich rewards, on manors and estates beyond his present holdings which, he had recently learned, were sadly ravaged by the war. He had been both surprised and angered by the news—especially since through an agent, he had leased an expensive house on London's Strand. She suspected that his resources had been more depleted than he had ever imagined, for he had done much complaining about even small expenses and was arranging now for the sale of his house in Paris, which she knew, he had once planned to keep. But it was not the time to be worrying about his losses. Not when she was watching the thrilling spectacle of Charles II returning to his kingdom!

It was thrilling and it was impossible not to be moved to tears by the sight of that approaching barge. Several men had crowded in front of her, but by standing on tiptoe, she could peer between their shoulders and glimpse the tall, dark man in the prow—the king, the king, the king—restored, his eleven lonely, anguished years of exile ended! Looking at him, she forgot her worries, forgot that she had been standing there close to five hours, that her feet ached, and that the noonday sun seemingly had borrowed its strength from the nearing month of June. Fortunately, her days in the small harbor town had helped her to become accustomed to its fetid smell, composed of refuse, human and animal excrement, tar, and stale salt water, which, combined with the body odors arising from the massed crowds about her, might well have proved overpowering. Several onlookers had already fainted, and one old man had died and been unobtrusively dragged away. She could wish she had not seen his sagging, empty face.

The barge was closer now. She could see the king more clearly—that his long, blue black hair fell into large ringlets, that his eyes were almost black under their heavy brows, that his nose was long, and that his upper lip was covered by a moustache. His skin was swarthy; he looked more foreign than English. Glenmore had said he favored his grandparents—Marie de Medicis and Henry of Navarre. He was magnificently dressed in shining white; some distance behind him was his fair young brother, James of York, in scarlet. There were other men around him, most of them young, all of them smiling and excited.

The boat was beneath the pier, a group of burly men were throwing ropes down. The people around Blanche were straining forward, she could hardly keep her balance, she was clutching Esther's arm turned rigid from excitement. Everyone was laughing and crying at the same time. She could feel tears on her own cheeks and as he mounted the steps to the dock, the cheers were deafening, loud around her, swelling to a mighty crescendo from the shore.

"LONG LIVE KING CHARLES, LONG LIVE THE KING, LONG LIVE OUR GRACIOUS KING!"

He was on the dock, under the canopy, he passed very close to her. She had an impression of bright eyes full of happiness that was close to ecstasy, darting eyes that saw everything and, amazingly, lingered for an instant on her face and were momentarily hard and searching before he, his brother, and their entourage passed by her.

It was very odd, for as she watched the mayor present his white staff and the Bible to the king, as General Monck handed him the sheathed sword symbol that England welcomed back her monarch, she felt chilled, and all her excitement had drained away. She had wanted to love the king, but instead, she felt intimidated by him, which was, she told herself sternly, utterly ridiculous and all in her imagination.

The ceremonies attendant upon his arrival were dispatched with amazing speed. Less than three hours later, surrounded by his friends and his military escort, Charles, his face flushed with pleasure, his black eyes even brighter by reason of his unshed tears, was walking toward the coach which was waiting to take him to Canterbury, where he would spend the weekend.

"Long live King Charles, long live the king," she cried, and in common with Esther and the other ladies about her, she blew him kisses, mentally upbraiding herself for her treasonous thoughts. He could not have looked at her as Glenmore so often had—with that hard, questing, desiring, disrobing glance! He was the king!

In later years, when asked to be specific about her memories on the triumphant progress of Charles II through Canterbury, where she, Esther, and Glenmore, still following in his wake, were present when His Majesty conferred the Order of the Garter on General Monck and knighted William Morice, she could not be entirely clear; nor could she give a really accurate discription of the happenings en route to Rochester from which the king had exchanged his state coach for the horse on which he rode to London. She could only recall disjointed fragments of a four-day journey which seemed compounded of noise, heat, color, and confusion.

There had been people who had run into the road just to touch his coach, just to assure themselves that it was real and not some vision sent to tantalize them. There had been a few who had railed and cursed His Majesty; one man in the rusty, black garments of a Puritan divine had fallen on his knees directly in front of the earl's horse, begging heaven to send lightning to strike the monarch dead. She would shiver remembering the earl unconcernedly riding him down, and the man pulling back half-trampled and bloodied by the stallion's hoofs. She had caught a glimpse of Charles's face once, heavy eyelids drooping, mouth turned down, exhausted by the rigors of his progress, only to beam into a smile at the touch of an aide's hand on his sleeve.

She could remember coming into London through the narrow, refuse-strewn, reeking streets where children, unmindful of the fly-covered dung, strew flowers on the road before the king's horse; and she could recall one little girl, running shyly up to him, her arms filled with roses, and how he had leaned down to lift her and set her before him on his saddle, while she cried shrilly, "You'll cwush my woses," at which he had kissed her lovingly, while all about him wept and applauded.

She could remember that there was wine instead of water in many of the city's fountains and that men were thrusting their heads beneath the flow and being drenched in its scarlet. Bright tapestries hung from the windows, and everyone wore their most vivid clothes, though there was yet a smattering of the sad colors, the grays, the purples, and the blacks favored by the Puritans. She recalled one young girl, in black with red ribbons in her yellow hair and wound around her waist, grabbing the king's booted foot and pressing her lips against its dusty sole. She had seen an old man in a garb stylish during the days of James I; such a spectacle he had been in his much-mended doublet and trunkhose, his high crowned hat tricked out with a bright green feather.

There had been jugglers and dancers and a tightrope walker performing perilously on a rope stretched tight between two houses on the way to Whitehall. There had been Gypsies, blind and crippled beggars stretching out filthy, palsied hands. There had been performing dogs, puppeteers, and peddlars selling trinkets against the pox and plague.

And over them and all about them there was London, with its narrow, cobblestone streets, winding crookedly between low, half-timber houses, most of them built a hundred years ago but looking almost new, their over-hanging stories, brightly painted, their plastered facades crisscrossed with carved oaken boards. There were tavern signs hung on rusty iron branches; she caught sight of three improbable green birds advertising The Three Pigeons; an even more unlikely fowl swung outside The Golden Cockerel. There were churches everywhere—impossible not to see and marvel at the great bulk of Saint Paul's which, though old, crumbling, and denuded of its once-magnificient spire, still rose above every other London building.

Even amidst the uproar, she was not unmindful of the stench rising from the streets, permeating the coach in which she was riding with Esther and Josette. At Esther's advice, she had brought a handkerchief saturated with musk, and she was heartily grateful for it. Though even its heady scent could not entirely combat odors from gutters heavy with the contents of slop jars, decaying garbage, and dead rats, or from the choking fumes that issued out of tannery furnaces and the chimneys of dye works. Yet, in a miraculously short time she had become used to it, for on that mad, astonishing, confusing, frightening, exhilarating day, it was impossible to concentrate on any one distraction. Everything was distracting, but wonderful too!

Towards evening, bonfires were lighted on neighboring hills, and there was singing and drunken reveling in the taverns and on the crowded streets, and she, with her companions, had come at length to an inn—The Turk's Head—and there she met the earl for a huge repast of beef pasty, gooseberry tarts, and pudding washed down with great drafts of canary wine; so that in the end she had scarcely any memory of climbing the dark, winding stairs to her bedchamber, and upon awakening in the morning was vastly surprised to find another man dead asleep across the foot of the bed she and Glenmore occupied.

* * *

Two weeks later, she was settled between Glenmore and Esther in the cushioned and canopied stern of the boat bearing them to Whitehall and the earl's impatiently-awaited audience with the king.

Stealing a look at her husband's profile, she saw that he was still looking very grim. He had been in a foul temper most of the time since they had arrived. More than once, she had heard him muttering to himself about the "ingratitude of kings." Furthermore, there had been his constant complaints about the cost of food, candles, furniture, servants, horses, and above all, houses in London, strengthening her theory that he had overspent. Meeting his hot eyes now, she hastily looked away, unwilling to let his mood spoil the excitement she felt about visiting the palace of Whitehall.

She had long wanted to see it. Her great-grandmother had been a lady-in-waiting to Queen Elizabeth. An observant woman with a ready wit, her stories still survived among the family. There were other stories about the palace. Blanche sighed, remembering that it was from a window in the dining hall that Charles I had stepped onto his scaffold and, ironically enough, it was in that same palace that his murderer Cromwell had died. An old man she had met in Saint Paul's churchyard, when she and Esther had gone hunting after books, had mentioned the great storm that had torn through London on that night. "It was the devil come for Oliver's soul," he had said solemnly.

Thinking of that old man, she shivered. Both his ears had been cropped. "One for Charles 'n' one for Ollie," he had told her, proudly producing the two broadsides that had gained him his punishments. London was a strange place, she was not sure she liked it. The streets were so dirty and so crowded that it was well-nigh impossible to force a passage through them, which was why they were going by river. Yet, it was little better.

Looking around her, she counted no less than fifteen wherries similar to their own, skimming past with loads of passengers beneath bright red, green, or yellow canopies, some with fluttering flags on either side. There were big ships too, with high prows and enough billowing sail to take them to the New World, where they might be going for all she knew, to places she had read about—such lovely, outlandish names—Jamaica, Surinam, Barbadoes. The sun, near its zenith, was reflected almost blindingly in the clear, blue surface of the river, and she was glad of the shade furnished by their canopy, even though there was a strong smell of fish about it.

Suddenly, one of the wherries passing too near sent a fine spray of water over them, causing the master, a short, plump, red-faced man, to rise and unleash a string of oaths dealing mainly with the parentage of the man piloting the other craft. These exchanges had occurred so often that not even Glenmore, who hated what he called the "insolence of the lower classes," took exception to them.

She doubted that he had even noticed the drops of water that were rolling down his face. His eyes were still fixed unseeingly on the shore. Obviously he was deeply worried, but she could not care. She was only pleased that it kept him silent. She had come to loathe the very sound of his voice.

"Oh, look," Esther, who had been eagerly scanning the horizon pointed toward the right, "there's Whitehall, my dear."

Blanche laughed, "But it's not white, it's yellow." Staring at the huge cluster of houses that went under the conglomerate name of *palace*, she shook her head, "I did not think it would be so vast."

"It is that," Esther said. "Oh, I do hope we'll not find it too much changed inside."

Glenmore, roused from his thoughts, grimaced. "It's not as it used to be, I understand. The Puritans did their best to do their worst. I've been told that they broke all the stained glass windows in the chapel and tried to scraped the Holbein frescoes off the walls."

"Oh, God," Esther raised her eyebrows, "were they thinking heaven would reward such zeal?"

"Heaven or their leaders—with extra rations and large draughts of beer," Glenmore said sarcastically. "It's a pity their names aren't known to Chancellor Hyde. He might have them drawn and quartered with the rest of the traitors come October."

"I've heard the king means to be fairly lenient in that regard," Esther said.

"Fairly," growled the earl. "Too damned fairly, I think. He'll execute only the regicides. Other turncoats, such as Monck, will be granted titles if you please."

"But if it hadn't been for Monck, Charles might be still cooling his heels in Germany," Esther reminded him.

"Someone else would have paved the way for his return. The people were of a mind to have him back, as you saw for yourself. It's not the General Moncks who should be so amply rewarded, but those who risked their lives and kept their faith in the Stuart cause, long after Monck joined Cromwell's staff."

Blanche had a moment of wondering why Charles had delayed Glenmore's audience so long. Had he an inkling that the earl's efforts on his behalf had not been entirely selfless? She bit down a mocking little smile and then turned her head quickly, fearing that from the sudden narrowing of his eyes, Glenmore might have guessed her thoughts.

Her fears were intensified as he drawled, "You seem in a fine humor, my love. Did you sleep well last night?"

She tensed. In the last few days, she had spent her nights alone, he having stated that he preferred his own chamber "to a cold wife in a warm bed." She shook her head vigorously. "It was monstrous close in there," she said. "I tossed and turned most of the night." Through her long lashes, she studied his face and was gloomily positive that he had indeed read her mind and was planning on the one retaliation he knew she would abhor the most.

Esther, on whom the import of the exchange was not lost, suppressed a sigh. She was conscious of an overwhelming urge to push Glenmore into the river. His continuous goading of the girl was not only ruining her life, it was warping her character. Hatred was an unhealthy emotion; it corroded and sometimes it corrupted. It was a pity. Under other circumstances, she could have been so happy; she was really so lovely, and on this day she looked particularly beautiful, in a gown of primrose silk, which made her hair seem all the brighter and enhanced the color of her eyes. She would be surprised if even the much-praised Lady Barbara Palmer could outshine her.

"Oh, Esther, look, the swans!" Blanche exclaimed delightedly, pointing toward the nearing quay. "Five of them and all in single file like soldiers!"

"Lovely," Esther agreed, glad that Blanche was smiling again.

Glenmore raised an interrogative eyebrow, "And what do you find so intriguing about swans, my dear?" he drawled. "Sure there are plenty of them in the Seine."

"Ah, but these are English swans!" She leaned forward impulsively to watch the progress of the stately birds.

"Come, you'll upset us," Glenmore chided as the boat rocked with her sudden movement. Pushing her back, he added, "Pray control yourself, my dear. You're not a child anymore, you know."

Esther stifled an angry protest as Blanche sank back in her seat, all the animation draining from her face. He reminded her of a cat with a mouse, letting it run free for a moment, then with a swift swipe of its paw, reminding the poor creature that it was totally in its power.

"There were swans in the lake near our home in

Dalkeith," she said to Blanche. "My brothers and I used to feed them with old bread crusts. You had to be careful of them, though, for they had bad tempers. I remember meeting one on a path nearby the river and having it rear back and hiss at me like an angry snake."

Blanche nodded. "Did it really? How unsettling," she commented in a tight little voice her eyes devoid of any interest.

Esther, clenching her teeth, abandoned any further attempt at conversation and, looking toward the shore, hoped they would arrive there quickly. However, though they were close enough to see the glistening patches of moss that coated the sides of the dock, there were a number of other boats headed in the same direction, and it seemed that they might have a long wait before their turn.

She had not counted on the combination of dexterity and rudeness that characterized their boatman. With a mixture of roars and well-placed jabs, he maneuvered their craft toward the steps, and in less than fifteen minutes they were up them and into the long, closed passageway that ended at the palace gates.

It was very stuffy inside, smelling of dampness, sweat, and urine. Furthermore, it was so crowded that Esther was momentarily daunted. "I don't see how we're going to get through," she remarked to the earl.

He gave her a cool stare. "We'll get through," he said casually, adding, "Stay close behind me." Taking Blanche's arm, he drew himself up to his full height and, with a look of studied insolence, elbowed his way through a mass of indignant but scattering people, in a manner that reminded Esther strongly of the methods employed by their boatman.

The palace proper was crowded too, with busy officials trying to force a passage through the masses of sightseers who were strolling leisurely around the small, narrow rooms. Glaring about him, Glenmore said curtly, "We'll need to go single file. If we're separated, join me in the Stone Gallery. You've been here before, Madame de Coligny, have you not?"

"Yes," she said.

"Can you find it?"

"Once I get my bearings," she replied.

"Good." He strode on ahead.

"Esther," Blanche plucked at her sleeve.

"Yes, dear?"

"Have you seen the queen's apartments? Queen Elizabeth, I mean?"

"Once or twice in the old days."

"Do you expect you could find them again? I'm told they're near the river."

"I'm not sure," Esther frowned. "This palace is a regular maze—"

"Come, let's try." Blanche's eyes were gleaming. "Mama has told me so much about them."

"Well," looking at Blanche's face, animated and happy again, she decided she could not refuse her, "we might try—and tell your husband that we lost our way, which we very well might do."

She had spoken partially in jest, but once they had traversed a number of a rooms and a network of small connecting passages, she stopped and shrugged. "I really don't know where we are, my dear."

"Come, let's go a little further," Blanche urged. "We're still near the river. Perhaps this way."

They came into a corridor, longer and wider than the others. At the far end, there was a curving staircase near a window. Looking at it, Blanche suddenly laughed and clapped her hands. "That must be the place! Mama mentioned that window and that staircase—Dudley's rooms were overhead, when he was Master of the Horse. Come." Without waiting for Esther, she picked up her skirts and sped down to the window. "Yes," she called. "There's the river and—" she pointed to a door, "there's where Her Majesty slept, I'm sure of it."

Reaching her, Esther looked about her, "Yes, this does look familiar, I believe you're right."

"I know I am. I could not be mistaken. Oh, such tales as my great-grandmother told—about secret staircases and concealing tapestries, but I'd best not repeat them here."

"No, most assuredly you should not." Esther lowered her voice. "You never know who might be about, and you mustn't forget that she was the present king's cousin and—" She suddenly gasped for the door to the queen's chamber had opened!

Framed on the threshold was a tall man dressed in a rich maroon cloth suit much bedecked with ribbons; his wide petticoat breeches were trimmed with tiers of lace. His black hair fell in thick waves over his shoulders, and his eyes, also black, were alight with mischief.

"And—what might an inadvertent eavesdropper hear about the king's august cousin Elizabeth?" he inquired softly. Moving into the hall, he came to a full stop, staring down at Blanche with unmistakable admiration. "Come, tell me my dear, for I am sure I should be much entertained."

Looking at him with horrified recognition, she took a faltering step backwards and then managed a deep, if slightly awkward curtsy. "Y—Your M—Majesty," she stuttered.

"Your Majesty," Esther echoed on a quavering breath, as she too sank down.

"Madame," he smiled at Esther, "please rise." Stepping around her, he took Blanche gently by the arms, half-lifting her to her feet. "Come, my dear, I vow you've turned white as a ghost. Or perhaps you feared me to be the ghost, coming upon you so suddenly from my cousin's chambers. I beg your pardon." Taking her hand, he carried it to his lips. "I should have given you more warning. You see, I'd gone to commune with her departed spirit—but how much more preferable to find a sprite instead."

There was laughter in his voice and a gentleness she'd not expected. "I—shouldn't have been here," she murmured. "I bade Esther—Madame de Coligny bring me here because I—I—"

"Because you too hoped to commune with a departed relative? Sure, it seems that this great-grandmother of yours would have much of interest to impart to me, as well—about concealing tapestries and secret staircases. But perhaps your knowledge will suffice. Pray tell me, what wickedness would you attribute to my virgin cousin?"

She blushed, "Oh, it was only the merest gossip, Your Majesty. I am sure that—that—" Meeting his dark glance, so close to her own, and feeling his hand still holding hers, she stuttered into silence.

His smile broadened, "No matter then, I'll not confound you further. But might one know your name, my dear?"

"I—it's—" For some reason, her tongue refused to obey her, and she felt as if her face were all on fire.

"Your Majesty," Esther stepped forward, "If I might be permitted—"

"But of course you might be permitted to reveal the name of this fair—this very fair unknown."

"Then, I shall present to Your Majesty, Blanche, Lady Marchmont, the countess of Glenmore."

"Glenmore?" he repeated with a slight frown. "You are wed to the earl of Glenmore?"

"Yes, Your Majesty," Blanche replied.

"Well," gently he released her hand and moved away, "I must make my compliments to the earl." He paused, looking at her quizzically. "Am I right in believing that he requested an audience with me today?"

"That's true, Your Majesty. He must be in the Stone Gallery even now," Blanche said.

"And left you and Madame de Coligny to find your way through this labyrinth alone?" He raised his eyebrows.

"No," she answered quickly. "I—expect he thought

we were close behind him, but I wanted to see the queen's apartments and I bade Esther show me. I ought to be with him by now. He'll be angry—" She broke off with a little gasp and twisted her hands together nervously, feeling like a fool for having blurted out an explanation that was far too long and far too informative. She knew Esther must be embarrassed at her awkwardness, and she herself was amazed at her own lack of dignity, acting like the merest child instead of a dignified married woman of six years standing.

"I see," he regarded her thoughtfully. "I'd take you back with me, but I think it better if you go alone, my dear. It will save comment in the gallery." He smiled at her. "I trust we shall meet again—and soon." Turning to Esther, he said, "Madame, do you know your way to the gallery from here?"

"Yes, Your Majesty, I do."

His eyes glinted with amusement, "You are to be congratulated, Madame de Coligny. Even I, in reacquainting myself with this palace, where I spent some years of my life, as you know, have been confused, and so I should imagine that Glenmore would not be so very angry, after all." Inclining his head slightly, he wheeled around and walked quickly down the hall, while the two women curtsyed, remaining in that position until he had disappeared around the bend.

Esther's heart was pounding, and she was swallowing air bubbles. Yet, if she had been asked, she would have had difficulty describing her reactions. Coupled with the natural awe she had felt in the presence of her king, was a trepidation which she could not explain, or perhaps she did not want to explain, but which lay in the way he had looked at Blanche, looked and touched and spoken. Getting to her feet, she turned to the girl, wondering what she might say, and saw then that she had tears in her eyes.

"My dear, what's the matter?" she asked gently.

"I—am so—ashamed," she whispered.

"Ashamed, love? Why?

"I—I said far, far too much—and to the king. He must think me moonstruck."

"I very much doubt if he thought that," she said dryly. "But—how unfortunate that we should choose this day to visit these apartments. Yet, certainly he was passing kind."

"Yes, he was very kind," Blanche murmured. "I'd not thought he would be."

Looking at her flushed cheeks, Esther was concerned anew. "I'd not refine too much on it, my love. His Majesty's known to admire many a pretty face."

Blanche looked up at her in some surprise, "That's not what I meant—I meant—"

"Meant what then, my dear?"

"He was not what I'd expected."

"Pray what had you expected, love? Some sort of ogre?"

Not wanting to confide her fleeting impression at Dover, Blanche said carefully, "He—he's different—that's all." Then meeting Esther's inquiring stare, she searched for an explanation that might satisfy her. "I thought he might be more like Louis, full of polite phrases, meaning none of them. He seems more honest—more human too."

"I am sure he's entirely human, though I am equally sure that in common with his Cousin Louis, he believes his right's divine," Esther replied, hoping that her implication would not be lost on Blanche. She added, "But we tarry here too long, we'd best be rejoining your husband, my dear."

The Stone Gallery was in another wing of Whitehall, lying the length of the old tiltyard where Queen Elizabeth had once staged jousting matches for the enjoyment and edification of foreign ambassadors and other dignitaries. Esther had seen it in the days of Charles I, when it had been more notable for his collection of fine paintings.

Quite a few of these were missing, she realized regretfully as she and Blanche came into an area even more crowded than the rest of the palace. Indeed, it was difficult to find a space to stand. Walking was accomplished only in a sort of mass, forward movement. Looking around her, she saw a few familiar faces, some so lean and gaunt and old that it was only too obvious what privations they had endured in the years of the Protectorate. However, most among the assembly were young, laughing and eager, and, she thought, curiously similar in appearance, their features stamped with that blend of wariness and ambition that signifies the would-be courtier. There were quite a few women present, most of them arrayed in magnificent gowns. Some of these dresses, however, gave evidence of having been packed away in chests for years, for the materials were creased and a closer look revealed tarnished gold threads and fraying silk. There was also a lack of the jewelry with which they had been wont to deck themselves a decade earlier, these having probably been sold, pawned, or confiscated. However, her quick eye noted some gowns which bore the unmistakable stamp of the French couturier, suggesting that there were many returned emigres.

"I cannot see Glenmore anywhere," Blanche remarked, standing on tiptoe.

"How can anyone see anything with all these people milling about. I suggest we try and make our way down to the far end, which will put us near the audience chamber. You see that red, velvet curtain? It might be that your husband's already closeted with the king."

"I hope so," Blanche said. "I hope he's not looking for us. I'm not in the mood to be scolded."

"He'd scarcely do it here," Esther soothed. "Come."

By the time they had reached their destination, Blanche was feeling very uncomfortable and not a little angry. In worming her way through the crowds, she had received a score of pinches from the men who looked at her with appraisals so frank that they seemed to strip her of her garments and leave her naked beneath their bold stares. Some of the looks she had seen in the women's eyes were equally appraising and determinedly hostile. For once in her life, she actually wanted to find Glenmore so that they might leave as soon as possible. However, he was nowhere to be seen.

"Perhaps he hasn't arrived yet?" Blanche frowned.

"I'm sure he has—" Esther began and broke off as the curtains over the doorway were swept aside by the two guards standing there. A woman, so beautiful that Esther blinked, entered. She was clad in a rich, pink gown which served to complement her masses of red-tinged hair and lend an extra touch of color to her creamy skin. Escorting her was a tall and frowning young man, who seemed to be looking through rather than at the assembly in the gallery.

As the pair paused on the threshold, conversation diminished, and a number of men bowed very low. Looking at the woman in pink, Esther was suddenly reminded of an old friend—Lord Grandison, Viscount Villiers, killed, she recalled, during the early part of the hostilities. She had his long, oval face, straight nose, and well-spaced eyes. Her full lips were a softer, more feminine version of his mouth. She swallowed a little gasp, remembering something Glenmore had told her, and she knew then that she was seeing Grandison's notorious daughter, Barbara Palmer, with whom the king was known to have passed his first night in London—and many other nights as well. The man beside her was undoubtedly her husband Roger. Esther felt sorry for him. No doubt that cold and distant glance had been carefully cultivated.

She breathed a deep sigh of relief and was inclined to laugh at fears which, she could now admit, had centered around Blanche's possible attraction for His amorous Majesty. Beautiful as she was, her defensive coldness would hardly intrigue a man as passionate as the king, not when he haw a vibrant creature like Barbara Palmer to share his bed. That she had already established a considerable ascendancy over him was proved by the deference with which she was greeted as she and Palmer moved through the room. They, at least, had no difficulty finding a space to walk. People actually fell over themselves trying to clear a way for them.

"Who is she?" Blanche demanded.

"Her name's Barbara Palmer, my love—" Esther began and hesitated, wondering if she would complete the identification.

"Oh," Blanche said in a low voice, "the king's mistress."

Esther started, "Where did you hear about that, my dear?"

"Glenmore told me," Blanche watched the pair. "He met her in Holland. He doesn't like her. He said she gave herself the airs of a queen in Breda. I expect she snubbed him. She is beautiful, isn't she?"

"Very," Esther agreed. "She comes of a good-looking family. Her father, Grandison, was a most handsome young man and—" she came to a sudden stop as Glenmore stepped through the portals behind them.

As his eyes fell on Blanche, they narrowed, and his lips twitched into a grim little smile, an expression Esther found unsettling, but it was gone almost instantly. Putting a hand lightly on his wife's shoulder, he said affably enough, "Ah, here you are, my dear. Did you lose your way, then?"

"Yes, we did," Blanche said. "We took a wrong turning. "We'd gone some distance before we knew it." She scanned his face a trifle apprehensively, wondering if her explanation had been given too quickly and too glibly.

She felt easier when he replied, "I've always thought it very difficult to find my way around. Yet, had you joined me sooner, I should have been able to present you to His Majesty."

She flushed, but managed to inject some regret into

her tone as she asked, "You've already seen him, then?"

"Yes," the earl replied, "there were others before me, but His Majesty was pleased to grant me special preference. His memory must be longer than I'd imagined."

"He has reason to be grateful to you," Esther said.

He looked at her for a moment before answering, "Yes, that's very true, Madame de Coligny, but my years in the service of two kings have taught me that gratitude's a debt that usually goes unpaid. However, I might have underestimated His Majesty. Though there's been no agreement—" He broke off, his eyes on a point across the room. "Ah, I see the Palmer woman and—she sees me." He smiled maliciously.

Following his glance, Esther saw that Barbara Palmer was indeed looking at Glenmore, and with an expression of puzzled resentment which actually seemed to be visited upon the three of them, but that, she decided, might be all in her imagination. She said, "She does seem a little out of countenance."

"She's unaccustomed to dismissals," he remarked ambiguously. He smiled at Blanche, "Come, my dear, it's time we were leaving." Offering her his arm, and with Esther at his other side, he moved ahead with an icy determination which brought them to the far entrance almost as quickly as Mrs. Palmer. She was still there as they passed, and Esther, who was nearest to her, observed another glance so full of virulent anger that she was amazed and shaken, wondering what might have passed between the lady and Glenmore, until she saw that the Palmer's eyes were bent on Blanche. On catching Esther's glance, the favorite tossed her head and turned away laughing.

The exchange had taken scarcely more than a second, but it left Esther full of questions, and with them was an amorphous sense of unease. She was intensely glad when they had regained their barge, and as the boatman started rowing, she hoped it would be a long time before they were required to return.

Yet hard upon this thought, the earl turned to Blanche, who was sitting quietly in her corner looking into the water, and said, "You seem pensive my dear. Are you sorry that you did not meet His Majesty? No matter, you'll have your opportunity tomorrow night."

"Tomorrow night?" she repeated, looking startled.

"We—the two of us are bidden to a supper and a frolic at the palace."

"A—supper and a—frolic. What might a frolic be?" she demanded.

"I've no notion of what it might entail, my love. There will be dancing, I am sure, but it's less formal than a ball. Still, I think it might be most enjoyable, and certainly it's an honor to join the king at supper." He looked over Blanche's head toward Esther. "Do you not agree, Madame de Coligny?"

Her heart was beating unaccountably fast, and she was swallowing air bubbles again, and again she had no explanation for her very real distress. Through stiff lips, she managed to say, "Who would not agree, my lord."

Chapter Five

Laughter ebbed and flowed around Blanche. She was seated at a long table headed by the king, headed by the king with Barbara Palmer beside him in a magnificent gown of golden satin cut so low that most of her bosom was exposed and the rest visible every time she leaned toward His Majesty, which, Blanche observed, was very often. She seemed in wonderful spirits that night and the king appeared to have eyes for no one else, though when the earl had led Blanche up to him earlier in the evening, he had given her a warm smile of admiration but not, much to her relief, of recognition. He had addressed a few polite phrases to her and to Glenmore, then, at the earl's prompting, they had drifted away.

Supper had followed fast upon their arrival, and they had been seated at table for close on three hours, being served course after course of fish, fowl, rich succulent meats, and fancy pasties to be washed down with quantities of wine.

Though there was more food coming—some admirable confections, quivering puddings, and great cakes, one in the shape of a crown with glacé fruits in the place of jewels—the diners were less enthusiastic than they had been earlier. Fingers were being washed in silver ewers, and forks were laid on plates that were being resolutely pushed away. The young man beside her, who had devoured a prodigious amount of pasty, was belching loudly and just as a disagreeable stench smote her nostril, the man on her other side laughed loudly, "Odd's blood, Harry, your strong foul wind could blow a ship to France."

Though this jest was among the lesser crudities of the evening, she blushed and quickly raised her napkin to her face for fear they might see it and hold her up to scorn. She felt extremely ill at ease in the gay assembly. All of them appeared to know each other very well, and she had the definite impression that a stranger such as herself was not welcome. If she had been able to join in the banter that was being flung back and forth across the table it might have been different, but she was not sure. They seemed mainly interested in topping each other's sallies, and some of these were so witty that she had the impression they had been coined at home and memorized for the occasion.

Not for the first time, she wondered why she and the earl had been invited. He was seated four places nearer to the king than she, and each time she glanced at him, she found him looking bored and impatient. His attitude did not surprise her, considering that he had very little interest in conversation for its own sake, and, having been absent from the king's household in Germany, he was no more acquainted with the people at the table than herself. Yet, certainly he had been eager to go and eager for them both to appear at their best.

He was richly dressed in black velvet, and he had insisted that she wear her newest gown, made for her just before she had left Paris, a blue shot silk which looked dark in one light and pale in another, depending how she moved. Contrary to his usual custom, he had supervised her dressing that night, making Josette nervous with his exacting demands concerning the arrangement of her hair. He had tried to insist she cover her face with the white lead so popular with court ladies, but this she had refused to do, having been warned by Ganymede that it was dangerous. Instead, her skin was whitened with crushed egg shells and heavily daubed with rouge, and she was wearing patches, which he had placed as expertly as if he had been one of the gilded young beaux, whose special prerogative it was.

She drew a short, frustrated breath. If he had allowed her the company of those young beaux, perhaps she would not feel so awkward now. The women who were present, she had counted five, seemed to enjoy an easy camaraderie with the men. They were just as witty and they flirted charmingly. Watching them, she felt sadly dull and, for once, it did not help to know that she could write poetry and prose as well as any man and could also read *Ovid* in the original Greek as well as Caesar's *Conquest of Gaul* in Latin. Neither writing nor reading the classics were accomplishments she needed here.

Darting a glance at the man beside her, she pictured the expression which might have adorned his plump and rather foolish face, if she had launched into her latest poem or quoted from Dante. No doubt, he would think her quite mad, but she wished she might do more than listen. So many of the jests and allusions were incomprehensible to her. A man might mention only a word to set the entire table to roaring with wicked laughter. Sometimes a mere look sufficed. Rather than being thought a cipher, she laughed too, and drank more of her wine because it was cooling. However, since it was also making her dizzy, she stopped it. Then, of a sudden, just when she was thinking she did not know what she would do if they were to sit much longer, the whole company rose and moved into the courtyard.

It was much cooler outside. There was a breeze that made the torches, burning in holders along the walls, flare brighter. Torches were not really needed, she thought, looking at a huge round moon. The sound of flutes and violins was in her ears, and turning in that direction, she saw a little band of musicians seated in a corner. With them was a girl in bright, loose silks and immediately the king and Mrs. Palmer came into view, she began to dance, whirling gracefully before them.

Blanche, watching her, smiled. She was very pretty but more than that, she moved so gracefully and so freely, as if she were really enjoying herself. With a certain surprise, she realized that it had been a long time, years, since she had experienced real enjoyment or since she had felt so free. The word *waterfowl* was in her mind. He had promised to show her where the bird nested and he—Rupert—had taken her among the rushes, where they had seen the nest, and there had been mud between her toes, she recalled that too, and she recalled the egg that had broken on the cobblestones and looking up, she had seen Glenmore, watching from his horse.

"My dear."

She started and turned to face Glenmore. "Yes?" she replied. "May we go now?" and was immediately angry with herself for having posed the question. It was better when she did not voice her wishes, for then he did not have the pleasure of denying them.

Predictably, he smiled. Predictably, he raised his eyebrows and shook his head reprovingly, "Go? But the evening's just commenced, my love. It would be an insult to His Majesty to leave so soon."

"Of course, I should have thought of that," she replied, though a glance in the direction of His Majesty assured her that he was still deep in conversation with Mrs. Palmer and patently unaware of anyone around him.

"However, my dear," the earl said, "I should like you to come with me. I am sent for by Will Chiffinch, an old friend, who has also expressed a desire to meet you."

"Very well." she said dutifully.

He looked at her closely, "You are a bit out of countenance, I see. I expect that's because you know no one as yet. However, you will in time, I promise you, for we may be much at court."

She did not find the prospect enticing, especially if he were to always be at her side. It was becoming more and more difficult for her to suffer his presence with anything approaching equanimity.

The young dancer whirled into view again, and Blanche watched her enviously, wondering wistfully what it would be like to be free of all the restrictions which her rank and marriage had placed upon her.

"Come, my dear," the earl took her arm. "This way." He led her across the courtyard and into a passage.

"Where are we going?" she asked.

"My friend will be in his rooms. He never joins the king at supper. He's much too occupied for that."

It was a long walk to Chiffinch's quarters. Blanche, following the earl through a maze of connecting corridors and traversing open courtyards, was reminded of her visit to the queen's chambers. It was in much the same location, hard by the river. In fact, on passing a window, she saw the bulk of the quay outlined in the moonlight.

"Come," Glenmore said impatiently, hurrying ahead to a recessed door. It opened so swiftly to his knock that she thought the servant must have been standing directly behind it. "Come," he said again, and she thought she detected a certain nervousness in his manner, but decided she must be imagining it, for Glenmore was never nervous.

She stepped into a long, low room lighted by candles in holders only on two tables. Still, even by that dim glow she could see it was amazingly cluttered. Books and papers lay on every available tabletop; there were more books on the shelves that lined one wall, and others were piled before them on the floor. There was also a large globe of the world mounted on a wooden pedestal. "Is he a scholar, then?" she demanded, looking at the books with a greedy eye.

"No," Glenmore answered. "He's by way of being a statesman, unofficially, however. Officially, he's the king's secretary."

"Is he—" she began and closed her mouth on the question as a tall, elderly man in a dark, plain suit emerged from an inner room. She had an impression of narrow, light eyes and a face devoid of any distinguishing feature. His nose was straight, his mouth neither thick nor thin, his chin slightly receding. She had seen a hundred similar countenances in the street. He walked softly and when he spoke, his voice proved also to be soft. "My Lord Glenmore," he said with more coolness than she thought might have been expected from a friend.

The earl, however, seemed to find nothing amiss in his reception. "Ah, Will," he smiled cordially. "It's good to find you here in these pleasant lodgings. My dear," he turned to Blanche, "this is Master Chiffinch."

"Master Chiffinch," she murmured.

"My Lady Glenmore," he bowed over her hand, looking at her so searchingly that she felt uncomfortable. He must have sensed her unease, for he gave her a reassuring smile. "Please, will you not sit down?" he invited, pulling a chair forward.

"Thank you," she accepted it gratefully, aware now that the long walk to his apartments had tired her.

"Well," Glenmore was pacing around the room, "you must have a great deal of work facing you, Will—with the coronation ahead and all."

"Yes, there's a deal of preparation before me, "the secretary acknowledged. "But first there's the matter of the regicides and their accomplices."

"Most are found?" the earl said. "Are they not?"

"Not all." Chiffinch replied.

Glenmore's eyes narrowed, "Would that be part of the reason that you've sent for me?"

Chiffinch nodded, "Part of it," he said. Looking at

Blanche, he added, "Would you have some wine, my lady?"

"No, thank you," she said quickly.

"Come, my dear, do have some wine," Glenmore urged. "Master Chiffinch and I must have a little discussion and it will make your waiting more tolerable. Still, we shan't leave you alone for very long, I promise you."

She was finding his attitude odd and evasive, but she did not care to probe into it more deeply. The prospect of being alone in this lovely, book-filled room was delightful. Yet, she was defensively careful not to sound too eager, as she said, "I shan't mind being left alone here, my lord."

"But will you have wine, milady?" Chiffinch repeated.

"No, thank you, sir. "She shook her head. "I've drunk far too much already. It's a wonder I'm not more light-headed, from it."

He gave her a small, closed smile. "As you choose," he said.

She had an impression that her refusal had displeased him, but possibly she had imagined that too. She feared that her years of living with the earl had made her overly suspicious of everyone.

After the door to the inner chamber had closed on the two men, she waited a few moments and then, taking a candle from one of the tables, she eagerly stepped to the bookshelves. On bringing her light nearer the titles, excitement was added to her eagerness. Evidently Master Chiffinch was a scholar as well as an omnivorous reader, for there were works in several languages. She was familiar with Montaigne's *Essais* and Ronsard's *Les Discours* and *Elegies,* but she had not probed the German text of *Volksbuch von Dr. Faust* nor had she read Montalvo's *Amadis de Gaula.* And there was Dante's *Divine Comedy* in an English edition, Marlowe's *Tamburlaine,* Tasso's *Rinaldo* and

D'Urfey's *Astree,* which she was about to read until she saw the *Predictions* of Nostradamus, which she had always longed to find.

Sliding it out very carefully, she carried it to a table and was beginning to puzzle over its obscurely worded quatrains, when the candle flame suddenly quivered in the draught from an opening door. Startled, she looked up to find a tall man standing on the threshold.

"Well," he said softly, "here's beauty at her books. And what would you be reading, then?"

His face was in shadow, but there was the gleam of diamonds on his fingers and surely he was uncommonly tall, and his voice . . . but how could it be possible that it was he, whom she had last seen in the center of that crowded courtyard, deep in conversation with Mrs. Palmer. Yet, certainly he was very like the man who . . .

He moved further into the room and then there was no mistaking his identity as he asked, "Come, my child, have you lost your tongue?"

"N—No, your—M—Majesty," she blurted. "It's only that—"

A single stride brought him to her table, "Nor have you answered my question, yet." Bending over the book, he laughed softly, "Odds fish, it's Nostradamus, that windy old bore, whose wisdom lies mainly in his power to confound." He smiled at her. "What are you doing in Master Chiffinch's rooms, all by yourself, perusing obscure oracles?"

"I—my husband brought me here," she stammered, still amazed. "He—he's closeted with Master Chiffinch."

"And left you to your own devices?" he demanded. "That must be passing dull."

"Oh, no," she said. "You see he has so many books."

Surprise flared in his eyes, "Are you really a reader, then?"

"Oh, yes," she told him. "I love to read."

"And you can puzzle out this ancient French?" he touched the book.

"Some of it," she said.

"My compliments," he bowed. "I doubt there are many ladies at court could give me a like answer. Still if you do not want to harm those lovely eyes, it were better that you did your reading in the sun." Closing her book, he continued, "Yesterday, you came to see my cousin's rooms and went away, I think, unsatisfied. How would you like it, if I were to take you to them now?"

"I—I—" she hesitated, hardly knowing what to reply.

"Your answer can be either yes, or no." he prompted with a smile.

She stared at him dubiously. "I—yes, of—of course, I should. It would be an honor, but—"

"That honor will be mine," he said, his hand on her arm.

"But—but my husband—" she cast a look toward the other door. "Shouldn't I tell him—I mean he'll wonder where I've gone?"

"Come, my dear, we'll not be far," he said with a hint of dryness in his tone.

Looking into his shadowed eyes, she was suddenly very nervous, yet that was nonsense, she decided, remembering his kindness of the day before. With a little smile at him, she stepped into the hall.

As he had said, the queen's apartments were not far. In an amazingly short time, they had gained the corridor where she and Esther had come. She had half-expected that it would be dark, but to her surprise, there were candles glowing in sconces all along the hall. She had scarcely started down it when he, in what seemed no more than two strides, had reached the far end and was opening the door near the stairs. "Come, my dear," he urged, almost impatiently she thought.

Quickening her pace, she came into a small, well-lighted room, sparsely furnished with chairs and one fine, ebony cabinet, inlaid with ivory and silver.

"This was my cousin's receiving room," he said, "and through this door's her bedroom. Did that naughty maid-of-honor tell your mother much about it?"

She laughed a little uneasily, "I did wrong in betraying her confidences, I fear."

"Her confidences?" He laughed. "Come, my dear, it's late for me to take reprisals. How did she describe it?"

"Well, she said it was small and with only a single window opening on the river, but it was always kept shut because of draughts, the queen being susceptible to chills and fevers."

"That's true. She suffered from the toothache, too."

"Yes," she said eagerly, "My great-grandmother said she had bad teeth."

"And fetid breath, besides," he added with the suspicion of a chuckle.

"She didn't mention that," she told him, almost sternly.

"Why did you pull such a face?" he asked.

"A—face?" she faltered.

"You'll allow my illustrious cousin, chills, fever, and bad teeth, but not bad breath nor belches, because they do not become a queen?"

"Nonsense!" she exclaimed, then gasping, put her hand to her mouth. "I didn't mean—"

"Come, my dear, you did," he laughed. "Do you think I'm a tyrant, who'll pike your head because you disagree? I'm afraid you've been taught to hold royalty much too much in awe. We're very human, I assure you. Only two years ago, in fact, there died a man in this very palace who'd proved that we Stuarts were human and as vulnerable as any other soul. That's a lesson you must learn and I must not forget, my dear." The laughter had fled from his eyes, and his face was somber. Then, he shook himself and smiled at her,

" 'Methinks, I see my cousin's ghost!' Would you know what I'm quoting?"

"Seeking out Romeo that did spit his body upon a rapier's point," she finished glibly.

"Ah, I should have guessed you'd know it," he approved. "And have you ever seen it played?"

She shook her head, "It's not done in France."

"Nor here," he said. "London's a dreary place without its theaters. I shall have them back and without delay. But we were discussing my cousin's chamber and your ancient relative's memories of it. Have you more that you can mention?"

"Well, she said there was a table all bright with silver and a bed of many woods, so cunningly inlaid you'd have thought they'd grown that way."

"That's true," he agreed. "Many woods and many colors, most ingenious. Come, you must see it, but first more light. It's passing dim in there." Picking up a pair of candleholders, he handed one to her.

The bed was even more magnificent than she had imagined from the description. The woods were fitted together to form a design, and on the headboard were the letters *E.R.* entwined with a lion and unicorn in ivory and gold. She had heard that the hangings were of India silk, but these were gone, and in their place was a golden damask.

"When I was a boy, I saw that silver table," he said. "But it's disappeared. Melted down, perhaps, or taken with so much else that belonged to us."

"Oh," she breathed. "I'm sorry."

"Not I, any more. At least, I am here," he said. "There was a time when I thought I'd spend my life in castles not my own. But no more of that, I've sworn to bury that dead past." He moved away from her. "Now my dear what about those secrets your great-grandmother knew, the concealing tapestries and the stairs."

"Surely neither of those are secrets any more," she said.

"I've no knowledge of 'em," he replied.

"She told my mother that there was a little door by the fireplace."

"Over here?" he questioned, moving into the shadows. "Come show it to me."

"I'm not sure where it lies," she protested, following him. "She only saw it open once, or thought she did."

"How can you think you saw a little door?" he inquired, laughing. "Are you still intent on protecting my cousin's reputation? I tell you, it's quite futile. All your polishing will not wipe away time's tarnish. Now show me where you think that it might be?"

Holding up her candle, she walked into the corner. "It would have been here, perhaps." She touched a row of carved Tudor rosettes by the fireplace. "One of these—she said it moved."

"Put the candle on the mantel and we'll see," he said. As she obeyed, he pressed and tried to twist each rosette. "Nothing," he said finally. "Perhaps the worthy Mrs. Elizabeth Cromwell found it before us and sealed it tight."

"Perhaps my great-grandmother mistook its location," Blanche hazarded.

"I doubt it. It's a good location for a hidden door. I wonder which of her lovers used it—Dudley, Alençon—there was even mention of Raleigh." He moved to her. "What did your great-grandmother say?"

"She didn't know for sure," Blanche said, starting from her corner.

"Well, it's of no consequence, is it," he said, "which of them crept into my late cousin's bed. They're all dust and ashes. But you are flesh, and such lovely flesh, at that."

Startled, she stepped back, "Your—Your Majesty—" she breathed.

His hand was on her cheek, caressing it lightly. "Not Majesty, now—" he said.

She tried to move away, but there was nowhere to go. He was too near and she was frightened. "I—please—" she whispered.

"Please?" he laughed. "Am I to take you at your word?" His arms were tight around her and vicelike in their strength. She could not struggle, she did not dare to scream, and in a moment she could not as his lips closed on her mouth. Finally, he released her, but it was only to lift her in his arms and bear her to the bed.

"The—the queen's bed—" she gasped in horror.

He drew back the coverlet, and sitting down, set her on his knee. "Ours for the nonce," he said, kissing her neck and then her throat.

Her head was whirling. She wanted to escape him, but he was too strong and besides he was the king and she—Confusedly, she realized that his fingers were on the laces of her bodice. How easily he untied them, as easily as Josette. She wanted to laugh at that, so odd to have a king undressing her with all the practiced knowledge of a maidservant. Now her gown was loosened and gently, very gently, it was being eased off her shoulders, down her arms, about her waist. With a little gasp she saw it fall in billows to the floor. He was undoing her corselet, managing that easily too. He had put her from him and laid her gently on the bed. He was rising. She cast a quick glance at the door. She could reach it in a moment and be outside, away from him, running down the hall, but no, even as she made the first, hasty movement she knew it was too late, for she was naked.

He was holding the candle just above her head. Its flickering light was reflected in his dark eyes. There was a look in them she remembered, "D—Dover—" she said, hardly knowing that she had spoken aloud.

"Did you call me—lover?" he demanded.

"No, you—you mistake me," she protested. "I only s—said—"

He set the candle down on the table. She saw that he was discarding his clothes too. Finally, he sat down on the bed and wound a strand of her hair around his finger, then bending his head so that his dark curls were spread on her breast, he kissed one of her nipples. "I pray you'll not be coy," he murmured.

Raising his head, he blew out the candle, but not before she had seen the hard, lean length of him and knew that the hair on his chest and belly was as black and heavy as that which grew upon his head.

Torn between shame and terror, she lay stiffly, scarcely daring to breathe, but then, as he moved closer, she could not repress a little frightened cry.

"Come," his voice was full of laughter, "What's amiss my dearest?" His lips brushed her unyielding mouth and then, he drew away. "Lord, Lord, are you a statue, then? A Galatea whom I must needs unstone?"

"Oh, M—Majesty," she sobbed.

"Not M—Majesty," he corrected. "You must call me Charles or— C—Charles, if you prefer." He kissed her cheek. "But I taste the salt of tears. My dear girl, why are you weeping?"

"Please, you must let me go," she entreated. "My husband will be wondering—"

"I promise you, your husband will not give us any trouble, dearest. We're quite safe from his wrath."

"But—"

"Trust me," he said.

"It's not right that you—that I—" she protested.

"Come," there was a tiny thread of impatience running through his tone, "that's enough of playacting, love. It was mighty entertaining for a while, but I'll have the matron not the maiden now." His fingers wandered delicately over her body, so delicately, so gently that she could barely feel them, and meanwhile he was murmuring endearments, little phrases, snatches of pet names, breathed into her ear. There was something soothing in the cadences of his voice. She was beginning to breathe more easily, but then his hands were moving downwards, squeezing between her locked thighs. With a gasp, she tried to elude those exploring, stroking fingers, daring to beat against his chest.

He caught her wrists, holding them easily, then they were pressed against his body and he was bearing down on her, crushing her so that she cried out. The hard weight was swiftly lifted and he began to kiss her, gentle little kisses that ranged over her whole body, bringing with them a tingling, an absolutely delicious tingling, a sensation she had never experienced before. Tentatively, she began to return his caresses, and she no longer tried to repel his invading touch. Quivering, moaning with excitement, she arched her body against him.

"Blanche, little Blanche, golden Blanche," he murmured, and kissed her on the mouth once more.

With a little cry of pleasure, she opened it to receive his searching tongue, then, at length, she lay beneath him once again, knowing his need and eager to match it with her own. His shuddering body melded, melted into her and she, breathless and dazed by passion she had never known before, climaxed with him into ecstacy.

She awakened in the early dawn to find him close beside her, his arm across her breast. She longed to kiss him, but she did not want to rouse him yet, for she wanted to think, and in the night there had been no time for thought or reasoning or knowing either. With a little shock, she realized that she did not know him at all, other than he was the king.

Stirring, he moved against her, but he did not awaken. She looked lovingly at his sleeping face. His long, black hair was tumbled all about it. She had not noticed the strands of white in it before. He had heavy features, she thought, and his nose was too long, but still he was handsome, no, not precisely handsome, but not plain, either. She was half-sorry that she could not see his dark eyes, but she found that his lashes were very long and slightly curling at the ends. Mentally, she traced the pattern of his brows. There were lines etched into his forehead, too deep for his thirty years, and there was a downward droop to his mouth. In repose, his face was sad, and surely, she thought with a wave of pity, he had reason to be saddened. Eleven years he had been exiled, a wanderer, ignored by those who should have helped him. Even his own cousin Louis XIV had turned him away, but that was not the boy's fault, it was his mentor Mazarin. Still, how humiliating it must have been for Charles to have been ignored by France. And there had been other slights, too. Thinking about them, she wanted to weep. Poor Charles, but not poor any longer, a king, again.

A king. She who had not known what it was to love had been taught that lesson by a king! It did not seem possible that the man who lay beside her, who had held, had loved her in the night was England's ruler.

"Mine, too," she whispered to herself, moving closer to him.

He was stirring now. Smiling at her drowsily, he stretched out a hand to fondle her. "Galatea—" he murmured, drawing her against him and beginning to stroke her body gently. "My golden Galatea, not stone nor marble any more?"

"Need you ask me that, Majesty—need you, Charles?" she said, winding her arms around his neck.

Something was tickling her awake, but she did not want to be awake, she only wanted to lie with her head pillowed on her lover's chest, but the tickling persisted and at length, she sat up and gazed into his laughing eyes. "It's late," he murmured regretfully. "It's very late. You've made me oversleep, my dear."

"Oh," she began to kiss his chest. "Oh, I love you Charles, I do."

He stiffened, "Come, I pray you'll not play me false quite yet, my Galatea."

There was a harshness in his voice that startled her. "Play you—false," she repeated.

"I've no need of these assurances—"

"But—" she started to protest.

"Hush," he put light fingers to her lips. "I find you charming, never doubt it. And if you tell me you are excited, transported, born to Olympus by Zeus's winged Zephyrs, I'll believe it and be glad. But there's no need to call it loving, Blanche."

There was a heavy feeling in her chest and a throbbing her in her throat. "But Charles, I do love you," she whispered. "I—I've never said the word before."

"Nor must you say it again—to me," he stated brusquely.

"But it's true," she cried.

"Why do you love me?" he inquired.

"Because—" meeting his hard eyes, she faltered. "I—I cannot explain it—"

"Supposing it had been another member of my court took you here and possessed you, much as I? Another, my Blanche, not the king. What would you have told that gallant in the morning?"

"But—it was not like that," she said. "You were so tender and so—so true."

He sighed, "It seems I mistook you, little Galatea. You've been six years married to that man. I thought you wiser—or perhaps you are. No matter, it's time that you go home."

"Home—" she repeated. "You're sending me away?"

His eyes widened, "Did you think I meant to keep you here?" he asked incredulously.

"I did not think—"

"Or thought too much?" he sighed. "Are you afraid of Glenmore? You need not be. It's all arranged."

"Arranged?" she questioned. "How—Charles?"

He smiled derisively, "When I am not Charles, my love, I am a king with certain convenient prerogatives. Complaisant wives have often mates who match them."

She shrank back. "He knew—he knew and—and might have even brought me to you?"

Meeting her stricken eyes, he flushed. "He did not tell you, then?"

"T—Tell me? N—no—he—he told me nothing." She looked at him in horror. "You—you thought I—I knew? You thought that I was only playacting when I—Oh, God, oh, God." Turning from him she thrust her face in the pillow so he should not see her tears.

"Oh, God—" he bent over her. "Then—I think I must believe you when you say you love me. I am too used to liars, my dear. I fear I've even grown to prefer them. Deceit can entertain me, honesty does not. I am sorry that you love me, my Galatea. Sorry because I've lost the knack myself." He kissed her gently. "Come. You must dress, my Blanche."

She felt the servants' eye her when she passed them at the door, but it did not matter. Nothing mattered. She was cold—cold inside and out. She stood in the front hall, looking wearily up the curving, marble stairs, and then she started up, slowly. A door slammed somewhere, there were footsteps that she recognized, and Glenmore was at the head of the stairs watching her. She had a sense that it had all happened before, and then she remembered Paris and the ball.

She continued climbing—looking at him with stony eyes. He was smiling. That was different. He had not smiled in Paris.

She was a few steps from the top when he said with an eagerness she found revolting, "He kept you with him all the night. Will he send for you again?"

"That's not for me to answer," she said contemptuously. "You're the whoremonger. I am but the bawd."

"You—" he began furiously, lunging at her. Instinctively, she clutched the balustrade, clinging to it, trying to avoid his flailing fists, and then, she was not even sure how it had happened, he had taken a forward step and slipped. She had one look at his paling face as with a cry he fell, plunging down the whole length of the stairs to the floor below.

Frozen, she looked blankly at his body and at the stream of dark blood that was slowly seeping from his shattered head.

Chapter Six

"I am heartily glad he did not die in winter." Esther forebore to cross herself for the thought, even though she imagined that her lack of grief was impious. Indeed, she had had little time for grief, her concern having been for the seriously depressed, if not grieving, living rather than the dead. And the living, meaning the widowed Countess of Glenmore, would have been hard put to make the long journey into Worcestershire if they had been forced to travel in December rather than July.

She shuddered to think what the roads they had been traversing for the last three days would have been like in winter. They were well-nigh impassable now, and that, she thought indignantly, was due to the deplorable way in which they had been neglected during the late Protectorate and before, if she were to be fair. Indeed, they had not really been well tended since the dissolution of the monasteries more than a hundred years ago. With these hostels had gone the abbots with their concern for traveling clerics, pilgrims, and others, who like themselves were forced to journey into the country. In their place were city governments, which meant that the road repair, once so carefully overseen by monks, was left to a lot of disinterested villagers, who would rather stand and gawk at passing vehicles than dig out stones and fill in ruts.

They had passed some of these just beyond London, gaping at their crested coach, while their picks and shovels lay on the ground and about them holes so deep that to run into them was to break wheel or axle. The travelers had been fortunate. Neither of these mishaps had occured but Tom Blane, their coachman, had lost his way twice due to the lack of signposts. One had blown down in a storm, they had been told at an inn, and had never been replaced these four years past, while the other had been gone longer than anyone remembered.

Then there had been the great discomfort of the coach. Even the cushions she had had the foresight to take hardly sufficed to keep the three of them from being buffeted about. Josette, poor lamb, had sustained a bad bruise over her eye and another to her knee, while in rounding a bend some five miles back, Blanche had been thrown heavily against her corner. It would have been better for her to have gone by horseback, but her present condition precluded riding such a long distance.

Esther was heartily glad that Blanche's mother and grandfather had arrived in England earlier in the month. Their estates had been restored to them much more quickly than those of many others, and they were in residence at Carlisle. Blanche would be better off with her family. She was far too depressed to deal with the earl's tangled affairs, better to let her grandfather's lawyers handle them and salvage what they could. She wondered what the earl had done with his wealth; there was no way to find out where he had lost the bulk of it. She felt sorry for Blanche, who had been left nearly without resources, but the girl did not seem to care. She glanced at Blanche, half-drowsing in her corner.

She was very pale, and she did not look well. There were dark circles under her eyes, and she was bone thin. In her black gown and veil, she seemed the very embodiment of grief. Fortunately, Esther could tell

Audrey Carlisle that Blanche's anguish had its roots in the shock she had sustained when she had witnessed Glenmore's death on the stairs. Certainly, nothing would convince the lady that her daughter was in mourning, and she was sure that Blanche would never reveal the real cause of her depression.

Esther wished fervently that she could tell Blanche that she knew the source of her suffering, had guessed it from the earl's brusque answers on the night he had returned home without his wife. Contemptuously, she recalled his remarks about royal prerogatives. There had been no anger in his acceptance of the situation, only a gloating amusement, as if in acquiescing to the girl's debasement he had been revenged on her for his own repudiation. It was a revenge that carried with it considerable advancement for the cuckhold. She had heard that Roger Palmer might be elevated to a dukedom. Glenmore might have coveted a similar honor, but most likely he had done it for financial gain. She would never know, nor did it matter; what mattered to her was Blanche's state of mind. Her misery and shame was only too obvious for all she had said so little since her husband's death.

She had a sudden vivid image of the events following that fatal plunge. She had been further down the hall when she had heard his scream. Rushing to the head of the stairs, she had found Blanche coolly watching while the servants ran to his aid. She had said with an unsettling calm, "I believe he's dead, Esther. Have Tom and Miles take the body to his rooms, and send Diccon for the surgeon. I expect we must have the funeral soon, the weather being so warm now."

She had spoken in a cold, little voice, free from all inflection, and that coldness remained. Her mood, however, had seemed so close to abject grief that she had aroused pity in all the inns where they had stayed. Host after host had expressed sympathy for the poor young lady, such a tragic figure in her widow's weeds. She wondered what they would have thought had they been aware of the struggle she had had in getting Blanche to don that dark attire.

"I am extremely glad that he is dead," she had said candidly. "I will wear black for the funeral and no more."

What had convinced her in the end was Esther's pointing out the hazards of travel. Even highwaymen were known to respect a widow's grief. She had prayed that this flight of fancy might reinforce her arguments, and it had. Or was it merely that the girl was not in the mood to argue. She had been so listless and so lifeless of late that Esther actually feared for her health. She would have given much to know what had passed between her and her royal seducer. Had he been too cruel or, possibly, too kind. She recalled that encounter in the corridor. From the way Blanche had looked at him, she had been afraid that she had been all too taken with his undeniable charm. Was it anger or love that plagued her now?

"Esther?" Blanche said suddenly.

"Yes, my dear?" she answered quickly.

"We're drawing near it. There's the abbey." Clutching the strap, she pressed her face against the window, looking eager for the first time since they had started from London.

Leaning forward, Esther saw the shattered walls with their empty arches and the tall grass growing between the flat, crumbling stones which had once formed its floor.

"Ah, *mon dieu,*" Josette murmured, "crossing herself," *Quelle barbarie!*"

"*Mais, très ancien,*" Esther soothed, feeling sorry for the little maid, whom she suspected of having a lover in London, so regretful had she been at leaving.

Blanche, however, usually alive and sympathetic to such nuances, had no comforting words for Josette. Probably, she was not even aware that the girl had spoken. Hands tightly clasped, she continued to gaze at the passing scenery.

Watching her, Esther was considerably cheered. She had not realized how much Blanche had yearned for home. Perhaps once she was back in the region where she had spent her earliest years, she might regain her spirits. After all, she was young and at least she was freed from the restricting, the hateful, hated presence of Glenmore.

"We're approaching the forest, Esther," Blanche said. "There are the copper beeches and the oaks. I'd forgotten how great and tall they are."

"Lovely," Esther said. Actually, as they penetrated into the dense woods, she was intimidated by their darkness. The trees grew closer together, and the soil beneath them, black and clotted, looked as though the sun had never penetrated through the thick curtain of leaves to dry it after the rains. Every so often, she saw a clump of massive boulders, and at one point, she heard the gushing of a stream.

"I seem to remember that there's a waterfall a little higher in the woods," Blanche told her. "And there are all manner of deer and hare and foxes too. Look—" she pointed.

"A clump of bellflowers." Blanche's eyes gleamed. "I remember something else. Once I rode here with my father—and I made him stop and pick a great bouquet of them to take home to mama, but they withered before we arrived."

"Wild flowers always do," Esther commented.

"I seem to think that's what mama said. I think she laughed and asked him, 'Why'd you bring me all those paltry weeds, Charles and—and—" she suddenly shut her lips tight and sank back into her corner.

Esther, seeing her pale, set face, turned cold, "My dearest Blanche," she began gently. "I know you've suffered, but—" she paused at a quelling look from the girl. There was something forbidding in her expression, as though if Esther were to reveal her knowledge, it might provoke estrangement. Seeing it, she grew silent, too.

Did that mean that she could not even mention her father, Blanche wondered. Did that mean that every time she heard the very name of Charles, she would see his face behind her eyes, his sleeping face beside her, his dark hair tousled, and his lashes long against his thin cheeks and while she, all unwilling, watched, he would awaken smilingly and smilingly reach for her, pulling her close his downy chest. She could yet feel the pressure of his hand and the lean hardness of his body—and the thrust of him against her and the beautiful aftermath, when he lay exhausted in her arms. She blinked, wanting that all too persistent image to fade and leave her with the peace she needed if ever her heart were to heal.

She drew a long, shuddering breath. She had tried so hard to hate him, but her hatred and her contempt were all for her silly self, which had stubbornly refused to stop caring, stop loving, stop needing a man who could not love nor need, but only picked a pretty bloom and turned it to a weed.

She smiled mockingly. Grief had evidently given her a talent for bad verse. It was better than nothing, she thought bitterly—for she had not been able to write a line since she had come back from Whitehall. She felt Esther's questioning eyes on her and wondered how much of the truth she knew. She wished now that she had not asked her to accompany her back to Carlisle. To look at her was to remember that moment in the corridor of Whitehall. He had been kind then, and gentle. She had believed . . . She shook her head, she would not remember. Hanging on to her strap, she looked out of the window again to find they had left the woods and were turning off toward the right. There should be a corridor of chestnut trees, she thought, and then she saw them. With a little surge of excitement, she exclaimed, "We're almost to Carlisle!"

Half in anticipation, half in fear, she watched as they passed through the trees. Had it changed, she wondered. Her mother had sent her no messages regarding that, but she would have had scant opportunity to write—they had only been home a fortnight. Ahead of them should lie the gatehouse and the bridge—and there they were, the gatehouse more weathered than she remembered, but really much the same. Then they were halting and a thin man was looking at them suspiciously, then nodding, and they were through, and the hooves of the horses clanged on the stone, and a glance showed the moat, mossy at the sides and reflecting the sunlight in its dark green depths, the sunlight and the wavering shadow of the bridge. She wondered if the school of carp still dwelt in it, the golden carp which Dame Alys told her lived a hundred years. No use to try and see them, they were already over the bridge and rising before them was the archway, flanked by its twin towers, vine covered as she remembered. She remembered too the birds which used to nest among the vines. It was amazing, how very much she was able to recall about this home. She had not seen it since she was six, yet she was finding it more real than all the other places she had lived during the ensuing years.

They were in the vast courtyard, and she had glimpsed the long mullioned windows of the hall, then with a further shaking of the coach and a snorting and stamping of the tired horses, they halted near the huge scarred oaken door, fashioned from one immense tree found in the park two hundred years ago—or even more.

The steps were being placed by the coach door. Tim, one of their grooms, was opening it. She crawled out, not heeding Esther's caution to be careful, and jumped down them, looking about her excitedly. There was the well and there, the grating over the unused dungeons far below.

"Blanche—child."

She blinked and found herself clasped in her mother's tight embrace, and there was her grandfather, leaning on his staff and smiling at her. Back of them was a slim, young woman, who was staring at her curiously. She had an impression of fiery red ringlets framing a sly fox face and was startled, knowing her to be her cousin Venetia, whom she had not met for years. When she had seen her briefly in London, Audrey had not mentioned that Venetia would be with them, but that was very like her. Dutifully, she smiled and nodded.

"Cousin Venetia," she murmured.

"Cousin Blanche," the girl moved forward, smiling. "I did not think you would remember me."

"But I do." She did not altogether like her smile but forgot it, for everyone was talking at once. The words pounded into her ears. She felt she must escape them. There were too many diverse sounds around her: the hooves of the horses stamping on the stone, the rattle of the reins, the exhortations of Josette, as she shrilly supervised the unloading of the panniers containing madame, the countess's clothes. She felt a little lightheaded and at the same time, oddly detached, as if she were standing outside of herself, looking at the scene from some great distance.

"Child, you seem near collapse. Come inside," Audrey said.

Blanche, coming back from her distances, stared at her mother in surprise. There was an unfamiliar note of compassion in her voice. "I am tired. It's been a long journey," she admitted.

"And it's at an end." Audrey's hand was gentle on her hair. "Welcome home, my darling."

"Home—I am home at last," she whispered.

"You are." All at once tears stood in Audrey's eyes. "I shan't let you go again so soon, I never wanted it, you know."

"You—didn't?" she asked.

"Never," Audrey said. "Now come with me."

She suffered herself to be led into the hall. It was much as she remembered from before, the old banners hanging from the gallery and in a corner, the battered suits of armor her ancestors had worn at Agincourt, during the Wars of the Roses and on Bosworth Field. Over the mammoth, stone fireplace, smoke begrimed from four centuries of burning was the betusked muzzle of a gigantic boar, slain in the nearby forest by her great-great-grandfather. His mother had worked the tapestries that hung on the far wall. Gazing up at the vaulted ceiling with its curving, oaken beams which had been rudely carved at the orders of one Garth Carlisle, whose effigy lay in the chapel, his crusader's shield and spear at his side, his hunting dog beneath his mailed feet, she felt a sense of pride. She was no king's castoff, no bankrupt cuckold's widow. She was Blanche, a Carlisle of Carlisle.

She awakened just after sunrise the next morning and lay watching the brightening slits of sky in her tower windows, and then she glanced around the room again, admiring the oak paneling, which was the same color as her bed, with its slender, fluted posts holding up the square, carved canopy. Just across the room was the fireplace, edged round with painted, old tiles—Bibical scenes, she knew. She smiled. She was still surprised at getting such a fine room. In the old days, it had been reserved for distinguished guests. She hoped that she was not being considered in such a light. Yet, perhaps she was, since for nearly six years she had been the Countess of Glenmore.

She frowned, wishing that she could repudiate the title, but that might happen only were she able to exchange it for another. And that would never do, no matter who came courting. She had had enough of marriage and of men too. She was convinced of that. Something stirred in her mind, but determinedly she put her memories aside, silently crying out her defiance to that dark face which, like some invading incubus, appeared unsummoned to torment her.

"I'll not have it," she whispered. "Galatea's stone again. Galatea's no more. I am Blanche of Carlisle."

"And how will Blanche of Carlisle fill the years

ahead?" another prodding demon in her mind demanded.

She had the answer ready, and she gave it with a smile, "Write, write, write. I shall write and with none to stop me." She winced, as she thought of her precious manuscript, her novel, in a thousand pieces on the floor. There was a chance she could write it again, but she was not sure she wanted to. Perhaps she might try a play. She wondered if the library were still intact. She was afraid it might not have survived the depredations of the Puritans, since they had the reputation of destroying all volumes that did not dwell on godly subjects. Once thinking about it, she was moved to go and find it. She was glad it was early for there would be none to stop her, none to talk.

Slipping from her bed, she dressed hastily, and moving quietly across the room so as not to awaken Josette, who was sleeping in the dressing room, she came into the hall and impulsively started down it. Then she stopped, realizing that she was not quite sure where the library was located. It had not been one of the rooms she had visited often when she had been a child. She had been confined mainly to her nursery and to the gardens which was why the circuitous route she finally followed brought her through the garden door.

She was not disappointed by her error. The morning air was cool against her face, and as she breathed it in, she smelled roses and other scents, each lovlier than anything that she had smelled in London. Moving away from the door, she started toward the gardens and then stopped in consternation. Her memory had given her an image of three sloping terraces, bisected by a broad, stone staircase. Each landing had been marked by a large, marble urn, filled with shrubbery, and at the bottom, a stretch of patterned flower beds circling a tiered fountain. The paths between the flower beds had been flanked by clipped yew hedges, and there had been massed rosebushes near the fountain, but what confronted her now was almost total desolation. The hedges had grown high, and behind them such flowers as had survived their blighting shadow were half-hidden by encroaching weeds and wild grass. The fountain basins were broken, and the unpruned rosebushes tangled into one great thorny mass.

Tears filled her eyes, as memory once more intervened to show her those paths grown smooth again and her young parents strolling on them. She saw her father stop to pick a rose and, bowing, hand it to her pretty mother with the words that its color was not near so bright as her own tawny hair.

Her father, her father who had been a Charles. It was odd that the name did not bring her the pain that it had produced before. There was a reason for that, she knew, as she now knew herself.

"Blanche of Carlisle," she murmured once again and realized she had known a similar feeling once before. "Where and when?" Concentrating, she traced it to her last great quarrel with Glenmore. She had achieved self-knowledge then, only to lose it to her king, but she would not lose it a third time. She was resolved on that, and thus she could remember her young father—Charles, Charles, Charles. The name *did not* hurt her anymore, for it was coupled with the dear ghost who strolled among those vanished roses in the garden.

"Good morning, Cousin Blanche!"

Startled, she turned to find Lady Venetia approaching. "Good morning, cousin," she replied. "You're up early."

"Oh, yes," Venetia acknowledged with a smile, adding importantly, "I developed that dreadful habit in Cologne. Charles is such an early riser."

"Charles—the king?" Blanche questioned through stiff lips.

"Oh, indeed yes, the king." Venetia's smile was nearer a smirk. "He had all of us up at the most unearthly hours. Poor Buckingham used to try and argue with him, but to no avail. And Barbara—There were times when she looked as if she'd not slept for a week, which probably she hadn't." She laughed lightly, and fastening her narrow, green eyes on Blanche, she asked slyly, "Tell me, my dear, is she still such an eminence at court?"

"Barbara—Palmer?" Blanche inquired reluctantly, hating to mention her name.

"Of course, my love. There cannot be another Barbara in his life, although there's been a Lucy and a—" she paused, looking at Blanche closely. "Or is there something I've not been told? Is pretty Barbara put aside?" She paused again, "Dear me, cousin, you are looking very disapproving. Am I shocking you, talking that way about the king? But sure he's not altered his habits at Whitehall?"

Blanche swallowed. "I know little of his habits. I've been only twice to court."

Lady Venetia made a little moue. "Oh, I know, poor child," she said commiseratingly. "My heart quite aches for you, having to leave London so soon. Such an unfortunate accident, especially for a general, you always think they should die in battle, but he'd retired from the field, hadn't he?" Without waiting for Blanche's muttered affirmative, she rushed on. "He was quite old, I understand. I shouldn't want to marry an old man. There was one offered me when I was fifteen and papa was almost of a mind to have me take him. He was quite wealthy and my dowry sadly depleted, but I told papa, I should rather cast myself into the Rhine. We had an argument, but of course I won. I always do. And now he agrees with me that was entirely fortunate that I waited." She gave Blanche an arch look, "But will you not ask me why?"

Blanche felt almost inundated by the flow of words and besides was totally incurious, but obediently she asked, "Why?"

"Because of Yule!" Venetia said triumphantly. "My dear, the most beautiful young man and at my feet! He came late to Cologne, a few months before papa left for Rome and sent me to London to wait for Cousin

Audrey. To think that I almost missed him! Such a stir as he created among the ladies! Fat Anne Hyde was quite enamored, but he had eyes for none but me. She's well into her sixth month, you know. So foolish of her to bed with York. She was sure he'd wed her and so he might have done, if his brother'd not been recalled. I shouldn't think there'd be a chance of it, now. No doubt James will be angling for a princess. Charles is already. A friend who's still in Cologne wrote me that they'd already proposed some one of the Hanover line, but he just laughed. I'm not surprised. He found the German women dreadful frumps and sadly dull."

Blanche wanted to put both hands over her ears or, better yet, thrust her hand against her cousin's busy mouth, but of course, she could do neither. "Did he indeed?" was all she said.

"Oh, yes," Venetia nodded. "Some at court would have it, he'll bed any woman who crosses his path, but actually he's much more choosy. Furthermore, he could never twist his tongue around that barbarous language and since he dearly loves to talk—Should you like to go with me to visit a witch, cousin?"

Startled by her lightning change of subject, Blanche stared at Venetia in consternation, finding her half-laughing, half-intent. "A—a witch?" she faltered.

"Shhhhhhh," Venetia put her fingers to her lips, "not so loud. We mustn't alarm those who are likely to take fright. Are you afraid of witches?"

"No—I don't think so. I've not thought about it much. Why?"

"Because if you're not, let's go." There was an edge of excitement in Venetia's tone. "There's an old woman who can read the future, so I am told. She's not far from here either. She lives in a little stretch of woods. I can get the directions, if you're game to go."

"Is she thought to be a—real witch?" Blanche asked.

"That's what Betty says, who works in the scullery.

She read her future and much of it's come true, so she told my maid Gretchen, who whispered the whole to me. Do let's go and see her, cousin. At the very least, it would be an adventure, don't you agree?"

There was an urgency in her voice that did not escape Blanche. It was coupled with a certain hesitancy, as if Venetia were torn between curiosity and fear. She said, "I've never seen a witch."

"Nor have I, but if—if she's as wise as Betty says, perhaps she'll tell me when Yule will come to me. I've been waiting for him. He should've been here, before now. I pray nothing's delayed him on the road. It's a long ride from Yorkshire."

"He's coming all the way from Yorkshire?" Blanche asked.

Venetia grimaced, "Yes, that's where he has his estates. They were recently restored for favors rendered to the king." She shivered. "It's monstrous cold up there and far too close to the Scottish border for my fancy. I shall want to dwell in London when we're married, or if not London, proper, Chelsea or Lambeth. I'd also like to know when he means to offer for me."

"He hasn't, yet?"

"Oh, he will. He's given every indication of it. Else why would he come dashing out of the north just to see me? I expect you'll say he hasn't come yet. But he will." Venetia's tone was less confident than her words. "I would just like to know when. Will you come with me to consult Dame Alys?"

"Dame Alys!" Blanche exclaimed. "Is that the name of your witch?"

"Yes, Dame Alys Martin."

"But I know her," Blanche cried. "She used to be my nurse."

"Really?" Venetia's eyes gleamed. "I'd heard she'd served the Carlisles before the civil war. Oh, that's lovely. It's much better if you know her."

"I never knew her to be a witch."

"Perhaps she wasn't then," Venetia replied. "The devil seems to take them only when they're old."

"The devil? Nonsense!" Blanche exclaimed indignantly. "She'd have nothing to do with the devil. She's most devout."

"Well, I don't think she's a black witch," Venetia allowed. "She makes herb teas, brews medicines. I think she might make charms against the smallpox and the plague, but that's all."

"That sounds like her," Blanche smiled. "She'd a little planting of herbs in our gardens and grew others on her windowsill. Mama said she could cure a headache just by touching. Oh, I should like to see her again. I didn't think that she was still alive."

"Well then, let's go," Venetia urged. "This morning after we've supped. I'll get directions from Betty. Only you'd best not tell your mother."

"Why not?" Blanche asked. "She'd not object."

"She might," Venetia frowned. "I've heard her say she doesn't believe in witchery."

"I'm not sure that I do, either," Blanche said. "My father never did."

"There were many witches in Germany," Venetia told her. "And many executions. They burned one in Cologne. In the public square. I saw it. It made me very queasy."

"You—you saw it?" Blanche shuddered. "How could you watch such horror?"

"I was in a crowd. I couldn't get away," Venetia shrugged.

"I'd have closed my eyes then."

"Well, I did, most of the time. It didn't take long. She didn't make much noise either. I think she fainted or maybe she was strangled. They do that, if you can afford to pay the executioner."

"Please," Blanche protested faintly. "I—I'd as lief not talk about it any more."

"Oh, very well, if you're squeamish. Anyhow, let's go and see this Dame Alys. If she can really see the future, there are many things I'd like to know. Wouldn't you?"

Charles. Angrily, Blanche thrust that persistent image from her mind. "The future holds very little interest for me, but I should like to see my old nurse."

"Good," Venetia smiled. "We'll tell them we're going walking as indeed we must. It's on the north edge of the estate, some little distance into the woods." She put her hand lightly on Blanche's shoulder. "I'm so glad you're here, cousin. I've been lonely for someone my own age. And I am glad you're coming with me. Even if we learn nothing, it will be such fun!"

It was a beautiful morning, so beautiful that Blanche almost forgot their mission. It was lovely just to be walking through the English countryside again. Everywhere she looked, she found something to please her—a cloud of white butterflies over the harebells in the meadow, a robin singing in a nearby tree, a clump of daisies in the hedgerows, bright poppies here and there among the high grass. She had an urge to climb a stile and run barefoot through a field. She had an urge to climb a nearby oak, but whenever she showed the slightest tendency to dawdle, Venetia pressed her to hurry.

Her cousin walked quickly, indifferent to her surroundings. There was a tenseness about her that increased with every step. As they neared the woods, she said breathlessly, "Betty tells me that the cottage lies on the other side of a small stream. There's a wooden bridge spanning it, and we're to be careful how we walk on it because it's very shaky." Moving under the shadow of the trees, she looked about her nervously. "It—it's very dark. I—I can hardly see." She shivered. "I—I don't like the woods much."

"I don't know why," Blanche said. "They're beautiful. Listen to the birds! There must be thousands of them about."

"The—the maids say that they're h—haunted,"

Venetia told her. "They say there's a demon hunter with a pack of ghostly hounds who rides through them at midnight and if—if anyone should see him—"

"They would be very surprised," Blanche found she could actually laugh. "Come, cousin, you can't believe these silly tales. Ah, I hear a stream gushing, don't you?"

Venetia cocked her head, "Yes, I believe I do!" she replied.

They found it quickly and one at a time negotiated a swaying, sagging wooden bridge, which ended in a little clearing.

"I don't see—" Blanche began and then added in a small, shocked voice, "Yes, I do. There's the—cottage."

"I—I don't see any c—cottage," Venetia's qualms had returned.

"By that withered tree." Blanche pointed at what appeared to be a jumble of timber, but which proved on second glance to be a little hut propped against a high boulder. Several trees grew around it, no doubt providing a barrier to the winds, but their entangled branches also kept out the sunlight, leaving it in perpetual gloom.

Moving closer to Blanche, Venetia stuttered, "It—it *l—looks* like—like a witch's c—cottage."

Blanche laughed contemptuously. "If she's a witch, the devil's not housed her very well."

Venetia crossed herself. "P—please, I pray you'll not m—mention the d—devil," she begged.

"Oh, don't be silly," Blanche chided her. Moving closer to it, she was relieved to find that its bit of yard was very neat. There were flowers growing near the door, and under the skeletal branches of a withered oak lay neat rows of small, green plants. From their aromatic odors, she knew them to be herbs. A path marked by flat stones led to the door. Impulsively, Blanche ran up to it and knocking on it cried, "Dame Alys—Dame Alys!"

After a moment, a quavering old voice asked, "Who calls me?"

"It's Blanche," she answered tremulously. "Blanche from Carlisle castle."

"B—Blanche? Little Blanche?" The door was pulled open and an old woman looked out at her incredulously. "Blanche, Blanche, my baby—" she mumbled.

Blanche felt a lump in her throat. She remembered Dame Alys as a plump, bustling, rosy creature, but the woman who stood before her was sadly wasted. Her skin, seemingly grown too large for her diminished body, hung on her in great folds and, in spite of the warmth of the day, she was swathed in several tattered shawls. Blanche blinked away her threatening tears and flinging her arms around the woman, kissed her withered cheek, "Dame Alys, dearest Dame Alys," she exclaimed.

"Blanche, my sweet love, let me look at you?" Dame Alys shook her head. "Ah, but you've grown bonny, my little lass. I knew you would. You gave great promise of it, even when you were in your cradle." She hesitated, staring at her out of eyes that were singularly blue and piercing, "Beautiful but sad. You're in mourning cloth, but that's not why you weep. What's amiss, my angel?"

Startled, the girl stepped back, "N—Nothing, I—we—" She looked over her shoulder at Venetia, who still lingered far down the path. "My cousin told me you were here. She wants to consult you. I only came because I longed to see you, again."

Dame Alys raised an gnarled old hand and gently patted her cheek. "You came to see me, my own, but also you too want to know what is hidden in the storehouse of the future. I can tell you some, not all, but it will be to your advantage to hear what I have to say."

"Please," Blanche protested softly, "it was my cousin who wanted you. Let me fetch her."

"I'll speak to your cousin in good time, but I am

told to take you first. Come in." Clutching her arm firmly, Dame Alys drew her inside.

As Blanche entered, she heard a plaintive "meow," and saw a white cat streak across the dirt floor to crouch on a quilt-covered, straw pallet in the corner.

"That's all right, Grizelda," the old woman soothed. "She's wary of strangers," she explained. "Many who come here don't like cats.'

"I do," Blanche said. "I love all animals." Tears stood in her eyes as she looked around the tiny room with its meager furnishings and only a small brazier for warmth. Plants were everywhere, some in pots on the one table, others hanging from the rafters, and still more on the floor. Yet, despite its crowding and its size, it was marvelously neat and clean. The furniture was lovingly polished, and the mats that covered the floor were newly clean.

Indicating a battered bench, Dame Alys said, "Sit down child."

Obeying her nurse was a habit she could not break. She sat down, saying, "I'll tell my mother you're here. She'd give you your old room back again. I know it."

Dame Alys placed a small bowl of water in the center of the table, and making the sign of the cross over it, she closed her eyes and muttered words that Blanche could not understand. Then, looking up at her, she said gently, "This is my room and the forest is my castle."

"But you must be so cold in winter," Blanche protested, remembering Dame Alys's large, sunny room at Carlisle.

"I've charcoal to warm me. Don't fret, love. I am very well."

"They—they call you a witch. It's dangerous to—"

"Not dangerous to me," Dame Alys interrupted. "The people hereabouts are very kind. I've known most of 'em, you see, since they were in their cradles, and they know me. They know I've not harmed anyone. Besides, they prize the potions I can give them and more than that, they prize the sight."

"How did you come by the sight?" Blanche asked.

"I've had it my whole life, my mother before me. She was a Scotswoman. They say there's many that have it in the highlands. Now you must be silent, love." Pulling a stool up to the table, she sat down and stared into the water steadily. "Ahhhhhh," she breathed and still staring, began to speak in a low, monotonous voice. "Poor child, poor child, you've had great riches, but sorrow's been your portion, sorrow and very little love. There was one, I see, that early went away, but will not stay away forever. There was another, who possessed you and died, but alas, not soon enough. As for the third, a man in a high place, who knows not what he has lost. Do not fret about it, child. Do not fret, it was not to be. I see a meeting and a wedding soon, but I warn you—" she stared at Blanche almost fearfully, "I warn you that there's danger in the old made new. You must remember what I've said, but I see you'll not recall it, until its far too late." She shook her head and said regretfully, "I wanted to bring you only happiness, but I must tell what I see. I see happiness. Yes, there it is, but mixed with it—much sorrow. You must be strong, very strong. Ah, I see something else!" She smiled. "You have a gift, a great gift and you've not used it, yet. You must. You must! With it will come your heart's desire, but there's danger, too—No matter, there's always danger, always death in life. You must be strong."

As she paused, Blanche, who had been listening half-fearfully, half-sceptically, said, "You see marriage, Dame Alys, but it cannot be mine. You must be referring to my cousin's wedding. I myself shall never marry again. Not ever."

Dame Alys's withered lips twitched into a slight smile, gone almost immediately. "You'll marry, my child. And there'll be children." She stared into the water. "There's a son already."

Blanche bit down a smile. So much for prophecy! "There's not," she contradicted. "I'm barren."

"The boy is coming, the seed is sown."

"No," Blanche exclaimed, "It—it couldn't be. My husband and I, we—" she gasped and felt her face burn. "It's not true."

The old woman gave her a pitying look. "It's true enough, my love. My sources never lie." Earnestly, she added, "And I beg you, child, heed me. Your life is like a tapestry woven in golden threads and black. Either could form the larger pattern, I pray you, let it be the gold—"

There was a sharp rap on the door. Looking up quickly, Dame Alys shivered, "Ah, there's death—death begging admittance."

"No, no, it's my cousin, Lady Venetia. I'm sure of it," Blanche soothed. She rose quickly, grateful for the interruption, "I'll let her in and you'll see."

"No, bar the door! Bar the door and keep her out!" the old woman shrilled.

"Blanche—Blanche." There was anger and impatience in Venetia's tones.

"You see," Blanche told her triumphantly.

Dame Alys got slowly to her feet. "Yes," she nodded resignedly, "I see. And I am told to let her come. There's no bar nor latch that will keep death out."

Blanche, opening the door, looked into Venetia's angry eyes. "You've been a long enough time, I must say," she snapped.

Blanche flushed, "I didn't want to come," she apologized. "But Dame Alys insited and—"

"No matter," Venetia interrupted impatiently. "Will she read for me."

"I shall," Dame Alys sighed.

"I'll wait for you outside, cousin," Blanche said.

"No, no, please stay," she urged.

"Yes, do, my darling," the old woman added tremulously.

They were almost equally wary of each other, and for as little reason, Blanche thought. However, she said kindly, "As you choose," and sat down on the pallet in the corner near the white cat, absently patting its head and tickling it under the chin.

"Ah, what's that—beside you?" Venetia gasped.

"It's a cat—Grizelda," Blanche looked at Dame Alys. "She doesn't seem to be afraid of me anymore."

"She knows her friends," the old woman said.

"Ugh," Venetia shuddered. "I hate cats."

"They are God's creatures," Dame Alys said mildly.

"The devil's rather," Venetia rasped. "What can you tell me?"

"I will look and see. Please sit down."

Blanche was angered by the hardness of the pallet. It was not fair, she thought indignantly. Dame Alys had given the Carlisles good service. She had not only cared for her, but for her father before her. She deserved more comfort in her old age. She would have it too, Blanche vowed. She would see that her old nurse received a new mattress, linen, warm blankets, and such help as she might accept and still retain her pride.

Watching her as she stared into the bowl, Blanche shivered slightly. She was glad enough to have found Dame Alys, but all the same, she wished that the circumstances had been different. If only she had not yielded to Venetia's persuasions. Dame Alys had warned her that she would forget her words, but she wished she had never heard them to forget. However, it was too late for wishing when they were whirling through her head. All of them had proved daunting, but the most frightening was the thought of the child she might possibly be carrying. She ran a nervous hand through her hair. She could not be pregnant. She was barren, otherwise she would have borne Glenmore his coveted heir.

"No, no, no, that can't be true," Venetia's voice was loud and out of control.

Startled, Blanche looked up and saw her cousin glaring into the old woman's startled face.

"You're lying," Venetia accused.

Dame Alys shook her head. "My waters do not lie," she retorted. "I tell you what I see in them, that's all."

"You see lies, lies, lies!" Venetia screamed. "I'll bed with no old man. I'm to be the marchioness of Yule, I tell you." Leaping to her feet, she knocked over the table, shattering the bowl and sending the burning candle to the floor.

With a little cry of fright, Dame Alys quickly stamped out the flame. Directing a sharp look at Venetia, she said coldly, "You will be pleased to leave my house, mistress."

Venetia's green eyes narrowed. "Did you imagine, I should stay longer to listen to your lies? She ran to the door. "He'll marry me, old witch. Not all your spite will keep him from me. Yule is mine!" Head high, she strode out, slamming the door behind her.

Dame Alys, picking up the shattered pieces of her bowl, was trembling. Pushing her gently aside, Blanche retrieved the rest, and putting her arms around her, she held her close. "You mustn't be frightened," she said soothingly. "My cousin's only angry."

"It wasn't spite," Dame Alys said. "I—I told her what I saw. She—she'll be my death, I feel it." She added piteously, "I—I don't want to die, not yet."

"Nor will you," Blanche assured her gently. "Her threats are only empty words. I'll tell my mother what happened. She'll deal with her, I promise you."

Finally, she succeeded in calming the old woman, and kissing her, she gratefully left the hut. It was a pleasure to come into the open air, a pleasure to get away from Dame Alys as well, she thought ruefully. She had a horrid conviction that her visions might prove true.

"Blanche!" Venetia called to her from the clearing.

Crossing to her, Blanche said coldly, "You ought to be ashamed, the way you treated that poor woman."

"My dear, Blanche," Venetia sighed, "I pray you'll not scold me, though I know you think I deserve it. I was angry and—and besides she frightened me."

"How?'

"It—it was as if she were ill wishing me," Venetia faltered. Then, with a sudden flash of fury, she hissed, "I'd not put it past her, that evil old crone! How could you touch that pesky cat? Don't you know that it's her familiar?"

"Enough," Blanche exclaimed. "She gave you what she saw. I'm sure I've no more reason to like what she told me, but I know she spoke honestly."

Curiosity flamed in Venetia's narrow eyes, and they grew narrower still, "What did she tell you that you didn't like?" she inquired.

Blanche looked down, wishing that she had not been so frank. "Many things," she said evasively.

"Many—and you'll not say what they were?" Venetia prodded.

"She said I'd get married soon."

Her cousin raised her eyebrows, "You found that unpleasant?" she demanded incredulously. "Unless, she told you it was to another ancient." Her face darkened, "As she did me."

"She didn't tell me who he'd be." Blanche replied.

"But of course, you must get married, once your mourning period's ended. You need no witch to tell you that," Venetia declared.

"I'll not marry again," Blanche said firmly.

"No?" Venetia laughed mockingly. "I'll lay you odds, you do."

"I tell you, I shan't!" Blanche cried.

"But what else is there for you to do?" Venetia demanded. "Unless, you've a notion to enter a nunnery."

"I shall become a writer," Blanche said firmly.

"A—writer?" Venetia's mouth dropped open. "Why?"

"Because I must." She suddenly remembered Dame Alys's words concerning her gift. "Dame Alys told me

I would, but I do not need her predictions. I've always known I would."

Venetia shook her head. "I can't see that life for you, cousin. Ink-stained fingers, parchments, quills, and sand? You're quite good-looking, you know. You were meant to grace some lordly establishment, and I am sure you shall." She laughed dryly, "That's my prediction."

Blanche shook her head, "I shan't. I mean to do exactly as I choose."

"Then—you laugh at Dame Alys's water-gazing?"

Blanche hesitated, then taking a deep breath, she said defiantly, "Yes, I most certainly do."

"Good," Venetia startled her by applauding loudly, "you have your quills, dear Blanche, and I, my Yule."

It was amazing, how easily she adapted herself to the life at Carlisle, where one day was very like the next. Unlike her mother, who fretted and cried "monotony!" and whose only diversion beyond the running of the household seemed to be closeting herself with Esther and discussing such bits of court gossip as had penetrated their isolation in Paris and London and was currently sifting through the village, Blanche welcomed the sameness of her days, for she could still count each hour, which was not darkened by Glenmore, a novelty.

As she had feared, the library had been pillaged by Cromwell's men, but her grandfather had begun to restock it, the work being overseen by his secretary, David Peel, a self-effacing man of fifty-odd, whom Audrey privately called the Stick. It was a name that suited him. Even Blanche who loved him could agree. Brown of complexion and so thin that his skin seemed plastered to his bones, he walked stiffly and his fingers, twisted by arthritis, looked like the bent twigs of some old tree. However, encased behind his narrow, fleshless forehead was an amazing fund of knowledge, which he was glad to share with Blanche.

Unlike Venetia and her mother, he did not decry her

ambitions. She had shown him a few fragments of her writing and he had praised it highly, saying to her one day, "In my estimation, you have a talent for speech. Have you thought of writing plays?"

"I've thought of it," she said. "I should like to try a tragedy."

He smiled, "That's to be expected."

She was a little angry at his tone. "Why?'

"Because you're young. The young believe in absolutes."

"The young know tragedy sometimes too," she said.

He looked at her pityingly, "Yes, that can be true, but it's best to write about it from the distance of some years. Still, you should do as you think best. The important thing is to do it, to write a little each day, which I think you do. And do you keep a journal."

"Off and on," she said.

"You should be consistent. Writing's a discipline."

He had other practical advice, suggesting that she trade her quills for pencils. "They do not answer like ink. They're less bright and they smudge, but you'll find them to your liking for you may carry them anywhere." He had given her pencils, and she had begun to keep her journal once again. Again, at his suggestion, she wrote in it before she went to sleep, and in the morning jotted down what she could remember of her dreams.

"Many poets have found their best inspiration in their dreams," he had told her.

On a Thursday morning of the last week in July, when the dawn was only a glimmer of pink on the horizon, Blanche, who had been awake for an hour, lay staring at her journal, not wanting to touch it or the pencil by its side. She was feeling very queasy and for the second time that week! She could not imagine what was the matter with her. She had never felt that way before. She was worried and she was disappointed. She had meant to spend the whole day in the library composing dialogue. She had started on her play. In common with Hroswitha, she was using an old classic as a guide, *Iphegenia in Aulis*. It was exciting to translate it from the Greek and then change it to modern English. She had made up some wonderful speeches for Clytemnestra. She hoped Peel would agree. At least, that had been her state of mind when she had gone to bed. At the present moment, however, her interest in that Attic mother and daughter had dwindled sadly. She felt almost as if her sickness had not only emptied her stomach but her mind as well. She drew a little frightened breath, wondering if she might have contracted some dread disease—the falling sickness or perhaps the plague. If there were only some remedy she could take.

She sat up in bed, remembering Dame Alys and her herbs. When she had been little, her nurse had often dosed her with potions which had made her feel much better. Perhaps she might also be able to tell her what was wrong. If she went immediately, she might not need to waste the whole day.

A half hour later, she came down the steps that circled her tower. She did not want to meet her mother and explain where she was going. Though Audrey had been sympathetic to Dame Alys's plight, she had chided both Blanche and Venetia for their expedition to the woods. "You never know what vagabonds might be lurking in them," she had cautioned, adding sternly, "Please don't go near them again."

Reaching the ground, Blanche was about to make her way back to the gardens and beyond them to the fields, when she saw a horseman riding over the bridge that spanned the moat. He was silhouetted by the rising sun, a slender figure astride a huge, white stallion. As he came nearer, she saw that he was clad in a leather coat of a golden tan, which was much the same color as his flowing, bronze locks. His face was thin and brown, lighted by golden eyes. His nose was straight, his mouth full and mobile, topped by a thin moustache, lighter than his hair. It was a handsome face, but more than that, it was one she knew. She stood very still, while he rode up to her, staring down at her, quizzically at first, then with incredulous delight.

They spoke simultaneously.

"Rupert!"

"Blanche."

He pulled his horse to a stop and swung down from his saddle, winding the reins around one arm and using his other arm to encircle her waist and draw her to him. "My love, my dearest love," he cried joyfully, and kissed her.

Chapter Seven

It might have been six minutes, not six years. She hardly noticed that he had grown taller or that she had to reach up to put her arms around his neck as she returned his kiss and gave him another. She did not protest when he took her to the stallion, put her in the saddle, and swung up behind. It was only when he turned his steed around and headed back across the bridge that she said, "Aren't you taking me inside?"

"Not yet, my Blanche," he said.

"We—we ought to—to—" she began.

Drawing her close against him, he rested his chin on her curls. "There's no *ought*, not any more," he told her firmly. "I came through London last week and asked for Glenmore. I'd heard that he'd come home. I wanted to see you at any cost—and I was told of his death. That's why I'm here."

"Where are we going now?" she asked breathlessly.

"I passed through a forest on my way. Let's go back and lose ourselves, as we used to do." Boyishly, he added, "May we, Blanche?"

She was dreaming. Surely, she was in her bed and dreaming. Tentatively, she touched his hand and found it warm and real. "On one condition," she said softly.

"What's that?" His mouth was close to her ear and his breath fanned her cheek.

"If—you'll show me where the waterfowl nests and find for me another egg."

"Oh, Blanche, oh, Blanche, my love, my love." His arms tightened about her and his voice broke, "I—I feared you might have forgotten me—"

"No—never in my life, my dearest."

Glenmore was not dead. He had never lived nor had anyone else whom she had known. Charles was only a shadow. The world was Rupert. That was what she thought, when she could think again, but there had been moments when she had not thought at all. Their coming together had been so natural and so beautiful. Once they had left the highway and tethered the horse, close to the little pool that lay beneath the waterfall, there had been no questions and no words; neither had there been shrinking nor shame.

Now, lying close against him, she spoke her thoughts aloud. "It was so natural," she murmured.

"Natural, yes," he responded almost solemnly, his face against her breast. "Like the foxes and the deer."

She did not need to ask him what he meant, she knew, knew too that nothing she had ever experienced had been like this. The world had been forgotten—there were only themselves upon the knoll that overlooked the waterfall. Lazily digging her bare toes into the damp turf, she watched the foaming spray as, forming into a silvery stream, it fell into the pool. Her eyelids were weighted. Moving nearer to her lover, she pillowed her head on his chest and went to sleep.

The awakening, when it occurred, did not take place in the forest, but later. Every moment in the forest had been beautiful. In after years, when she thought of it, she could hardly believe it had happened quite that way. Indeed, even before they had reached the castle, even when the shadows of the trees still patterned the road behind them and he had reluctantly lifted her to the horse's back, she could hardly believe that she had lain with him upon the spiky grass, upon the crackling leaves and tiny stones, and afterwards had bathed naked with him in the pool. But she did believe it because her skin was tingling and her hair was hanging damply on her neck.

In after years, she would remember that she had been nervous when she had seen the arch between the two towers. She had not wanted him to spur his horse and canter through, but before she could protest, they were in the courtyard. Then, all unmindful of anyone who might be watching, he lifted her from the saddle, kissing her lingeringly before he set her down.

From the shadows, near the door, she heard a harsh sound and turned to see Venetia, hurling herself toward them, loudly screaming, "Yule!"

Standing close to Rupert, clinging to his arm, Blanche tried not to shudder as she looked into her cousin's furious face. She should have remembered that Rupert's family name was Yule, but she had never called him that, never thought of him that way—he had been only Rupert. She was not jealous of Venetia. Without his telling her, she knew that he had never loved her. She could even feel sorry for the girl when, paler than her white lace collar, she looked past Blanche to cry defiantly, "Yule, I was wondering when you'd come for me." Into the silence with which he greeted this statement, she dropped another question, "Were you this long time in Yorkshire?"

"I've been to France and back," he said stiffly, his arm tightening around Blanche.

Venetia's eyes were on his arm, and at her side, her hands were clenched into talons. In a small, tight voice, she said, "You went to see your brother, the priest. I expect. When we parted, you mentioned that you might."

"I saw him," he told her.

"Was he well?" she inquired jerkily.

"Quite well."

"Well, that's well." Her light laugh was not successful. Then abandoning all artifice, she whirled on Blanche, crying accusingly, "You knew Yule and did not tell me. Why didn't you tell me?"

"He—was not known as Yule at—Diamant," Blanche said. "He was—just Rupert."

"Diamant!" Venetia rasped. "That was years and years ago. You were only children, then."

"Not children," Rupert said. "We were only younger. We knew our hearts."

She glared at him. "Why did you never tell me so?" she cried. "Why did you lead me to believe—"

"I led you to believe nothing, Venetia," he said gently.

A harsh sob shook her. "It's not true. You—you told me you—you'd come for me to Carlisle."

"I said—I would come to see you at Carlisle," he corrected. "As a friend, no more. There was no understanding between us, Venetia."

"There was—there was," she wailed.

"There was none, Venetia. You've mistaken me and for that I am most sorry. I wish there were some way I could make amends, I truly do—but—"

"You can wed me, as you promised."

"I never did," he said.

"You lie!" she screamed. "May I be damned to hell forever, if you do not." She took a hasty step toward him, then with another strangled sob drew back and ran inside.

He turned a troubled face to Blanche. "There was nothing between us. I—sought her out in Cologne because someone had told me she was a connection of the Carlisles. I hoped to hear some word of you. I never gave her reason to think that she and I—"

"I know," she said. "She mentioned that the man she loved had not yet offered for her."

"She—" he broke off, and looking over her head, he stiffened, and with a touch of hostility said, "My Lady Carlisle."

Seeing her mother approaching them, Blanche took his hand and led him to her. "Here's Rupert, mama." she said simply.

It was the happy ending, so beloved of playwrights and romancers—the parted lovers reunited, Audrey Carlisle reflected. Scanning their radiant faces, she wished that she might share their happiness. Unfortunately, she had been at the hall window when they had ridden in. She had watched Venetia meet them, and just a moment since, she had tried to comfort her when she had come sobbing through the corridor. She had never liked Venetia, but still she felt the situation could have been handled with more grace, more gallantry as well. Rupert had known Venetia was at the castle. He could have restrained his ardor and not embraced her daughter where anyone might see. Either he had been completely thoughtless or carefully thoughtful, she was not sure which, but whether he were ingeniously gauche or purposely conniving, neither attitude pleased her. Still, since there was nothing else she could do at present, she forced a smile and hoped she sounded cordial when she said, "I bid you welcome to Carlisle, my dear Rupert."

"But you cannot flout conventions like that," Audrey said sharply. She had been saying much the same thing in different ways since the discussion had begun. She had brought forth all the arguments she knew and Esther too had done her part, but nothing either woman had said had had any effect upon Blanche or Rupert. They sat close together in the drawing room, their hands tight clasped and their eyes, occasionally meeting, filled with the same dazed and dreaming look. You would have thought, Audrey decided bitterly, that nothing existed apart from themselves and, in a sense, perhaps it didn't.

Blanche said, or rather repeated, what she had been saying for the past hour. "I am not in mourning for Glenmore. I'm not sorry he is dead. I hated him, as you know. I'll not let him stand in my way again. I'm no longer twelve. I need no one to tell me what to do."

"But not even to post the banns, child," Esther remonstrated gently.

Rupert said, "But you see, Madame de Coligny, we do not want to wait. It's been nearly seven years already." He gave the two women a charming but determined smile. "We must be married tomorrow."

"Yes, tomorrow." Blanche agreed.

"But child, there are settlements and—"

"I have very little left," Blanche said. "I've told Rupert that."

"We can provide you your dowry," Audrey said dryly.

"It's not needful." Rupert told her.

"Of course it is," she snapped. "You've not discussed your own financial state, my lord. Has the king restored your estates in full?"

"He has," Rupert asserted. "I've broad holdings in Yorkshire and property in Scotland too."

"Please, mother," Blanche rose. "Let us have no more talk of money. I tell you, I'd have wed him if he lived beneath a hedge."

Rupert's look was loving, "And I'd wed you—if you were begging at my gates."

"It's fortunate that neither of you is forced to make good that boast." Audrey remarked dryly, ignoring her daughter's outraged stare. She wished that Tony had not taken to his bed with an ague which kept him too fretful and feverish to add his voice to her arguments. Possibly, he could have commanded more respect, but she doubted it. Actually, she could not blame them for their stand, and if she had been placed in their position, she might have done the same. But she was rather sure she would not have taken Rupert for her lover. She had no reason for her feeling other than his conduct in the courtyard. Certainly he was personable. Indeed, though he was yet something short of twenty, he seemed much more mature and capable, but thinking on it, she had liked him better as a boy, but why? She did not know and she really had nothing on which to base her conclusions other than the fact that he was too masterful, too demanding, too eager to fly in the face of all convention and claim his bride. However, given the circumstances, would not all men have acted in the same manner? She smiled wryly. Were she a lawyer, she could have argued for both sides and left the judge and jury as confused as she herself. Still, darting a look at Esther, she found the woman looking as troubled as she herself felt.

"I should like it if Blanche and I could be married in the chapel at Carlisle," Rupert said almost wistfully.

Meeting his eyes, Audrey found no wistfulness in them. Indeed, she thought his statement could be interpreted as a threat. Given her estimate of his nature, she was sure that he was quite capable of bearing Blanche away within the hour were she to offer further objections. She did not want to do that. Long ago, she had estranged her daughter completely by separating her from Rupert. Even now there was a coolness between them and a tendency on Blanche's part to favor Esther. She had the chance to redeem herself and, in a sense, to reclaim her daughter, who, she had the feeling, might have need of her one day. Forcing a smile, Audrey said, "Of course, you must be married in our chapel, else there'd be no priest of our faith'd dare preside. We'll send for him immediately."

"Mama!" Running to her, Blanche threw her arms around her mother, and then she embraced Esther too. Seizing Rupert's hand, she said joyfully, "Come, we must tell Mr. Peel!"

"Mr. Peel?" he inquired.

"In the library. I'll show you."

When the two had left the room, Audrey turned to Esther. "I do not like it, though I am not sure why. He's handsome, charming, titled, rich—"

"Yes," Esther agreed. "He's all of those, but she

needs more time to think, and he'll never give it to her."

Audrey started. "You noticed that?"

"Yes," Esther sighed. "I am disappointed. She's loved him a long time, you know."

"Yes, I know," Audrey said dryly. "Yet, I wonder if it's Rupert she loves or the idea of Rupert, her lost suitor. It's the stuff of romance, Esther, and he does present a most romantic appearance too. When I was young, I had a head full of ballads and the *Morte d'Arthur*. I used to stand at my window and look down the road, hoping a knight would come a-wooing me. They were all so brave and bold and impetuous. I could actually see myself being carried off on his saddlebow. I did not look to have my dreams fulfilled by Blanche. They never said what happened to those maidens once they'd wed those impetuous and brusque young men." She frowned. "I wish there were some way to stop her."

"I don't think that's possible," Esther said. "And perhaps it's just as well. He's not the man I would have chosen for her. However, it's obvious that he loves her, and she needs loving now."

"Would you mean particularly now, more than at another time?" Audrey gave her a searching look. "Esther, I've had the feeling there's something you know about my daughter that you've not told me."

"No," Esther said too quickly, "I'm only thinking of Glenmore. He was very cruel to her, you know."

"Yes," Audrey studied her hands. "I'm all too aware of that. It was a great mistake, that marriage. That's why I'd not have her make another. But there's so little I can say. I'm afraid my maternal feelings developed much too late and—" She shrugged, "Perhaps I am borrowing trouble. I hope so, since the wedding's tomorrow. *Tomorrow*! That allows us very little time for preparations, especially if I'm to give a wedding supper. Come, Esther, let's see the cook. You can help me in the planning, if you will." She hurried out.

Esther followed slowly. She was of two minds about the marriage. Rupert's domineering manner reminded her unpleasantly of Glenmore, but perhaps it was only assumed for the occasion. He was charming, and it was obvious he adored Blanche. Actually, her reasons for approving of the match were more valid than her vague objections. She thought of Whitehall and the king. She was sure Blanche had not forgotten either. If she were to stay on at Carlisle alone she would only brood, and she had been looking very peaked lately. Furthermore, she was a girl who was clearly meant to be a wife. She needed loving and she would have that from Rupert. "It's definitely for the best," she muttered. "I wish them happy."

Peel was not in the library.

"Oh," Blanche exclaimed disappointedly, "I'd wanted you to meet."

"Why?" he inquired. "Is he my rival, then?"

"Rival?" she repeated. "I told you he was old."

"I feared you might have become accustomed to old men," he said lightly.

She shuddered and looked startled, "Never."

"Poor Blanche, poor Blanche," he kissed her. "Was it so terrible, then?"

"Yes," she answered in a low voice.

"What was he like?" he asked curiously.

She moved out of his embrace, "I pray you'll not ask me. He's dead and I do not want to think of him again."

"You shouldn't," he agreed. "Who is this Peel?"

"He's grandfather's secretary and librarian. See." She pointed to the shelves. "He's bought all those and will be getting more to replace those which were lost during the occupation of Carlisle. He's made some wonderful choices."

"Has he?" He slipped his arm around her waist again. "Are you a reader then, my poppet?" he asked with an indulgent smile.

"A reader and, I hope, a writer, too. You remember that I used to make up poems."

"Oh, yes," he said, kissing her. "But you're a female."

She did not like his tone. "Mr. Peel tells me there are many women writers now."

"Are there? I wouldn't know. I fear I'm not a scholar. I've had little time for books these past years." He smiled at her. "I hope that doesn't disappoint you."

"No," she assured him quickly. It occurred to her that she knew very little about this man she was so soon to marry. She was a trifle daunted by this realization, but put it quickly from her mind. He was Rupert, her lost, her only love, and that was all that mattered. Yet, she did ask, "What have you been doing all these years, my dearest?"

"Traveling in the service of the king, negotiating with statesmen in France, Spain, and Italy." His eyes sparkled. "One day I shall take you to Italy, my love. It's my hope that I might be appointed to the ambassador's staff in Rome, or perhaps in Paris, but not yet. I must needs finish getting my estates in order. My poor castle suffered considerably worse damage than Carlisle."

"Oh, that's a pity," she said. "What happened to it?"

"Some parts of it were shelled. And then it was occupied by some of Cromwell's troops. They stabled their horses in the main hall and used the rooms upstairs as their latrines—" he grimaced. "They also managed to destroy most of the furniture, and they pulled the tapestries down. Some of them were five hundred years old; the castle itself was built six hundred years ago. It's hard by the sea and there are moors beyond it. It might seem gloomy at first, but once the alterations I've been making are finished it will be lovely. At least, I hope you'll think so." He looked at her a little anxiously.

"Oh, I know I shall!" she exclaimed. "I can hardly wait to see it. Let's go there soon."

"We will," he promised. "It's a long journey. I hope it will not tire you."

"Not with you at my side," she whispered.

"My love," he kissed her gently. "Tomorrow's far too long to wait. I would we were wedded and on our way this very moment."

"Oh, Rupert, Rupert, Rupert, Rupert, Rupert—" she caroled.

He laughed, "So many Ruperts! Why?"

"Because I love to say the name, I always have, and now, now you're here to answer to it."

She had paced the length of the corridor, then tried the great hall, and then the courtyard, but finally she found him alone in the gardens. She was breathless when she reached him, breathless and weeping. "Rupert," she clutched his arm.

"Venetia," he gave her a troubled look. "I am sorry for all this, but we never had an understanding, never. Why did you say so?"

"Because *I* understood we did," she sobbed.

"Venetia," he repeated. "We were friends and nothing more."

"You—you promised you'd come to me at Carlisle," she accused.

"Yes, I did make such a promise, but that was my only promise. I never led you to believe there was anything else between us. I'd not be so cruel."

"You are cruel!" she exclaimed. "You've spoiled my life. I—I want to die."

"Come, my dear," he put a brotherly arm around her, "You're talking nonsense. You're a young and good-looking, with many ways to please a man."

"And I pleased you," she hissed. "Don't pretend I didn't. Oh, Rupert, I could make you happy, far happier than Blanche. I've not come to you from an old man's bed, an old man who, according to all I've heard from Cousin Audrey, used her hard."

He flushed darkly, "Enough!" he said sharply.

"Ah, you don't like the idea of taking another man's leavings, do you?" she jeered.

"Be silent!" he commanded between clenched teeth.

"It's true," she cried. "I am a virgin, all untouched. You—you could take me now and see. Take me, love, please." She fell to her knees and clutched his legs. "Please, Rupert, please."

He freed himself gently. "My dear," he said uncomfortably, "don't humble yourself this way. You don't understand what's between Blanche and me."

She raised a face so full of hate that he was almost frightened. "I understand. I understand that I've been cursed. That old woman with her evil eye. She cursed me and turned you away from me. That's what happened and—if I'm cursed, so are you. You'll find no joy in this marriage. It was the devil's doing!"

He sighed, "You sound demented, Venetia. Come to your senses, please. I wish you nothing but well and if you were wise, you'd do the same for us and forget this daft talk of devils!" He turned away from her and strode back into the house.

She threw herself down on the grass, crying loudly, "I am accursed, she cursed me. She wanted him for Blanche. It was her doing—that damned witch!"

In spite of her misgivings, Audrey was pleased by her daughter's appearance. Blanche, she thought, had never looked more beautiful than on the day of her second wedding. She had doffed her mourning clothes and wore a gown of rich white brocade, delectably Parisian in its cut. Josette had wired Blanche's golden hair into ringlets, and her throat was encircled by a necklace of large pearls that glowed against her creamy skin like a row of little moons. Rupert too, in rich brown silk with his shirt and breeches trimmed in a gold lace that was almost the color of his eyes, looked very handsome. They were certainly an attractive couple. Even Tony Carlisle, brought from his sickbed and patently disapproving of the proceedings, could agree to that.

Still, she was very glad that the wedding party was restricted to the five of them, for she was sure that their neighbors would be shocked by the suddenness of her marriage. Certainly such a thing had never happened before, but, in a sense, she had no one but herself to blame, for if she and Tony had not forced the child into Glenmore's arms . . . She sighed. Esther had told her all that Blanche had suffered. It had made her very unhappy, the more so since Blanche herself had never confided in her.

At least, Rupert would be kind. He was of a good family, and he had loved her for a long time. Furthermore, she should not decry the flouting of convention, she who had even defied the dictates of her church to become the mistress of her husband's father. Yet, thinking of her wedding to Charles Carlisle, she felt sorry for Blanche. It had been lovely, all their friends were in the church, and afterwards, the feasting, the merry-making, the dancing and the drinking—and Charles spiriting her away and . . . She blinked those memories back. At least there would be a fine wedding supper with pasties, tartlets, and creams. She frowned, wondering why she was so nervous and so frightened, almost as if there were something pending. An image rose in her mind, a dark cloud on a summer's day; but that was only in her head, for a glimpse through the windows of the chapel showed her only brilliant sunshine, and now, the ceremony was beginning.

At high noon, when the wedding started, Venetia was walking across the fields, hardly knowing which way she was going. Her hair hung in damp tendrils about her distorted face. Occasionally, she flung herself down, wailing out her anguish and rising with straw and burrs caught in her tangled locks. At the edge of the road, she met several people from the village.

Looking at her, they were amazed, knowing her for one of the gentry from the castle; glancing into her wild, green eyes, they were also frightened, especially when she fell down again and lay writhing on the ground like one possessed by devils. They were even more frightened when, on asking what ailed her, they were told she was plagued by devils. These had been sent to torment her by an old woman who lived in the woods, a witch. Yet, if they were frightened, they were also very sympathetic. No one doubted her story. Had not the minister been preaching sermon after sermon on the prevalence of witches?

They knew the witch she meant, and though they were surprised that the woman in question would turn malevolent, they agreed it could happen. As everyone knew, she had unusual powers, and furthermore, they had the living, breathing evidence before them in the person of the poor, bewitched young lady.

They brought Venetia to the minister's cottage. The good man was away on a call, but his wife put her to bed and they all waited until he returned, some two hours later. As they waited, they grew even more frightened, for the victim did not cease her writhing and screaming. They were extremely relieved when the minister finally came back. He agreed that she was indeed bedeviled and lost no time in placing the blame upon the witch of the woods.

There was a large crowd by then, for the news had spread quickly. Among the new arrivals were many who could cite other horrid experiences with the witch. One Goody Rudd recalled the day the old woman had passed her house and, stopping by the fence, had remarked on her fine cow. Immediately afterwards, the poor beast had sickened and her udders had dried. At the time, she had not blamed the incident on the witch, but now she thought about it, it seemed most likely. There was also Ellie Bray, who weepingly recalled that she had obtained a potion from the old woman, guaranteed to unite her with her lover. Instead, he had left the village, promising to return soon it was true, but it had been close on two weeks since she had seen him, and now she was sure they would never meet again!

Yet, there was Tom Harper, a farmer, who begged them to show mercy, reminding them that the said witch had provided many of them with herbal cures and soothing remedies. He also mentioned that she had been well beloved at the castle, when she had been nurse to Master Charles and later to his daughter Blanche. At this the poor creature on the bed sprang up and ran around the room, before falling shrieking to the floor.

Everyone looked at him accusingly, asking if he were in league with a minion of the devil? He paled but still dared to suggest they should not depend on word of mouth alone, even if that mouth belonged to a woman of the gentry. "The witch must have a fair trial," he insisted.

They were all in agreement about that. They wanted the old woman to have a fair trial, a trial by water. That always had proved effective for, as all the godly knew, water would not receive a witch but would keep her bobbing like a cork upon its surface. Some of them hurried to the village pond to prepare the ducking stool, while others started for the woods.

They had been at table for close on three hours and still the wine went round. "Health and happiness!" Audrey and Tony both cried.

Dazedly, Blanche raised her glass and drank, drank to the young man sitting next to her at the long table. He was blurry: the others, her mother, Esther, and her grandfather, were too. She had had too much wine and she felt very strange, as if she were floating, but she was very happy, an emotion still new to her, one she had never really known, except—except for that night with Charles. She frowned, not wanting to think about him, besides it had not been real happiness, because he had said something that had negated all the rest, something about love, but she did not really remember. She moved her chair closer to that of her husband. Her husband? But she had planned never to marry again. Raising her glass tipsily, she said, "I will write. I will."

He laughed and kissed her on the lips.

She frowned at that. She had the feeling he did not think her writing important, but it was. It still was. She told him solemnly, "I've written half a play and—" he kissed her again, stifling her words. "No, Rupert—" she said, when he raised his head, "you must listen to me—I," but he kissed her hard, and then what she had been about to tell him did not matter any more, because she was overcome with a great desire to be alone with him, upstairs in bed, alone. . . .

There was a clamor in the hall. Someone was making far too much noise, crying out loudly that there was trouble in the village. The sound came closer, it was in the banqueting hall. She wished that he would not shout so loud. His voice was harsh and abrasive. It was spoiling the golden mood of the occasion. She turned toward whomever it might be, a finger to her lips, and saw to her amazement that it was the Stick, quiet Mr. Peel, who never raised his voice. He was raising it now, loudly, and it was tinged with anguish and he was speaking about "the pond—the pond—" and then he said, "the witch."

"Oh, Lord," Audrey started up, "they've taken some poor old creature from the roads, no doubt. We should send our men to stop them."

"No," Mr. Peel contradicted. "It's Dame Alys, who used to work here—I knew her when I was a boy."

"Dame Alys—" the name penetrated through the clouds of wine in her head. "Dame Alys, did you say?" She jumped to her feet.

"Love, what is it?" Rupert rose with her.

"Dame Alys—in the pond?" she cried. "We must

stop them—She's too old. Oh, God, how did they come to take her?"

"She was accused," Mr. Peel said. "I did not get the whole of it. They were too frightened and too angry."

"I must go to her," Blanche cried.

"No," Audrey protested. "I've seen witch mobs before. There's no arguing with them until they've had their way. You'd not be able to help her."

Rupert, looking at Blanche's frantic face, said, "Come, my love, we'll go together."

"Best let us send men from here," Audrey cried.

"Let them come with us," Blanche began to cry. "It's Dame Alys, mother. You know she's no witch. She's frail—if they put her in the water she will die. Come, please—we waste time in talking!"

Dame Alys was weeping because they had strangled Grizelda, which they called her familiar. She had brought the white cat up from a little kitten, saving it from drowning at the hands of the baker's wife. It had been such a scrawny kitten, not expected to live, but she had sheltered it in her bosom and it had grown apace and had been such company. It had slept close to her at night, warming her greatly when there was no fire. It was like her child, she who had never had a child but only cared for other people's children. She was thinking more of that than of her own peril, for when she had seen them come bursting into the clearing, she had known that the red-haired girl had accused her, knew too that she had been waiting for this to happen, had always known it might, since she had called upon her powers of seeing. These had earned her bread and tea, when she might have been thrown on the mercy of the parish, but she had always been aware that they might be her death, but, the tears rolled down her face anew, she had not wanted them to be the death of the white cat. If only the beast had not stayed close to her skirts and spit at them when they came running toward her. It was a strange thing for her to have done, because she was always a shy cat, afraid of strangers, usually dashing beneath a bush or into the cottage whenever they appeared, but this time she had stayed and spit and had been grabbed and strangled as easily as if she had been a chicken. The poor little white body had been tossed at her feet with the remark that the devil might claim his own.

She was very tired. They had made her walk such a long way. She was not used to walking anymore; her joints were so stiff. She had stumbled often and they, lifting her ungently, asked why the devil did not come to save her. They had provided their own answer, saying that the Lord was on their side, keeping her Satanic master at bay.

Among the crowds, she had caught glimpses of faces she knew: Diccon, whose baby she had cured of colic. Mary-Ann, who had bought a love potion from her and swore it had brought her Will, her husband. Then, there was Peter, whom she had watched while Margery, his mother, had gone off to the fair. Peter, who had put his little arms around her and kissed her because she had fed him sugarplums. Now he looked so angry, and he muttered that she had witched him with those same plums when he was small. Ellen had begged her to look into the water to see if her soldier would return, and the old woman had said he would. Ellen had given her a fine chicken when he came and would have had her to the wedding feast, except that Alys was too ill to come. Yet, now they all looked at her with such fear and loathing, talking of the devil and swearing that they had known that she had sexual congress with him in the woods.

The baker and the blacksmith taxed her with her dealings and said they would spare her the ordeal were she to confess to having slept with Satan. "Is it true," someone screamed from the crowd, "that his organ is as cold as ice?"

They screamed other terrible questions at her, filled

with such obscenities that she wanted to close her ears. But when she tried to raise her shaking hands, they pulled them down and went on with their interrogation. Then, finally, when she could hardly crawl, they were at the pond and there was a coil of rope. She knew its significance but was much too weary to care.

It was odd how afraid she had been at the thought of death and now was afraid no longer. It would have been very lonely in the cottage without Grizelda, patting her on the face for her breakfast in the morning. She had been such a comfort, poor white cat.

The red-haired girl from the castle was there. Her harsh, accusing voice hurt the woman's ears, and when the girl screamed that she was cursed, it seemed to Dame Alys that with such disheveled hair and flaming eyes that she was the real witch, and Alys was frightened of her and wanted the good Lord to protect her, but it seemed that he had turned his face away.

They tied the rope around her waist, securing it with a strong knot. It was very tight. She could hardly breathe. Someone near her must have noticed that for he said, "It's too binding. You must loosen it." They did not heed him.

"Swim the witch!" someone cried.

"Yes, swim her, swim her—" they shouted in unison.

"Have you anything to say, old woman?" It was the minister who had asked. She had never liked him. His sermons were so full of death and damnation.

"No," she said.

"Swim her, swim her, swim her," screamed the mob.

When they lifted her to the stool which would tip her into the pond, she saw that the sun was a great, round red ball in the west, with shards of clouds above it, a creamy white they were, all edged with gold. It was so beautiful, and then she saw it reflected in the waters just below her and forthwith fell into that lovely molten gold.

* * *

Even before Rupert had reined in his horse, Blanche had jumped down and was dashing across the road to the crowd around the pond.

"Blanche, love, wait for me!" he called fearfully, hastening after her, but as he reached them, they had silently parted to let her through. As he followed, he saw that they were all silent or, if not entirely silent, they spoke in muted voices and looked at each other sheepishly. Some of the women were crying and a few of the men too.

He found Blanche crouched near a sodden heap of old clothes, or so it appeared until he saw the gray white hair, lying lank upon the grass. Kneeling near Blanche, he looked into the wan face of an old woman. Her eyes were barely open and her breathing was very shallow.

"Love, darling—" Blanche stroked the old woman's hair.

Her eyes opened widely. Staring at Blanche, she made an effort to smile. "Innocent—" she muttered. "The waters took me. They were kind—all golden."

"Dame Alys," Blanche was trying not to weep. "You—you mustn't talk—"

"Must—must," Dame Alys said urgently. "I see for you—" she turned her head, staring up into Rupert's face. "You—my—my sight tells me you are just wed to Blanche."

"Yes, it's true," he answered, surprised by her words and by the terror in her eyes.

"You must be gentle," she urged.

"How could I not be gentle with my love?" he demanded.

She did not answer him. She looked at Blanche, "I warned you, but you did not heed me, but I—I knew you would not—could not. I wish I could stay, but no—May God guide you and send you strength, my dearest, I—" her voice faded and though she tried to speak again, no sound came out. Then, with a long, rattling sigh, she died.

Blanche rose shakily to her feet and faced the mob. "Why?" she demanded hotly. "Why did you do it?"

There was no answer. In their fear of lurking devils, they had forgotten all that had passed before they had dropped the witch into the pond and brought forth a victim instead of a sinner.

Blanche clung to Rupert, "Take me away from here," she begged, "far, far away. I never want to see any of these murderers again!"

He kissed her tenderly, "Nor need you. I'll take you to our home as fast as we can ride. We'll go tomorrow, if you choose."

"I do," she whispered, pressing against him. She felt very cold. Death was an ill omen for a wedding day, but with his arms around her, that feeling vanished. He was Rupert and at last, she could call him husband.

Chapter Eight

The sky was gray and a cold wind was blowing through the yellowing grasses that stretched for miles on either side of a path too narrow to be called a road. Yet, it was being used as such by a great lumbering traveling coach, pulled by six large gray horses and accompanied by four outriders, two before and two behind. Bundled into heavy greatcoats, and with hats pulled down against the stinging salt-laden breezes, they cursed the filthy climate in words that were echoed by the coachman and the shivering grooms.

Inside the coach, Audrey Carlisle, hearing their plaints could also echo them, as, clinging to the strap, she braced herself against jolts which seemed to grow more numerous with every weary mile. Early March was a kinder month in Worcestershire; here in Yorkshire, it felt like winter. It looked like winter, too. She did not like it, all those miles of moors and now, as they turned and took the coast road, she had disheartening glimpses of wind-ravaged trees, their exposed roots looking like skeleton fingers, as they clung tenaciously to the rocky soil. Far below them, a gray sea plunged incessantly at the water-sculpted cliffs, as if it longed to batter them down and steal away the land.

Not for the first time or the tenth she wondered how her daughter had withstood this bleakness for five long years. Yet, she had and with no complaint. Indeed, after her first few months, she had written very infrequently. Audrey grimaced, the poor child had had little time for writing with four babies in as many years and a fifth expected, if she had not been brought to bed already.

The infants had come far too fast for Audrey's liking and she wished that she could have been with her to give her hints for controlling her fecundity, but it had not been possible for her to come. She had been much involved with improvements in the castle and then Tony had not been well. Later, she herself had had the smallpox; thank God, it had left her unmarked. Last year, when she had meant to go, there had been the dreaded plague ravaging through London and taking some toll in the countryside, and the roads were choked with people fleeing. It was less virulent now, though still abroad, but she was determined to see her daughter and the children.

Tony had wanted to go with her, but he was still weakened by his last ague, and she had refused to think of it. She smiled, he had sent her off in fine style, being worried about disasters on the road. She was touched by his solicitude, even more by his reluctance to let her go. He had even feigned a relapse but she had seen through it and teased him; but when he had come to the coach, she had unaccountably burst out crying and he had kissed her often which was very strange in him, for generally he kept his feelings hidden—as did she. She had almost been minded to dismiss the coach and stay, but she could not. She was worried about Blanche, though she was not sure why.

Certainly, she must be living the life she had always wanted with the man she loved. Possibly her worry was founded on her last letter, which had been very brief indeed. She had mentioned that she was expecting another child and concluded with the words, "Mother, please come, I long to have you see my children." Though the message was ordinary enough, it seemed to her as if it were a cry for help. She had said as much to Tony, only to have him retort brusquely that she was imagining things—which probably she was. Well, she would soon find out.

They were passing a ruined abbey, one of many she had seen on her long journey, but this one was different; it was older, she could tell that by the weathered stone and knew it must be Whitby Abbey. Blanche had mentioned it in one of her first letters. She had liked to walk to it from the castle, which meant, Audrey thought gratefully, that they must be nearing their destination. She recalled that Blanche had also said that the abbey had been pillaged by the Danes in the middle of the eighth century and had also asked her to tell Mr. Peel that she was writing a romance about it. Evidently she had changed her mind for her subsequent letters had not mentioned it again.

They left the abbey behind, and now, as they came over a rise, she saw the square outlines of a castle, stark against the sky, only to lose it at another dip in the road, but she knew it must be Yule. As if in answer to her guess, she was jolted even more as the coachman, with that habitual burst of speed that always marked the journey's end, urged his horses forward.

"Oh, milady, be we almost there?"

Audrey started. She had completely forgotten the presence of Rose, her young maid, who had been half-dozing in the other corner of the coach.

"Yes, we must be, my dear."

"I'm that glad," the girl sighed.

"I too." Audrey gave her a brief smile. She was a pretty child, not more than fourteen, with a mass of curly brown hair and bright blue eyes. She had caused quite a rivalry among Tom, Diccon, Hugh, and Giles, the outriders, and even crusty Arthur, the coachman, had looked with favor on her. But seemingly, she was quite unconscious of their interest and totally devoted to the concerns of her mistress, rare these days, when young and pretty servant girls were becoming hard to keep in remote villages, they being drawn to London town, where it was vastly more exciting.

Audrey stifled a sigh—to think of London was still to want to live there, for all it was noted to be growing dirtier and more unhealthy with each passing day. Still there was so much to do. One did not need to depend on fairs or traveling players or country balls, which, to her mind, were sadly dull. She had never been attracted to the local nobility. She much preferred the society one found at court, especially these days when people were welcomed as much for their wit as for their pedigree. Nor was Whitehall the only beacon, the theaters were open again and with female actresses upon the boards, a situation which had been denounced from all the pulpits and still set the conservative minded to grumbling. Audrey, for her part, thought it remarkably progressive; she had never liked seeing the prancing boys who enacted the Juliets and the Cleopatras. Their work always left something to be desired. Actresses must be far more satisfactory.

She laughed. Here she was thinking of London and meanwhile, they were at the other end of the world, or so it seemed. The coach was slowing now and they had come to a high wall. They stopped and she heard Arthur's voice, evidently identifying them. There was the squeak and scrape of gates being drawn back, and then they were rumbling up a long drive. Far ahead of them, she could see the huge gray facade of the castle. Unlike Carlisle, it ran to angles rather than curves. The keep was square, and the main part of the castle also square, ending in a newer wing of a different sort of stone, but still angular. The effect was uncommonly bleak, she thought, especially since the trees near it had already lost their leaves save for a few that clung to the branches, making them only seem barer. Finally, they stopped at the main door, which was deeply recessed under a Gothic archway. There were the usual shouts as the four young men galloped up behind them, and then the steps were brought and the coach door opened. Audrey climbed stiffly down, followed by Rose, who leaped out looking around her excitedly and then, shivering, drew her cloak tighter.

"Oh, but it is cold."

"It is that," Audrey agreed. She did not feel any warmer as she faced the gray stone buildings, nor did she care for the crew which had come to hold their horses. They seemed a rough and surly lot and for a moment she thought they must be foreigners, but then she realized they must be speaking a dialect, for ever so often, like seeing a currant caught in unmixed dough, an English word protruded.

"How do we get inside, milady?" Rose asked through chattering teeth.

Audrey looked toward the door and realized that she had actually expected to see Blanche come running through it, which was ridiculous, of course, for why did one employ servants. Still, there should be someone to greet them. Had no one heard the coach arrive? She started toward the door and then suddenly, with the swiftness of a shadow, a little boy came up to her. He was thin faced with bright, dark eyes and a shock of black, unruly hair. As he drew nearer, she saw that he was wearing a velvet suit which was much mended and that his shirt was frayed. He had a sensitive face which looked vaguely familiar even though he resembled neither parent. Possibly he was not one of her brood, though he was of an age for it being not much more than five, she guessed.

"Have you come to see my mama?" he inquired, fixing her with an intense, dark stare.

"If your mama's the lady of the castle, then I have," she smiled.

"Oh, I am glad. This is the third day I have waited."

"The third day?" Audrey repeated.

"Oh, yes. Mama was waiting before. She came out every day last week, but she's been brought to bed again. She will be happy. She's wanted to see you for ever so long and she said to me that she had a feeling you would come this time."

Audrey was confused by his words. Nothing in Blanche's letters had led her to believe that her arrival was so eagerly awaited. She said, "I've wanted to see her, too. Will you take me to her."

"No," he said quickly. "Mistress Digges must do that—and you must not tell that you've seen me. I was but to let her know."

"But—" Audrey started to say, but stopped, for the boy had darted away, disappearing around the side of the castle.

"Did you ever?" Rose exclaimed and then was silent for a tall, gaunt woman had emerged from the front door. She was dressed in a maroon gown which had been stylish a dozen years ago, and she wore a small lace cap over neatly braided gray brown hair. Her eyes were a pale blue, and she peered at Rose and Audrey with the squinting gaze of the shortsighted.

"And what might I do for you?" she asked in a surprisingly light voice for one with so large a frame.

Audrey, disliking both her appearance and her voice, said grandly, "You can take me to my daughter, my good woman. I am Lady Carlisle."

Without waiting for a response, she beckoned to Rose and, sweeping past the woman, went on inside, emerging into a hall which, like that of Carlisle, stretched upwards for two stories. It was paneled in dark wood which, midway toward the ceiling, was topped by plaster. There was a spread of antique weapons on one wall and a row of antlers on the other. Through an open door she glimpsed a flight of stairs, but what mainly interested Audrey was the roaring fire in the fireplace across the room. She and Rose hastened to it, and as they stood warming their hands, the woman, whom she presumed to be Mistress Digges, strode up to them, looking half-angry, half-discomfited.

"Your daughter—" she began in an argumentative tone, immediately interrupted by Audrey.

"Who might you be?" she demanded.

"I—I am Mistress Digges," she stuttered. "I—am housekeeper here and milord's away."

"That matters not at all to me. I am here to see my daughter, Lady Godwin. I presume we are expected. I sent her word that I was coming. Have the goodness to show my maid to our rooms and take me to my daughter, at once."

The woman opened her mouth, then closed it again, and opened it a second time, "I was not told of this—"

"Mama—oh, mama—" The words uttered in a tremulous voice, caused her to whirl toward the passageway. She gasped. Leaning against the wall was a woman in a faded, blue velvet robe. Her long yellow curls trailed lankly over her thin shoulders, and she stared at Audrey out of weary, dark-circled eyes, which seemed far too large in her wasted face. "Mama," she said again and, taking a few steps toward her, fell fainting to the floor.

"Oh, Your Ladyship," the woman screamed. "What be you—"

Whatever else she might have said was lost as Audrey rushed to her daughter's side and, kneeling, gathered her in her arms. "Child—what's happened to you?" she cried in horror. Glaring at the woman, she commanded, "Help me to get her to her room."

"Oh, yes—yes—" the housekeeper knelt beside her. "Here—let me carry her, milady."

"You fetch one of the men, please. My coachman or—"

The woman paled, "Oh, no, milady, I dassn't. Milord's forbidden it. I'll carry her. I often have. She's not heavy, not a bit." With surprising ease she lifted Blanche in her arms, and hurrying toward the stairs, she said, "I'll take her to her chamber. If you'll follow me, milady."

A thousand frantic words crowded to Audrey's tongue, but uttering none of them, she merely nodded and went after her, feeling as if she were in the grip of a nightmare.

Blanche's bedchamber was large and square, and its long windows faced the sea. Audrey could hear the ocean's distant roar, and it seemed to her that she could also smell it. The bed that Blanche had evidently just left was sadly tumbled and its pillows disarranged. "Wait," she commanded sharply, as Mistress Digges started to put her down. Smoothing the sheets and plumping up the pillows, she said curtly, "Now."

"Should I get some hartshorn, milady," the housekeeper asked deferentially.

"Yes, please." Audrey surveyed her daughter in distress. "She—she looks as if she were close to death."

"Oh, no, milady, the doctor says there's no danger of that, but it was a hard labor and a harder birth, poor little mite come afore its time."

Audrey, glancing to the side of the bed, saw an empty cradle. "And—the baby?" She was almost afraid to ask.

"Oh, milady," for the first time, the housekeeper seemed actually distressed, "he didn't live but a breath or two. I—I'll get the hartshorn."

"Oh, milady," Rose moved to the bed. "She does look mortal sick."

"Hush," Audrey said sharply. "You heard that creature. She says she'll not die." Sitting on the edge of the bed, she brushed Blanche's hair back from her forehead and put her hand against it. "It's cool," she said thankfully. "If she'd been fevered—but she's not." Her eyes fell on the sheets. Much to her amazement, she saw that they were badly worn and had been mended in at least a dozen spots. The pillowcases were frayed, as were the silken curtains of the bed. Looking around the room, she noted now that it was sparsely furnished with chairs and tables that were scarred and old.

"I do not understand it—" she murmured.

Blanche suddenly stirred and, opening her eyes,

clutched her mother's arm. "You are here! I didn't imagine it. Oh, why didn't you come sooner. I wrote so often, and you never answered. Did he tell you, then—and do you believe me a whore."

Audrey started as though she had received a physical blow. "What did you say? A—a whore?"

"Yes, that's what he calls me," Blanche sobbed. "And I told him—I told him—" she paused and swallowed. "He was so proud that I—I'd conceived so soon. You see—Dame Alys was right, but I forgot—Rupert arrived so suddenly, and I was so happy I didn't feel—sick anymore. I said it was not my doing, but he'd not credit it. I said it was my husband forced me to it—but he'd none of it, and now—he—he calls me whore."

Listening to the disjointed explanation, Audrey wondered if her daughter were quite sane. Then, becoming aware of Rose, she said hastily, "See to the luggage please, and get that creature to tell you where we stay."

"Yes, milady," Rose said reluctantly and hurried out.

Turning to Blanche once more, Audrey said gently. "Love, I could make no sense of what you said. Surely, Rupert who was so mad to have you that he wouldn't wait—surely he'd not call you—whore."

"He has and does," Blanche said with great distinctness. Her face crumpled, then and she added, "Look at me! Would you know me—I am old, old."

"Dearest, you are only tired. It was a hard birth, I'm told. You need to rest and time to recuperate."

"Rest, I'll have no time to rest. In two days or a week, he'll return to fill me with another child and keep the cuckoo from his nest." She laughed so harshly that Audrey winced.

"What is this talk of cuckoos?" she demanded.

"Rupert says—he says—" she paused, staring fearfully at the door.

Audrey looking in the same direction was almost

afraid she might find Rupert on the threshold, but it was only Mistress Digges. "You were a long time," she said coldly. "My daughter's awakened of her own accord. We've no need of the hartshorn. You may go."

As if she had not heard her, the woman came into the room looking at Blanche, "I fear milady's feverish," she said solicitously. "It were better not to disturb her more. If Your Ladyship will come with me, I'll show you where you're quartered."

"No, my mother stays here." Blanche cried defiantly.

"Come, lass—" Mistress Digges began.

"Did you hear my daughter?" Audrey demanded. "Please leave us—at once."

The housekeeper stood her ground, looking at Audrey coldly now. "I take orders from His Lordship and he said—"

"His Lordship's not here to give orders now and I very much doubt he'd bar the bedroom door against me. If he returns suddenly and is put out, you may blame me. Now go." She did not speak loudly but meeting her frosty eyes, Mistress Digges actually dropped an awkward curtsy and scurried from the room.

"Mama, dear mama," Blanche said softly. "You spoke as though you were a queen."

"And why did you not speak as I?" Audrey demanded hotly. "Has the marchioness of Yule become afraid of a common servant? For God's sake, where's your pride?"

"Pride's purchased at too high a price in this house, Mother," Blanche said wryly. "In the beginning I was proud. I told him he could believe as he chose and I went my own way. He was in his cradle then, but later it was different and she came and I had to obey her; I had no choice."

"No choice? Is she your jailer then?"

Blanche's eyes filled with tears. "When he's not here—because of Charlie, for if I am stubborn and I disobey, it's Charlie who suffers. She tells tales and he is beaten. I try to protect him, but Rupert'll not believe anything I say."

"Charlie." Audrey was becoming more and more mystified. "I feel as if we must have stepped into a madhouse, love. Who might Charlie be?"

"My son, my first-born son." Blanche wiped her tears away. "Mama, we must speak. I know I'm not making much sense. I can't when I'm trying to say five years of words at once."

Audrey glanced at the empty cradle. It occurred to her that she had not even mentioned the baby's death. "Perhaps we could talk tomorrow. You must be sore distressed. Your poor little boy. I am indeed sorry that you lost him, love."

Blanche looked toward the cradle. "They should take it away," she said vaguely. "It's not needed now." Then looking into Audrey's astonished eyes, she added, "He would have been very sickly, so I'm told. I am glad that God's seen fit to take him."

Audrey bit her lip. Blanche had spoken so indifferently, but her mother could not find it in her heart to chide her. Obviously, the poor girl was not herself, physically or even mentally she feared. It made her almost ill to see her child's vibrant beauty gone. She was only twenty-three but she looked a weary thirty-five and more. With a little shock, Audrey realized that if she had seen her own daughter on the road, she might not have even recognized her. "I wonder if I shouldn't let you rest," she said reflectively.

"No," Blanche cried. "Let me tell you what has happened. I must tell you before he returns. I never know when he's coming back, but usually he waits until the bleeding's at an end. I think he may this time. He said something about going to London, but I am not sure. He said so once before and returned too quickly."

"Too quickly?" Audrey frowned.

"I—had made arrangements." Blanche lowered her voice. "There was one in the castle might have taken us, Charlie and Arabella, away. There were only the three of us then. But he came back. That's why there's Mistress Digges, and no men about save in the stable-yard."

"And this 'he' you mention's Rupert?" Audrey said incredulously.

"Yes," Blanche sighed.

"I never liked him quite. He was always too impetuous, even as a boy—acting first and thinking later. He was old enough to know you couldn't have survived a week upon the roads and yet—but no matter, that's all past. Still I never thought him evil."

"He's not evil," Blanche said earnestly. "He—he says I—I killed all his trust. He says I only wed him—to mask my sin." She put her thin hands over her tired face. "It's not true, I didn't know—I loved him."

"Child, rest." Audrey begged. "I'll stay here while you do. And when you're feeling better, we'll talk again."

"No," Blanche clutched her mother's arm. "You must listen now, so you can tell me what I needs must do. You must listen so you can help me to understand him and myself. There's been none to talk to, and I am sore confused, and I've become so weak, I hate myself."

"Your condition's no fault of yours, my poor love."

"I'm not talking about that—or perhaps I am. You see, I've tried to resist him when he comes to me, but he's very strong and he can be tender too—and I think perhaps he's changed and now believes me. He's sometimes said he does, and for a while, he's Rupert, the way he used to be. And I am so lonely that I yield and we are happy for a little while and he's kind to Charlie, too—and then he changes." Her face darkened. "But that's at an end. He'll not delude me any more. Last time I fought him—until he overcame me. Oh, if I could get away, but there's Charlie and Arabella and Rupert, baby Rupert, such a little joy, and Owen who'll be ten months on Tuesday next. He's so good.

Mistress Thompson, that's his nurse, she says he hardly ever cries. I wanted to nurse him myself, but my milk went dry. Oh, you must see my pretty darlings, I love them all so much." For a moment, her lost beauty glimmered in her eyes and her cheeks were softly flushed, and then her weariness returned. "But I am so tired all the time, and I do not know which way to turn. Why did you never come before, mother? Why did you never answer all my letters. I wrote so many!"

"There were not many that I received, love. I had no more than five and I wrote many more."

"I didn't receive—Five!" She looked at Audrey aghast. "But I wrote dozens more."

"I never saw them," Audrey told her grimly. "Perhaps they were not sent."

"But why would he send some and not the others?" Blanche asked confusedly.

"Never mind that, my dear. Tell me about him. Tell me why?"

Blanche talked for more than an hour, and listening to that spent and weary voice, Audrey's fury increased. At first it was directed at Glenmore whose motives for coupling her daughter with the king she thought she understood. As one who knew Charles, he must have been aware that Barbara Palmer's husband was soon to be granted the patent for the title he now bore—the Earl of Castlemaine, with the estates and monies accruing. And Glenmore, they had learned, had gambled most of his fortune away. Rupert, however, had proved to be of a different mind.

Of course, she could understand his chagrin and his jealousy when faced with the child he had thought to be his first-born son. Blanche described his confusion with such clarity that it was easy to see how badly the episode had affected each of them.

"I was nursing him and Rupert, coming to the bed, was so morose and looked at him so queerly. 'He's a dark child,' he said. 'Black eyes and an olive skin—

with all the Godwins and the Carlisles fair. I am almost minded to believe in changelings, love.' And—and then I thought of Dame Alys and of my fears. I remembered how I had been on my way to see her when I met Rupert at the gates. I had had two mornings of sickness and I wanted a potion, but I did not know the rest. Yet, I suppose that I looked stricken when he began to question me and—and then because I was weak—I told him of the king and how Glenmore had arranged it."

"Why didn't you tell him he was Glenmore's child."

"Because I—I'd said we'd not lived together at the last. I thought he'd understand, but he did not. He went from the house. I did not see him for a day, but then he returned and seemed much calmer and lay with me, but in the morning pressed a coin into my hand and said it was payment for my services."

"And you said nothing back?" Audrey cried.

"Oh, yes, there was a furious quarrel."

Following fast upon it, she described a reconciliation. Audrey, though she could not approve, understood that Blanche, still loving Rupert, had wanted to appease him and atone for what she ashamedly confessed to be her "sin" in yielding to the king. Blanche had said, "I might have resisted him, but I didn't want to in the end. He—he was so kind."

"He has that reputation," Audrey said dryly.

Blanche turned her face away. "Do not talk of him. I wish to hear no more," she cried with a trace of passion.

"Very well, I shan't, but you must tell me the rest," Audrey urged.

It had been Rupert who had insisted on naming the baby Charles, so that Blanche would not forget his origins. "As if I could forget!"

As he grew older, his unfortunate resemblance to his real father became more obvious, and Blanche could see that Rupert resented him. "He is of two minds about the boy. Charlie is very bright and he loves him and Rupert is kind—"

"Kind?" Audrey interrupted.

"Kind to animals and to anything that's helpless. He's found foxes caught in traps and taken them home to tend them. He'll not join a hunt to kill a deer. And at times he seems both fond and proud of Charlie—but at other times—oh, he's so changed. He used to be so gay and laughing. He talked of how we'd go to court and later on to Rome or Paris, but afterwards, after Charlie came, he said he could not trust me at the court nor any place where there were other men. And so I've stayed at Yule."

"But surely you must know people here, certainly there's a society of a sorts?"

"I know no one. We stay apart. Rupert has meetings with the local squires, but most of the time, he's managing the estate, and I am always here and, of a truth, I've little wish to go about. I become so tired, mama, for either I am with child or recuperating, and there's another reason I'd as lief be alone. Each time I've been brought to childbed, he's stood at the cradle, scanning the infant's face so carefully that I am glad I know no one he can blame."

"The man's mad!" Audrey exclaimed.

"Sometimes I've thought so too," Blanche said wearily. "Mad with jealousy, perhaps."

"You—you've lived this way for five long years?"

"Yes," she sighed.

"How have you beguiled the time?"

"There've been the children, though they're mainly with their nurses. Still, I see them nights and mornings, and we walk about the gardens on fair afternoons or play in the nursery when it rains."

"And that's all you do? You've no say in the running of the household?"

"That's left to Mistress Digges. Yet, in a way it's been my salvation. I still have my writing." Her dull eyes lighted. "I—I've written a play. I've modeled it after Shakespeare, the form, not the content. I've no notion if it's worthy, though sometimes I believe it reads quite well. No matter, it's served to take my mind from my troubles. Without it, I—I fear I might have gone melancholy mad."

"And might yet, if you don't get away," Audrey said darkly.

"Oh, if I could, but it's not possible, mother. I could not take my babies. They're too small to travel as far as we'd need to go, and—"

"What?" Audrey interrupted. "You're resigned to this life? Where's your spirit?"

"Gone—with my looks, I fear. Oh, I've not always been so submissive. I told you what happened in the beginning. And even later, there've been times when I have burned to go. My babies, much as I love them, would be well tended by their nurses, and I have thought I'd rather be a beggar than a dweller in this cuckoo's nest, as he calls it at times to hurt me and, I think, himself as well. Oh, he's turned so strange, mama. And yet—I think—I know he loves me yet."

"He has an odd way of showing it."

"But you see, I hurt him so. He's very proud."

"He's a fool and might be a knave besides. But why do you talk of begging and why's this place so shabby. What happened to your jewels? Surely you could use them as barter—"

"I have no jewels. He took them all."

"And you made no demur?"

"He said he needed them to feed the children since he could not sue the king for more than he'd received when he came home. It's better now. The land's beginning to yield again."

"You could get money, if you chose. Charles has a father who could help."

"No—I'll never let him, never!" Blanche cried.

"Better to make him suffer for his bastardy all his life?—or do you believe your fine husband will grow more kindly with the years? Young Charles Fitzroy, who's Barbara Palmer's boy, will be a duke and yours might finish in the dust. Would that be fair?"

"Oh, God," Blanche groaned. "But what can I do?"

"You can leave him and take the lad. If you were fit for traveling, we'd go at once."

A gleam flickered in Blanche's dulled eyes, "Oh, if I might—" she breathed. "But it—it's not possible. I'm yet so weak—"

Audrey kissed her daughter's cheek. "Oh, my poor, poor child, I know it's not, but we'll manage it later, when you're better."

"But he'll have returned by then," she said distressfully.

"That coward, to be away and let you bear your travail alone—" Audrey began, then stopped abruptly. "I'll not tell you what I think of him. It would take too long and waste too much breath. It might be better were he here. I can deal with Rupert and I shall."

"Why, better?" Blanche inquired.

"Because that jade below and the other pack of varlets in the stable will be less vigilent."

"But if he lies with me—"

"He will not if you are in pain, I'm sure. Even if you improve, you must stress your suffering. Sure it will not be hard for him to understand, since the child is dead."

Blanche winced, "When I was told, I couldn't cry. Have I grown inhuman then?"

"Never think it, love. There's just so much suffering we can stand, and then there's a numbness comes to relieve it. It's a wonder you did not reach that point, years ago. Indeed, when I think on it, I can't see how you've survived at all."

"Oh," Blanche murmured gratefully, "you do understand."

"How could I not?" Audrey said indignantly. "But enough. Hear me. If he returns tonight or tomorrow morning you must pretend to be weak with pain, if it's later, you are prostrate with grief. You must moan and cry. Thus, if he has any heart, which I myself am inclined to doubt, he'll let you be." She paused. "Or better yet, I'll say you begged I sleep in here with you. I think he'll not dare refuse that. Then we shall evolve a plan."

"Oh, Mother, you give me hope, but almost I am afraid to hope; you put yourself in danger."

"I am not afraid of anything he can do," Audrey laughed. "It's I who set in motion these events which have brought you to this pass, and it's I who will stop them now." She rose from the bed. "Are you comfortable, love?"

"Yes," Blanche said, "I think I'll sleep now."

Audrey kissed her once again and left the room. She emerged into another chamber, evidently a sitting room, but sparsely furnished like the other and, since there was no fire, very cold. She was about to make her way toward the stairs when the child she had seen earlier rose up from a nearby chair.

"If you please, milady," he said softly.

Audrey said quickly, "But you must not call me milady. I'm your grandmother, child. And what would you be doing here in this chill room?"

"I—want to know how mama is. Mistress Digges made me leave her before I'd had the chance to do more than tell her you had come. She seemed very low."

"She's better, love, and will be better yet. I swear it," Audrey said decisively.

"Is she really?" the boy asked earnestly. "Will she get well? I—I'd not have her burned in—in flames." His lip trembled.

"Burned in—in flames?" Audrey frowned. "What can you mean?"

"M—Mistress D—Digges said that if—if she d—died, she'd go straight to hell. She said my little brother's there already, for there was none to baptise him. She—she said it was a judgement on mama, for she'd been very wicked. But I—I don't think she's wicked." He trembled and coughed, bringing up his hands to hide his face.

Audrey guessed he did not want her to see his tears. For her own part, she was aglow with anger, but it would not do to let him see it. She said, "Your mother's not been wicked, and as for your poor brother, he's in limbo, for though he died unshriven, he'd not lived long enough to sin. He'll not suffer eternal damnation, love. This Mistress Digges sounds like a canting Puritan, and sure she has a lying tongue. I beg you not to heed her." Patting his head, she felt his heavy curls—his father looked to have hair that weight and of that color, too. "Come closer to the window, love, and let me look at you," she said gently.

"If you please, I—I'd like to see mama."

"She's sleeping, my dear, but you may come back later."

"Later, I'll have to go to bed," he answered. "Mistress Digges—"

"Mistress Digges be damned," Audrey said impatiently. "The more I hear of her, the more I'm convinced she should be stood in pillory. Come with me and show me your brothers and your sister. I'd like to meet them. Will you?"

"Of course, I will, but—" he looked at the closed door.

Seeing the wistful expression in his large eyes, she capitulated. "Come, my dear," opening the bedroom door softly, she beckoned to him. He moved inside, but lingered just beyond the threshold.

"Who's that?—R—Rupert?" Blanche called fearfully.

"It's only I, mother."

"Charlie, come." Rousing herself, she held out her arms, and he hurried toward her but stopped short in his headlong rush and came to stand quietly by her bed, reaching out a tentative hand. "The lady says that you are better. I pray that's true."

"Yes, my dearest, I am. Much, much better now." She patted his cheek.

"Oh, mama—" his voice broke, and, climbing on the bed, he stroked her hair. "I have prayed and prayed that you should soon be well."

"And your prayers are answered, both our prayers are answered, Charlie, love."

Audrey felt tears prick her eyes. Her dislike of Rupert had already hardened into hatred, and it grew even more implacable as she looked at the beleaguered pair. It was incredible, she thought furiously, that Blanche should have suffered so much woe, when with her beauty and her undoubted appeal to men, she had seemed destined for a brilliant life at court.

Barbara Palmer, Castlemaine with far less to offer, was a reigning beauty, queening it even over poor Catherine of Braganza, Charles's childish bride, boldly parading her bastards *and* her husband's cuckoldry; while Blanche and her little boy suffered here alone. Truly, Rupert Godwin must be half-mad. She did not welcome his presence, but conversely she hoped to see him soon, if only to give him a piece of her mind! She sighed sharply. She could not do that, she realized, for it was his wife would suffer not himself. It was a sad law that made even the most unworthy husband the keeper of his wife! However, Blanche would not remain in his keeping. She would see to that. She felt a little touch on her hand.

"I'm ready to go now," the boy told her. "Mama ought to sleep."

She had been standing near the window, and as he moved toward her, the waning afternoon light fell on his face. She experienced a slight shock. He did resemble the king and of a truth, he already comported himself with all the gentle dignity of a little prince. Looking at his shabby clothes, her anger increased, but she managed a smile for him. "You're most considerate," she approved. "Now take me to the others, I must make their acquaintance, too."

* * *

The nursery lay in the tower; a large room furnished with two large four-poster beds, a cradle, and a plethora of little stools and tiny chairs. There were also toys and games. At a long table, spread for supper, there were two women, one middle-aged and the other in her late teens. Between them on a long bench were a bonny little girl and a smaller boy, while in the cradle lay a plump, rosy baby, fast asleep.

The two women rose and bobbed curtseys as Audrey entered. Looking at the older of the pair, a plump woman with small blue eyes and the firm mouth of a disciplinarian, she said, "You must be Nurse Thompson."

"That I be, milady," she replied.

"And you?" Audrey looked at the other, a rosy-cheeked girl, whose full breasts proclaimed her the wet nurse.

"I be Lydia Smith, milady," she said deferentially.

"I am Her Ladyship's mother come to see my grandchildren." She moved to the bench. "You must be Arabella then?"

She rose immediately and curtsyed, "Yes, I am," she acknowledged shyly, adding, "and this is my brother Rupert."

"Make your bow, Master Rupert." Nurse Thompson urged the boy, who was staring at Audrey, spoon in hand.

"No, no," she protested quickly, "let him have his supper, please."

"Charlie—" it was a whisper, "where've you been?" Arabella stared at her older brother. "With mama?"

"Yes," he smiled. "And she's much better."

"Oooh," the little girl clasped her hands. "I would I might see her."

Nurse Thompson frowned, "You b'ean't a-botherin' your poor mama, Master Charlie, after all that's been said."

"It was I who took him there," Audrey interposed hastily and was annoyed to see the nurse give her a half-suspicious look with a stern glance for Charles. She also noted, with a pang, that the younger children were all fair, Arabella much resembling her father, while little Rupert looked like Blanche. Seen in company with the three of them, Charlie looked very swarthy. It was a great pity, she thought, that in common with his father, he must needs take after his Italian kin. He would be a constant and unwelcome reminder to Rupert; more than ever, she was convinced that, like her daughter, Charlie must not remain there. Indeed, she hardly liked to leave him now, for she was sure from the nurse's attitude that he would be punished. Turning to him, she said pointedly,

"I hope I did not keep you too long away, my boy. You were most kind to bring me here. I thank you."

He looked at her gratefully. "It was my pleasure, grandmother," he replied as gravely as a boy of twice his years. "I'm glad that you've come to visit us."

"And I am glad to be here," she smiled. Turning to the others, she bade them and their nurses a good night and hurried from the room.

Once outside, she stood for a moment against the closed door, fighting another attack of fury. They were such lovely children! Her daughter could have been so happy, while instead she was made to suffer under a weight of guilt and misery for that which she could not have prevented if she had chosen. She shook herself. It did no good to regret the past. She needed to help her get away—but how?

"*Somehow*," she said aloud.

A lemon colored sun was shining through the windows when Audrey awakened. She blinked and sat up, rubbing her head. It ached, and no wonder, for she had slept very little in the night, between evolving and discarding plans for an escape and listening for the footsteps that might signal her son-in-law's return. Moving against her pillows, she grimaced, for she felt very stiff. Part of this she attributed to the rigors of her journey, and part to the hardness of the daybed she had insisted Mistress Digges place in Blanche's chamber.

Thinking of her conversation with the woman, she longed for the authority to send her packing! Such insolence as she had displayed! One would have thought her the lady of the manor, and for Blanche to be at her mercy! Looking toward the bed, she saw that her daughter was still sleeping. She lay so quietly that Audrey was frightened. Had she stopped breathing in the night?

Rising, she stepped hastily to the bed and, bending over her, was relieved to see the rise and fall of the covers on her breast. In sleep, she looked younger and less careworn. If she gained a little weight and her hollow cheeks filled out . . . All she needed was rest, care, and felicitous surroundings. To dwell in an atmosphere of doubt and disapproval for even a few months was debilitating, and poor Blanche had suffered for five long years!

As Audrey leaned over her, Blanche stirred and awakened. "Mama," she held out her arms. "Oh, I am not dreaming," she said again.

"No, my love," Audrey kissed her. "I've been here the whole night, and Rose is in the outer chamber. Which reminds me, what happened to little Josette?"

"Josette," Blanche sighed. "He wanted to send her back to Paris. He said she was my confidante and thus could not be trusted, but instead she ran away to London. There was a footman, who used to be in Glenmore's service. They'd been lovers. He wrote to me and told me they are married."

"Oh, God," Audrey ground her teeth. "If I could get you out of here, this minute—"

"If I weren't so weak," Blanche sighed. "When he returns, I fear—"

"You're not to be afraid," Audrey said determinedly. "I've said I shall manage and I will. Now, I want you to try and sleep some more. The more you rest, the better you will be."

"Yes, mama," Blanche dutifully closed her eyes.

Audrey dressed hastily and was about to leave the room when the door was thrust open and she saw Rupert on the threshold. Evidently, he had just come from the road, for his garments were dusty and his boots were muddied. Looking at his face, she was shocked. The disappointments and the frustrations he had experienced were clearly marked. Deep lines already scored his forehead and were deeply etched from nose to chin. In the space of five years, he had changed from a charming boy to a brooding and bitter man. If she had not known that his misery arose mainly from his wounded pride and his refusal to recognize the truth when it was told to him, she might have pitied him, but as it was, she had none left to offer.

Mindful of her instructions to her daughter, she came to him quickly. "Shhhhhh," she cautioned. "Pray do not come closer, Blanche is only now asleep. She had a wretched night and was much in pain." As she spoke, she advanced on him and he, being obliged to give way, backed into the other room. She quickly closed the door and stood in front of it.

He glared at her. "Still I want to see her. Will you let me pass, please?"

She did not move. "Not yet, my dear Rupert," she said gently. "Wait until she's awakened. She needs her rest. She had a hard labor and, as you must have been told, the baby's dead." She lowered her voice. "You have my sympathies. I am sure it was a most grievous disappointment to you."

He looked down. "Yes," he said tersely.

"But still, you've much to compensate," she continued, smoothly. "Four such beautiful children."

"Four?" He gave her a lowering look, saying resentfully, "Sure you know better than that, my lady. You must have known too that she had a bastard in her womb before she wed me. No wonder you and your father-in-law were in such haste to accept my suit."

Audrey put her hand behind her, leaning against it purposefully; for if she had not, she knew she would have been hard put not to strike him. In a tone, she struggled to keep even she said, "You were the one in haste, dear Rupert. And, as for the child, I knew nothing about it at the time and nor, I am sure, did Blanche. Furthermore, being well acquainted with the character of her late husband, I am positive it happened just as she explained it to you."

"Are you indeed," he said between his teeth. "You think a man who was so mad to possess her that he wed her when she was twelve because he was jealous of a mere lad, would willingly thrust her into the king's bed? You are easily deceived, my lady."

"You didn't know Glenmore in his later years," she reminded him.

"His later years numbering—six more?" he inquired derisively.

"Much can happen in an even shorter span of time," Audrey replied, and then because she could no longer restrain her anger she added, "I find my daughter sadly changed, my lord, and that I attribute solely to your cruelty."

"My cruelty?" he laughed mirthlessly, "I've not been cruel. I've but indulged her lusts."

"You've treated her as your whore and not your wife," she flared.

He bit his lip. "She's my wife because I'm wed to her by a priest of the Holy Church and I may not unsay my vows. She's my whore because I count a bastard a bastard, no matter who begot it. She married me for her own good reasons and it's only right that I use her now for mine!"

Words bubbled in her throat and crowded to her tongue; she longed to spew them out at him, but she dared not. She would only harm Blanche's cause. She said, "I am sorry that you think as you do. My daughter came to you, not in guilt or fear, but because she'd loved you all her life. I think it was not she who's proved unworthy, my Lord Yule."

His hands had knotted into fists, and his face was white. For a moment, she feared he would strike her, but instead, turning on his heel, he strode from the room. She sighed with relief and was about to return to Blanche when she heard a muttered curse and the sound of a slap, as Rupert said harshly, "What are you doing out here? Eavesdropping as usual, you misbegotten brat!"

Hurrying into the next room, she found Charlie lying on the floor with Rupert standing over him, glaring down at him. Giving Rupert a withering glance, she knelt by the little boy, "Why?" She shot the question at him.

"This is your fine—prince," he said in a choked voice. "A sneak and—"

"I'm not," the boy cried. "I—I came to see mama."

"You came to listen as you always do," Rupert shouted. "You shouldn't be allowed in this house. You belong in the stables and by God, I'll put you there!"

"You will do nothing of the kind!" Audrey retorted.

"You'll give no more orders in my house, Lady Carlisle. I want you to leave as soon as you can pack. I didn't want you here, nor will I have you stay."

She was filled with dismay. An apology trembled on her lips, but looking into his hard eyes, she knew it would be useless. He had much against her, including that moment long ago, when she had stopped him and her daughter at the door of Diamant. Then, suddenly, a wild plan whirled into her mind. She said, "Very well, I'll go and take the lad with me. He's nothing of yours—but he's my grandchild. I'd be glad to care for him."

He hesitated, a curious look upon his face, it seemed compounded of regret and frustration. Then, he shrugged, "So be it. As long as you're out of here."

"I shall be—and within the hour," she replied, "if

you'll be good enough to see my coach is ordered and send my girl to me."

"Very well," he agreed and strode on out. Her heart was pounding, and her other self inside her head was repeating, "It's madness, madness, madness," but she ignored it. Looking at Charlie, she saw to her relief that though his cheek was reddened, he was not crying. "Child, go and get your warmest cloak and have your nurse pack some clothes for you, then come back here immediately."

"I'll not leave Mama," he said.

"You'll not need to," she whispered. "Trust me and say nothing. Only do as you are told."

His eyes were full of a precocious wisdom. Nodding, he left her.

Audrey went back to Blanche and found her awake, "R—Rupert's here?" she breathed.

"Yes," Audrey said, "but no matter. Can you walk, my dearest?"

"I—I am not sure." Blanche faltered.

"Try," her mother urged.

Slipping from the bed, Blanche moved toward Audrey; she was obviously weak, but her steps were firmer than they had been the previous day. "I can," she said. "You've instilled new strength in me."

"And I must instill more, because we're leaving, now."

"Now—but—but—" Blanche's eyes were filled with fear.

"Listen to me, my love. If you can get down the stairs and out to the coach, we'll be safe."

"But—"

"Listen to me, Blanche. Your husband's ordered me to go in the hour and I've said I'll take Charlie with me. There'll be no time for you to bid farewell to your other babies, and I'm sorry for that, but as your life and his depend upon it, you must come with me. Your husband's half-mad I think, and may grow madder still. I'll not leave you at his mercy."

"Charlie will come with us?" Blanche asked.

"He must. Are you game, child?"

"Yes, but—but my darlings—" Blanche hesitated.

"You cannot think about them now. They have their nurses and are safe. He'd not harm his own. I can't say the same for Charlie. He hates him. I saw it for myself."

Blanche tensed, "He—hurt him?"

"Yes."

Blanche moved forward. "Badly?" she demanded.

"No. He struck him and ordered him to the stables."

"He—he's often threatened that. He did not mean it."

"Are you defending him?" Audrey cried incredulously. "He meant it this time, I can assure you, and probably because of me. I'm sorry for that, my dear, but never mind that now. My Rose is of your size and she's brought a warm, hooded cloak. I'll have you wear her clothes, and the hood will hide your face. Then, you'll lead Charlie and I'll instruct him to cry and say he'll not leave his mother. That should prove a convincing touch."

"But what of Rose?"

"She'll meet us on the road. I'll have one of the outriders pick her up. All of this is a great risk, but I think it's worth it."

"But if he comes to my room?"

"I don't think he will. I said you were tired and sleeping. I stressed your pain and grief. I've the feeling that will keep him away. He is all confusion, and I believe he loves you overmuch, my dear, but it's a love you do not need. And—" she paused, as they heard a knock on the door.

"Oh, God, it's Rupert," Blanche whispered.

"No, I think not." Audrey moved swiftly to the door and opened it to Rose. "Ah, you're here."

"Yes, milady." She looked surprised. "Are we going then?"

"Yes—and here's what you must do."

* * *

She had never worked so quickly as she did in the time allotted her. With Rose's help she dressed Blanche. The clothes were too big, but the cloak proved all enveloping, and they were much of a height. If only Blanche could negotiate the stairs. She was still so weak. She had a moment of real panic when Charlie joined them, carrying his little knapsack.

"Oh, mama," Blanche shook her head. "I must see my babies. Could they not come to me?"

"And their nurses too?" Audrey demanded. "No. We can't chance it."

"But I—I might never see them again—my pretty darlings—Oh, God, how can I leave them?"

"You must think of Charlie," Audrey said sternly.

She looked at him. "Yes—I must," she said in a stronger voice.

Finally they were ready, but as they started for the door, Blanche stopped, "Mama, the bed—We must make it look as if I'm still in it."

"Yes, you're right," Audrey agreed. She rushed to it and thrust the pillows beneath the covers, but as she started to draw the curtains Blanche said hastily, "Don't. I never do."

"That's a pity." Audrey sighed and stiffened. "Hssst, do I hear something in the outer room?"

"Shall I look?" Charlie whispered.

"No, wait." For a moment she ceased to breathe, and then she could say, "I think I am wrong. Perhaps it was the wind."

At Audrey's suggestion, Blanche moved along the wall of the outer chamber. To her anxious eye, she looked close to fainting, but finally they were in the hall and fortunately, the staircase was only steps away. She started to take her daughter's arm.

"No mama, I'm your maid," Blanche whispered. She came down the stairs very slowly, too slowly for Rose by far. Audrey had never felt more desperate. Every moment she feared to see Rupert, but he did not come, and then they were at the threshold of the hall, the long, long hall.

She murmured a Pater Noster and followed it with a quick Hail Mary, as Blanche came after her. Charlie, bless him, had a shoulder for her to grasp and did not even tremble when she did. She was still walking slowly, but she did not falter. Inwardly, Audrey applauded her. She might be weak and depressed, but that same strength that had kept her going all these years had not failed her now—she would not give in.

They were nearly across the room. Oh, God, they were approaching the front door. Out of the corner of her eye, she looked through the window and saw the coach without. She was glad it was not a courtyard like Carlisle. An open space was better. There were some of those raggle-taggle stable boys about, but they were at the horse's heads. Would Rupert see them off? Or would his conscience, provided he still possessed one, keep him absent? She thought he might feel guilty, and that he acted as he did in spite of it was part of the agony she had read upon his ravaged face. She could not think of Rupert and his actions, not now. They were nearing the door. She blessed his dictum against manservants. Never had she seen such an empty house. Mayhap Mistress Digges would assert her independence and stay away as well. No, her heart plummeted, she had appeared and stood waiting for them near the door. Was she eyeing "Rose" suspiciously?

Seeing her, Charlie, bless him, began to wail, "Oh, Rose, please, please, don't make me go," he sobbed. "Mama will miss me so!"

Audrey stepped forward, her hand on Blanche's arm. "Now, my dear Charles, you're not to plague us," she said tartly. "It's not Rose has the say, but I."

Mistress Digges was smiling broadly. "Farewell, Master Charles," she said in a way that made Audrey long to hit her. She dropped the barest curtsy, "Farewell to you, Milady Carlisle," she added with an edge of triumph to her tone.

She had opened the door, and the salt-laden winds from the sea were blowing in their faces. She darted an anxious look at Blanche and saw her clutch her hood and hold it tight about her head—and she was stepping out. She had stumbled, but Charlie pushed her back, saying quite crossly, "Don't push me, Rose. I'm going."

Lord, Lord, but he was uncommonly bright, as became a king's son or a Carlisle. Audrey said, "You mustn't push him, Rose. He's hurrying as fast as he can." She paused in the doorway and turned back to Mistress Digges. "Will my Lord of Yule not favor us with his farewells?" she inquired coldly, inwardly amazed at her own audacity.

"My Lord is resting," Mistress Digges said insolently. "He had a long ride this morning and is vastly tired."

"So be it," Audrey shrugged, and because she wanted the door slammed in her face, she added threateningly, "Do not think he's heard the last of me. I shall sue the king when I return to the city, and I shall fetch my daughter home, whether my lord wills it or no."

As she had anticipated, Mistress Digges shut the door. Audrey ran to Blanche, staying close behind her as they came up to the coach. Rose had alerted the grooms, and one of them lifted Blanche and Charlie inside. Audrey climbed the steps, the door was slammed, and the horses plunged forward. They were bowling down the long drive, they were at the castle walls, the gates were being opened. She could hear the familiar crunch and scrape. They were through and out upon the road; there was the sea glimmering in the sunlight. Of course, she would not dare breathe until they had put long miles behind them. No, she was forgetting Rose. Had she made her way to the gate, or had they seen her, stopped her, questioned her? She could not take her eyes from the window, she could not even look to see how Blanche was faring for they were still in danger, still he could come riding up with his crowd of uncouth stable lads. They were slowing. . . . Why, why, why?

"Why are we stopping?" Charlie demanded.

"We must pick up Rose, my darling," she said steadily because, of course, that had to be the reason.

They had stopped. Blanche had not uttered a word. Had she fainted? Audrey darted a look at her and caught the gleam of her eyes in the darkness of her hood. Her one hand was entwined with Charlie's, the other was tight upon the strap.

The men were shouting. She heard laughter in their tones. The door was pulled open and little Rose, also laughing and windblown climbed inside and crouched upon the floor. A few moments later, the horses had sprung forward once again.

"Lord, I had a rare time," Rose told them. "I crawled out a window below the stairs, and at first I couldn't find my way, but then I went through the kitchen garden and there was a bad place in a fence—and here I am." She looked anxiously at the silent Blanche. "How's milady?" she demanded.

"I am all right," Blanche whispered. "Only suppose he comes for us. His horses are fleet. He could catch up with us so easily."

"The men are armed," Audrey told her grimly.

Blanche shook her head, "They—they must not hurt him," she protested.

"They won't unless it's unavoidable," Audrey replied.

"No," Blanche cried frantically. "My babes—he's their father. They'd be all alone."

"Hush, mama," Charlie put his hand on her arm. "It's not happened yet."

"Oh, love, my little love," she whispered brokenly.

Pushing back her hood, she bent and kissed the top of his head and Audrey saw her cheeks were wet with tears. Was it weakness, she wondered or sorrow over those she had left behind—or could she still love her Rupert? If he were to follow them, what would happen? Would she yield and let him take her back? Back to what? To death, perhaps?

They were leaving the sea road. And there were the long, yellowing fields they had passed yesterday. The outriders were shouting at each other, as they had shouted yesterday. She frowned. Did she hear a certain warning in their voices? She strained to listen for sounds of pursuit but heard only the rattling of the coach wheels and the thud of their own team's massive hooves. Did she also hear another sort of cry? A wild howling like a beast in pain, a maddened beast. The sound was clearer now, borne on the wind perhaps.

Blanche stiffened. "Rupert," she mouthed, "on his white stallion—coming to the castle gate—and we found the waterfall." Her voice trailed away and her hand fell limply from the strap.

"Blanche!" Audrey made a grab for her while Rose quickly pushed her back against the seat.

"Mama," Charlie cried. "Is she—"

"She's only fainted, dearest," she soothed. She was glad she had fainted. "Charlie, move aside," she said urgently. "Rose, help me ease her onto the floor."

At her instructions, they lifted her down and covered her with the cloak, while Rose, taking her vacant place, looked boldly out the window.

Moments later, the sound was louder, and a man rode past them, his face like a mask of tragedy Audrey had once seen carved upon an old theater door. Then, he was out of sight. There was a momentary slowing down, then a shot rang out.

Increasing their speed, the horses leaped forward. They passed a fallen horse and rider. Audrey saw him try to rise and fall back upon the ground. His angry cry was in her ears, and then, he was far behind them.

Audrey, looking down at Blanche, was glad that she was still unconscious. With a certain defiance in her tone, she said loudly, "Thank God that she is free from him at last."

Chapter Nine

"If I had but known—if I had but thought—" Audrey said desparingly. They had been summarily turned away from another inn, with the host and his wife looking so wild that Audrey had almost been afraid they would mark crosses on the door of the coach—so terrified of plague were they, for all it was known to be decreasing and had been since the middle of the month.

Yet, looking at Blanche, she could not altogether blame them for their fears. In their three days on the road, she had grown even paler than she had been at Yule. Indeed, she seemed to be all one color and that, as yellow as her hair. There were moments when Audrey had even thought it would have been better to have left her daughter behind, for at least she could have rested. No, not with that madman about. She would have suffered as before, and in her debilitated condition, there was no telling what would have happened. He might even have succeeded in killing her. She wondered if that had been his intent. A strange and horrible revenge indeed, to use his potency and her fertility as the instruments of murder. She was inclined to think that a flight of fancy on her part, for many women were in similar straits, a baby every year. However, they did not all bear them in such an atmosphere of suffering and contempt. She did not like to think on what her daughter's life must have been for the last five years.

She darted a look at Blanche, who was lying in her corner, holding onto the strap. That was a good indication since it suggested a will to survive, but she looked so unhappy! She had said more than once that she had hated to leave her other children behind. She hoped that was the cause of her sorrow, rather than the abandoning of her husband. She had insisted that she had grown to hate him, but there had been a curious lack of conviction in her tone, and there had been an expression of actual pain in her eyes when he had pursued them—pain, not fright. Could she have wanted him to come, wanted to be rescued? It wasn't possible, not after the way he had treated her, unless her years with Glenmore had warped her nature and left her with need for pain.

She had heard of such things happening, had even known a woman who had craved the lashings her husband had given her. Audrey winced. She could not believe her daughter similarly afflicted. No doubt, it was her weakness coupled with the jolting of the coach that was affecting her. Which brought her back to her present problem; where could they find shelter for the night? Already the sun was descending, and the countryside that she saw from her window was passing wild. Certainly, they would not dare travel after dark with the roads so bad and the chances that the horses would go astray and lead them into a ditch or even over a cliff. She could only hope that they would soon be passing another inn, but if they didn't? . . .

She was still pondering the problem an hour later when the sun, flanked by oblong stretches of graying clouds, had dwindled to a dying, scarlet streak across the western horizon. They were nearing one of the many ruined abbeys that they had seen upon the road. This one, more solid than the others, boasted a tower which had, somehow, escaped the bludgeons of King Henry's men. The multicolored sky, seen through the crumbling arches, was a lovely sight, she thought, and then her eyes strayed toward that tower once again. Was it possible that they might shelter there? It would be cold, for sure, but she had brought coverlets aplenty, since you never knew what you might find at a country inn; also they had flasks of ale and wine, and there would be grass for the horses to crop. They could make do, at least until sunrise. She tapped the roof of the coach.

It had been a magnificent structure, a miniature city once, and to see its empty arches and its roofless passages and the great gaping hole where once the altar had stood was to feel a constriction in the chest and a pain in the throat. But Audrey, with Rose and grumbling Arthur followed by Tom and Diccon, the other two outriders remaining to guard Blanche in the coach, could not dwell upon the wanton destruction that had left thousands of clerics homeless, had robbed the poor of almshouses and travelers of safe hostels on the lonely, thief-infested roads. Thinking of the bands of thieves and beggars that still roamed those roads, Audrey hoped they would not find any lurking among the ruins. Arthur had suggested that they might. He had also mentioned that many of the abbeys were known to be haunted by their ousted nuns and monks. However, even he had seen the wisdom in tarrying somewhere for the night. Now, if only the tower proved to be as solid as it had seemed from the road!

It stood at the far end of the ruins, and reaching it was a matter of walking very carefully over ground strewn with the rubble of a hundred years of pillaging. Abbey stones had gone into the foundations of cottages and into larger halls, but many more remained—fallen pillars and fragmented floors. She was forever saying, "Be careful where you step," especially to little Charlie, who, freed from the confinement of the coach, danced ahead of them like a sprite, she thought, with his thick black curls streaming behind him in the wind.

Then, suddenly and with a little cry, he disappeared among the pillars that must once have formed the north aisle of the church.

"Charlie!" Audrey started forward as Rose, paling, ran ahead with Arthur and Diccon close behind her. Then, all three of them came to a jolting stop. Charlie had reappeared, and with him was surely an apparition—an old bent man in a worn brown cassock, a rope around his waist and a dangling rosary attached. He wore rough leather sandals on his bare feet, and his white hair was carefully tonsured.

Arthur crossed himself. "Sure and it must be the devil, milady," he muttered between chattering teeth as Audrey reached his side. "The d—devil as a m—monk."

"Yes," Rose had begun to sniffle, and even the outriders, who professed to fear neither man nor beast, were looking pale.

Arthur, she saw, was backing away. In another moment he would be running. She put a hand upon his arm and found it was trembling. "If he's a devil, he's a very old and toothless one. I could not envision a toothless devil, Arthur," she whispered.

"The devil comes in many guises, milady," he said seriously. "And very often as a monk. He could not be living for all that dwelt in this place are dead, a hundred years ago or more."

"One hundred and twenty-four years," she thought to herself, for the last of the monasteries had been suppressed in 1541. Probably he was some harmless lunatic, but even that thought was daunting. She was not of a mind to tangle with a madman. However, there were several of them and only one of him, and if he were not the devil they were certainly safe. Armed with that conviction, she stepped forward boldly, but before she could address him, he said in a cracked, old voice, "I bid you welcome to Frontley Abbey. I am Father Matthew."

His accent was cultured, his voice gentle, but obviously he was mad. Still, she said with a duplication of his own courtesy, "I thank you, father, I am Lady Carlisle. I was not aware there were any monks remaining."

"Oh, there aren't," he assured her. "There's but myself. The others are dead, long, long ago."

She frowned. If he were not mad, what was his story? "You live here, though?" she asked.

"Yes, I am sure my being here must seem very strange to you. I've been in residence for the last five years only. Before that, being a chaplain to a Papist family which was scattered by Cromwell's order, I was prisoned and tortured." He held up a hand and she shuddered to see that it had been badly mangled and was a mass of scars. "I thought I should die there but the good Lord let me survive; so when I was freed, I came here to finish out my days where I might thank him. Now the boy has told me you are looking for some shelter. I have such and would gladly share it with you, though I must tell you, it's not very grand."

"Oh," she whispered. "I think God must have guided me here."

"Of course, he did, milady," the old man gently answered.

She was more than ever sure of it, when they brought Blanche from the coach into the tower. As she had anticipated, it was habitable, and the priest had made himself a home in a large room on the second floor. It was not very grand, certainly it was a veritable monk's cell, sparsely furnished with a small table, a few stools, and a straw pallet in the corner. It had been very cold when they had entered, but there was a brazier stocked with sea coal, which, though it did not generate much heat, had taken away the chill. The old man had insisted that Blanche and Charlie take his straw pallet.

"There are many places I can sleep, and indeed I do not need much rest. I spend a great deal of the night in meditation and in communing with the past. It's very close to us in this place," he had told Audrey gently.

Audrey was glad he had not expounded this particular theory in the presence of the servants. Arthur especially was still loathe to spend a night among what he stubbornly contended were haunted ruins crowded with a host of demon monks. However, finally they were all situated in various niches sheltered from the winds. Audrey, lying in another corner of the tower room, closed her eyes and felt satisfied, for Blanche had fallen asleep quickly. She had done well, she thought drowsily, for if God had guided them to this sanctuary, it was God who had aided her in removing her daughter from the clutches of her lawful husband. She had had some qualms about that, she realized now with some surprise. One did not come between man and wife, that was the teaching of the church, but it was for the best. Yet, what would happen in the future? She could not think of that. She would leave it up to God.

From where she lay, Blanche could see a veiled moon. There would be rain in the morning, she thought, and she stifled a sigh. It was dreary at Yule in the rains, dreary and cold, filled with the dampness of the sea. The children would be fretful at not being able to play in the gardens, and she was still too weary to entertain them with the stories that they loved so much. Then—with a little start—she realized that the three of them were many leagues away.

The watched moon grew mistier yet through her tears. She felt as if she had left part of her own body behind and, of a truth, she had. She had not been able to bid them good-bye, and he would tell them . . . She drew a tremulous breath, she knew exactly what he would tell them—that falsehood which would seem the truth he had always sworn it to be. "You love that boy more than any of mine," he had accused her bitterly.

It was not true. Or at least, it would not have been

true, had he not treated Charlie so cruelly from time to time, punishing her through him. Why hadn't he believed her? How could he have stopped loving her so quickly, when she . . . She moved restively on her pallet, not wanting to face that particular fact. Yet it remained, and she needed to examine it. He had only to give her a kind word and she, like some chastened hound, would crawl to him upon her belly and humbly lick his shoe. Her lip twisted at the image, and she had only contempt for herself—for that self that reached out loving arms and drew him to her bosom and, each time, forgot the contemptuous words, the angry sneers, hoping against hope that his wounded pride had finally been healed.

It was the same self which had seen his blanched face framed briefly in the carriage window and had actually wanted him to stop her headlong flight and bring her home. Yes, she had wanted that and had even been resentful that her mother had managed to separate them so neatly, as neatly as she had done all those years ago, when she had caught them on the stairs. It was ridiculous of her to couple those two disparate events. Save that the three of them had been involved, one was nothing like the other. She had to be glad that she was free of him and of that hateful loving, or loving hatred, which had sapped her energies and made her old before her time. Still there was a pain in her heart when she thought of their children, and it was no consolation at all for her to realize that they were young enough to forget her quickly and that he would see they would. There was a little movement at her side. Charlie was stirring in his sleep. She would have kissed him, but she did not want to awaken him. Lovely, at least, to have him near her in the dark. It was because of Charlie that she had come away, and it was he she needed to consider now.

She remembered what her mother had said about commending him to the care of the king and bit her lip, recalling what Rupert had been quick to tell her about Charles's many "bastard brats." It had been said to wound her and it had. Yet, she could not but believe her son was very special, so sensitive to her every change of mood, so responsible and protective too. She had often wondered, looking at that little face which so resembled a picture she had seen of the young Prince Charles, if the king himself had been like her boy when he was small. Even though their coming together had lasted but a night, she felt she understood him better and respected him more through what she saw in his child. Had Rupert guessed that? Had it increased his resentment of the boy? If only he had troubled to know him as she did. She wished she could sleep. Her memories were becoming too painful for her—but sleep was very far away.

She stiffened, for she had seen a shadow framed in the moonlight on the floor, a robed shadow. She shuddered, thinking of those demon monks she had heard Arthur mention to her mother. It was approaching her and kneeling by her pallet. She could hear breathing. She relaxed a little. She had never seen a ghost, but she did not think they breathed.

"My dear, I thought you were wakeful and I see you are."

Startled, she looked into the moon-touched face of the elderly priest who had given her his bed. "How—did you know?" she whispered.

"I feel many things. I've brought you something that may soothe you. It's not bad tasting and it will relax you."

"Oh, how very kind you are."

"Here," he said. "I'll hold it to your lips. Just lift your head a bit."

She obeyed and felt the liquid cool against her tongue. It had an odd, sweet taste. She sipped it then said, "I think of meadow grasses."

"There's a bit of grass in it," he told her. "And other herbs. The monks of Frontley used to brew it and give it to the weary travelers who stopped here, centuries ago."

"How do you know that?" she asked curiously.

"I've read about it. Some of the books of Frontley found their way into the library of the house where once I served as chaplain. I think you'll sleep now."

"Thank you, father," she said gratefully.

His hands rested lightly on her brow, "God be with you, my daughter, and may he send you peace." He left as noiselessly as he had come.

She felt peaceful and comforted. There was something in his gentle manner which stirred a dormant memory of someone she had known. A name came to her . . . Peel, David Peel. Yes, he did remind her of her grandfather's secretary! Was he still at the castle? If so, he must read her play!

Sick as she was, and in the wild flurry of leaving, she had not forgotten it. She had carried it beneath her cape and it was under her pillow now, five years of writing, which she had shown to no one, but which she must certainly give to David Peel. She wondered what he would think. He had always advised her to write what she knew, and this, of course, was a historical subject. Yet, it was what she knew.

She smiled bitterly. It had a heroine with whom she was much in sympathy: Adeliza, a young French countess, forced to leave her true lover and marry the aging king of England, Henry I, who craved an heir. Alas, she had remained barren.

Into the lines of that play, she had poured her soul. And she had more in common with the queen, she thought, for on the death of her husband, Adeliza had married her old lover—the only difference being that they had lived happily, or so the chronicles said.

Would David Peel like her play? Suddenly, she longed to be back in her grandfather's library, listening to Peel's wise comments. She knew he would be honest. Her heart began to beat faster—she wondered how long it would take to get home—she wished the coach had wings. And then she smiled. She, who thought she had lost all hope, had begun to hope again. She . . .

She slept.

They *had* been guided to the abbey, Audrey thought, because after leaving it everything was easier, Blanche's spirits were marvelously improved, there was even new color in her cheeks. The horses were swifter, the roads less bumpy, and though they had run into a heavy spring rain, they were not stuck in any mire. By the time they had left Yorkshire, the weather was much milder, with only one day of rain and that in Shropshire, less than twelve hours from home. Furthermore, they passed into Worchestershire on a day which surely must have been borrowed from the coming April, since it was marvelously mild and the winds tamed from lion to lamb. In the early afternoon with the merest fluff of clouds, there were the twin towers of Carlisle.

She felt as though she had been away two years instead of only two weeks. She was out of the coach as nimbly as a sixteen-year-old and in Tony's arms, half-laughing, half-crying. As before, he did not hesitate to reveal his happiness at her safe return, but kissed her in full view of the household, which had congregated to welcome her; and numbered among it, the ubiquitous Mr. Peel, about whom Blanche, for some reason, had inquired most solicitously. But she could not think of any of them—not even Blanche—for Tony had whispered ardently, "Enough of this, my Audrey, I'll not let you go again—unless I come with you."

"Nor will I go again without you," she answered, knowing now how much she had grown to love him, knowing too that she was loved in return.

On a morning in late April, Blanche awakened to find her room bright with sunshine. Through the window, she could see the ash trees brave in purple blossoms, the oaks and elms a tender green, and buds upon the Judas tree. It was lovely, she thought, to awaken and find greenery rather than the great expanse of sea. Yet, she had loved the sea before coming to Yule. She moved restlessly. She did not want to think of Yule nor Rupert, not now when she was beginning to feel herself again. It had been difficult, more difficult than she had imagined, to be alone, she who had been used, when waking in the night, to hearing Rupert's breathing. He had always been a restless sleeper. In the morning, the covers were invariably tangled into a knot, and sometimes she, even lying as close as she could to her side of the bed, had found him clutching her, only to have him awaken, glare, and pointedly draw away.

He had not liked to make love to her in the mornings, but only in the darkness. He had made it clear that he did not want to look at her. Once the truth about Charlie had been realized she had ceased to be a person to him and had, instead, become only a convenience. Yet, on occasion . . .

She sat up, clutching her knees. She would not think about him, would not wonder why he had failed to pursue her. During her first fortnight at Carlisle, she had expected him almost hourly—expected him and feared his coming. Certainly, she was glad he had not come; she had not wanted trouble nor had she wanted the father of her children to suffer the indignity of being turned away by the servants. Probably Rupert, aware that they must have orders to repulse him, had purposely stayed away, or perhaps he had no wish to see her more. She hoped that was his reason, for she did not want to see him. She was relishing her freedom. Only . . .

Only she could not stop thinking of her children. She missed them dreadfully. Were they well? She knew they must be, for their nurses were attentive and dependable, and they had taken charge of most of the care of them. Yet, on occasion, she had had noticed things that had escaped their scrutiny—such as when Arabella had the colic and they had mistaken it for mere fretfulness. Also she was prone to colds and especially if they dressed her too warmly and forgot to remove her cloak once she came inside. That was often to happen for she was active and prone to laugh and elude them. She had such an infectious little laugh, and even at four it was sure she would be a beauty—she had her father's eyes but larger and a greeny gold. Had they left the coral beads on Owen's neck—he was restless and they did say that coral kept a child from falling. As for little Rupert . . . But it did no good to think on them or to fret about their nurses. If only she had been more friendly with the two women, she could have written surreptitiously, no, for neither one could read.

She flung back the covers and slipped out of bed. She would find Charlie, and they could walk in the garden; he dearly loved being outside. She smiled, thinking of him. He was so much happier here and so petted by her mother and her grandfather that she was afraid his head might be turned, but it needed turning after Rupert's treatment. Her face hardened. She resented that even more than his behavior toward herself. She wondered that she had borne it so long. It was as well she was away—even though she had been forced to leave her babies behind, for sure they would have been taught to hold her in contempt and before they were much older. They were better with their nurses. As for herself, if she were not entirely happy, at least her health had improved. She was much stronger and she looked more like her former self.

She sat down at her dressing table and picked up her mirror. There had been a time when she had avoided looking at the pale face that had stared back at her. Now, she had no fear, the hollows around her eyes had nearly vanished, and her skin had lost its horrid, yellow tinge. As for her hair, once more it fell in shining locks about her shoulders. Of course, she looked older, but she was old, near twenty-five, a dignified matron.

She put her mirror down. She ought to be a dignified matron, she, a mother of four, but instead she was a pensioner again, dependent on the bounty of her family. To all intents and purposes, she and her little boy were beggars, unless she did as her mother advised and brought the matter to the king's attention. She winced, remembering Audrey's oft-repeated words, "Lady Barbara's children are dukes and duchesses; Charlie could have a similar title and estates as well from his father. Blanche, you must sue for them. He'll give them to you. He's more than kind to all—those who have a claim upon him."

Audrey had been about to say "his mistresses." Blanche knew that, but she had not been Charles's mistress and her knowledge of his reputation, also gleaned from Rupert, led her to believe he would not even recall an encounter that had lasted only a night. There must have been many such; besides there was no chance of approaching him as yet, even were she of such a mind. The plague still raged in London—she could not expose her son to its dangers nor herself, neither. She was not entirely well. Until the time when she was forced to give serious thought to Charlie's future, she would be patient, and she could write.

She expelled a long, hissing breath. The self who counseled patience had little in common with the other self, who was at present pacing the chambers of her brain, seething with frustration. Mr. Peel, as she had hoped, had seized upon her manuscript eagerly, but as yet had given her no answer as to its merits. He could not. He was out of the castle on business and had been for two endless weeks! It was amazing, she thought, remembering the swiftness of the events that had brought her from Yule, that her life was suddenly at almost as complete a standstill as it had been in Yorkshire.

She was still suffering that same frustration an hour

later when, with Charlie, she walked through the gardens, restored now to their former beauty. Hedges cunningly cut, coiled around patterned flower beds, and in niches all along the walk stood statues brought from Diamant. In spite of her pleasure over the changes, she wished that these had remained in France, or to come upon one or another of them was to remember similar encounters when in the company of the boy, Rupert. She wondered how long it would be before she could stop walking with memory.

"Mama, look!"

"What do you want, darling?" she asked.

"Come here," he commanded.

As luck would have it, Charlie had found a pool, ringed about with cedar trees, another, more painful memory of Diamant. She had not seen it on their other walks—she wished she had not seen it now. "Let's go another way," she called.

"But it's like a looking glass!" he cried. "Please come."

She could not refuse him. Moving to his side, she willed herself to look and not see Rupert. Why, she wondered, was hate as strong as love and equally able to people the landscape of the heart with ghosts, for of course she did not see Charlie's vivid little face reflected in those depths. She could liken herself to a prisoner, who, released from his dungeon, still feels the weight of his absent gyves. She was about to turn away when she heard her name called and at the same time glimpsed a third reflection in those waters, not a handsome boy, but a worn, craggy face, creased into a broad and unaccustomed smile. With a little exclamation, she whirled toward Mr. Peel!

"You've come back!" she cried unnecessarily.

His smile grew even broader, "Indeed I have my dear, and only wish it might have been sooner, for I've much to tell you."

Her heart was thumping. He would not be smiling if

he had not liked what he had read. Still, she was almost afraid to ask, "Did you—read—"

"Your play," he finished quickly. "Yes." He shook his head.

Her spirits plummeted. Why was he shaking his head? Obviously, his smile was meant to reassure, to comfort her or perhaps to encourage her to write another, better work. "How—did you find it?" she pursued, adding quickly, "I—I know it must be full of errors, but—"

"Nonsense, my dear. It's fine—very fine in character and perceptions, extremely sensitive. I only wish the theaters were open to receive it now. Yet, soon they must be. The plague's decreasing and the people will want to be diverted from the dismal spectre of death—"

She stepped backward. Her knees felt weak. "You—you think it—belongs in a theater?"

"Doesn't every play of merit?"

"Every play of merit." She savored the words and felt almost as though she could taste them on her tongue. "I never thought—"

He was not attending to her words. "I'd like to think that Mrs. Jennings could do justice to your Adeliza or perhaps Mrs. Knepps, though she does not have quite the depth," he mused. "It's a fine part for a woman and well that we have women now to perform it—"

"To perform it," she repeated ecstatically.

"And for the young hero, Kynaston's one choice. A handsome young man, adept in comedy and in tragedy as well. Sometimes a bit too mannered for my thinking. His gestures can be effeminate, but of course since he was a reigning tragedy queen that's not much to be wondered at. It's odd we did not have women long ago upon our stages. Think how it would have gladdened Shakespeare's heart."

She was only half attending now, "Mademoiselle de Scudéry makes her living by her pen. Would you think that I—"

"There's every chance you could. You've given me a great surprise. The work you showed me years ago had considerable merit, but you've grown immensely as a writer, both in style and form. You have great insight into your characters—and certainly you know a woman's heart."

She flushed, "Yes, I think I do." Inadvertently, she stared into the pool. "Yes, I know it."

He gave her a measuring look. Even without being aware of what must have transpired in the last five years, he could imagine she had suffered much. Indeed, he had been shocked at the change in her. When he had first seen her, she had been a widow, true, but blooming in spite of her black clothes, and glowing whenever she had looked at the young man, whom, much to his own personal regret, she had married so suddenly. Since her return, she had been going about in bright silks, but colors could not conceal the mourning spirit that dwelt behind her eyes, adding a certain weight both to her movements and her speech. In the two weeks he had been gone, her appearance had mightily improved, he was glad to see. Her beauty shone forth again, though not in all its youthful vibrancy. There was still an air of melancholy about her, which was apparent even now when she was obviously so gratified by his approval of her work. Considering her, he sought for a description and emerged with one he thought appropriate. Her trials, whatever they had been, had left her with a chiaroscuro of the spirit, but that he could not decry. A writer needed both light and shadow in one pen and she had both. She should do well, if she were not impeded by the burden of being a desirable woman. He found himself wishing quite fervently that he might guard her from another serious error. Perhaps by giving her a sense of her own true worth, he might.

He said, "My dear, I have friends in London who must see your play. However, first we will have to make a copy, and I have some few minor suggestions that might improve it in certain ways. If you'd care to listen to them—"

She clasped her hands, "Oh, yes, I will, I will. Only tell me when you will be ready to begin!"

He smiled into her lovely, eager face, "Now," he said succinctly.

"She's my wife, mine, bound to me in holy wedlock, her place is at my side!"

Those words had been going through Rupert's mind for the five days he had been on the road. The repetition of them helped to strengthen his purpose and keep him in the saddle for, though he was loathe to admit it, he was damned uncomfortable. His leg, where he had wrenched it, when they had killed his horse, was aching badly. Most of his discomfort centered in the knee. It was hard to bend it for the amount of time he was riding, harder to straighten it out when he dismounted. Rivulets of perspiration poured down his face, and his shirt clung damply to his back. It was past time for him to stop, his mare wanted watering and grain. The flanks of the poor beast were heaving overmuch, and there was the white frost of sweat upon them. He had seen an inn and knew he must halt there, but being so near to Carlisle, he resented each delay.

He had already been forced to let more than a month go by while he nursed his injury. In that time, his anger had grown apace, fed each day by his children's endless questions. He had never expected that they, with their nurses presiding over most of their waking hours, would miss her so. After all, the eldest was only four and Rupert, a few months past three, but the two of them had clamoured loudly for their mother; and surely baby Owen was more fretful than he had been before, though he, of course, could have had no notion of her flight.

Her flight!

Thinking of the clever way he had been outwitted, outguessed, outmaneuvered, his fury returned anew, and the mare's head jerked where he had unconsciously pulled the snaffle rein, jamming the bit hard against her sensitive mouth. "There, there, my poor beauty," he murmured, patting her wet neck. He loved his horses and never willingly abused them. He thought then painfully of Geraint, the stallion, dead upon the road. Geraint had been his particular favorite. It was on his back that he had come riding up to Carlisle, all those years ago.

His harsh laughter rang out suddenly, startling a flock of blackbirds, causing them to fly wildly, haphazardly up from the nearby field—he could compare them with his scattered thoughts. Why, he asked himself, should he so love the steed which had brought him to the woman, who had deliberately deceived him, not once but twice. A trembling Mistress Digges had described her swathed in that hooded cloak. "It must've been her, sir. There weren't no other way for her to go."

Thinking of Audrey's stratagem, he ground his teeth, and his hand tightened on the reins again. He could have called her to account for her trick. The magistrates would uphold him, coercing his wife to leave him, and at such a time! He thought of Blanche's pale face, seen for a second in the coach window. She had looked more dead than living. "Pale as thy smock," where had he heard that drift of words?

At the play. Othello mourning the wife he had slain from mistaken jealousy. Blanche had always called his own jealousy mistaken. She was herself mistaken in dubbing it jealousy when it was righteous wrath! She had lied! She had pretended to love him and the living proof of her deception had been with him every day; every day to see that little face with its dark Stuart features. The son whom he, out of pride, had acknowledged to all outsiders as his eldest, a throwback in coloring to his Norman kin. Had they believed him? It little mattered now.

She had been so pale. In her dangerously weakened state, she might not have survived the rigors of the road. That was the thought which had been tormenting him for the past month and had grown more hurtful over these long, weary miles. It was madness, madness for her mother to have snatched her from her bed, especially now, when there was yet plague abroad. Only yesterday, he had met some men with wagons in which all their possessions had been piled. They had been fleeing London which, they said, was still a pesthole, though the doctors had contended that the winter blasts had killed the disease.

There had been one overturned cart he had seen, and nearby a poor swollen wretch, dying, his body already covered with hordes of feasting flies. He shuddered, wishing even now he might have stopped to give him the water for which he had called so piteously, but instead, he had been craven like all the others and spurred his horse onward quickly.

What if Blanche were also dying, a plague sore on her swollen body, a stiff white corpse in a common grave? . . .

"No, he assured himself quickly, blinking away a sudden moisture in his eyes. He would have some word on it. They would have had to tell him. He peered into the leafy distance; Carlisle was not more than four hours away. He longed to spur his horse and cover those remaining miles, but that would get him there after dark, and besides his mare was spent and the inn just yards ahead. Prodding her gently, he turned her toward that goal.

He was surrounded by hostlers, and over their heads, he spied the smiling host. There was a pert maid passing, her full, white bosom generously displayed, a warm and lusty armful whose hot eyes beckoned him, ranging greedily over his person, while the tip of her tongue played over her full, red lips.

As he dismounted, he grinned sourly. There had been many like her at many inns in recent years, girls whose bodies he had used of a night; they had come as easily to him, as Blanche had to her king. Their faces were fused in his mind. They had no identities, no more than Blanche had for her king! He thrust her angrily from his thoughts and limped toward the door, hoping it would be cooler inside, his knee was hurting damnably, his foot swollen inside his boot. He needed to sleep, and by God he'd not spend this night alone.

She had been polishing her final act. It was amazing how the little suggestions Mr. Peel had given her clarified the text. With his encouragement, she was actually beginning to think of her play in terms of a production, daring to weigh the talents of a Mohun, never seen by herself but described by Mr. Peel, against a Betterton, whose work she had heard praised more extensively. Then, there was Mrs. Knepp and . . . Suddenly, she heard the clatter of hooves in the courtyard and, without knowing quite why, hurried to the window and there froze. Rupert was below!

He had anticipated trouble at the gatehouse, but had found the keeper dozing in the sun and rode past him, demanding of a servant lounging in the courtyard to fetch him Lady Yule.

Occasioned by his worry and his impatience, his manner had been abrupt, an attitude he meant to quell when she appeared. The door was opening. He tensed expectantly, but as he might have guessed, it was her mother who appeared. She looked at him as angrily as he felt towards her. "Well, my lord, what brings you here?" she demanded coldly.

His passion triumphed over his discretion as he said loudly, "I presume my wife's with you. I've come to fetch her."

She lifted her chin and narrowed her eyes. In her face, he saw something of Blanche, but how much more beautiful the daughter than the mother. How much more gentle, how much more kind. Oh, God, he had to see her! She said coldly, "My daughter *is* home, my lord, and here will stay. I fear you've had your long ride for nothing."

His fury rose again but was diluted by relief. She was alive then, not dead, as he had feared. "You'd no right to take her from my keeping. You could have killed her," he accused.

"I did not take her, my lord," she corrected. "She came of her own free will and gladly."

"Coerced by you!" he accused.

"Not by me, but you," she responded contemptuously. "Better my giving her a chance for life than your killing her by inches, as you have tried to do."

"I—" he started to retort and stopped. There was no defense he could offer save that he had not meant to harm her, only to keep her at his side, prisoned by her pregnancies, committed to none but him. That decision had worked against them both, since in making it he had given up all plans for a career in diplomacy, being quite unable to face the man who was his king.

It had been a madness on his part, an anger which even he could no longer understand. It had been the reason that sometime in the night he had tossed the clinging woman from his bed, giving her money to soothe her wounded vanity and shutting the door upon her. He had fallen weeping on the floor, realizing at last what he had tried to hide even from himself, his old love for Blanche. And he knew that he had felt it before, when he had first seen those bunched pillows on the bed. No, before that, long before, but pride had not let him acknowledge it. He had always loved her, loved her now, needed her, wanted her. And looking into Audrey's implacable face, he could not conceal his desperation as he said, "I must see her. At least, let me see my wife."

"I do not think that would be wise," she replied firmly. "Now I suggest you go, else I will call my servants."

"I've told you I must see her," he repeated, moving toward her determinedly.

"And I say that you will not!" Raising her voice, she called, "Diccon—Hugh—"

"Mother," Blanche said behind her breathlessly, "Don't. I'll see him. I'm not afraid. Do not keep him standing in the courtyard. Ask him to come inside."

Hope struggled with amazement as he heard her voice. He could not see her in the darkness of the doorway, but she sounded stronger, and there was an unfamilar note of authority in her tones which even Audrey must have recognized, for, sounding less certain than before, she said. "I don't think it would be—"

"Please," Blanche interrupted. "It's better so."

"Very well," Audrey said crisply. "You'll come inside, my lord."

At Blanche's insistence, she left them in the hall. Looking at her, his relief increased. She was still pale but it was not the pallor of sickness; her face had filled out and her hair was shining. With a shock, he realized he had forgotten how beautiful she had been, had been and was again, but there was a difference about her now, a coolness that confounded him.

All the way from the inn, he had been rehearsing this moment in his mind, how he would beg her pardon and plead for her return, but facing eyes that seemed to look through him rather than at him, he could not find the words. Instead he said stupidly, resentfully.

"You seem to have been faring very well."

"Yes," she said composedly.

"What have you been doing?" he frowned.

"Writing."

"Your scribbling, I suppose."

"Yes," she said.

"You might have sent a letter. You might have let me know that you were well."

"How could I be sure you'd receive it, my lord. So many letters my mother wrote to me were lost."

"She lied!"

"I think not, my lord."

There was an icy glitter in her eyes that he had never seen before. The cadences of her voice—they were icy too. Here was a Blanche whom he had never known. She frightened him. Out of his fear, he spoke, "You're coming home with me!"

"No," she said.

"You need not be afraid of punishment. I—"

"I'm not afraid, my lord," she interrupted gently.

He could see she spoke the truth. It was craven of him to use the argument he now produced, but there had to be something he could say to reach her. "The children—" he paused and swallowed. "They cry for you."

She shook as if she had been struck by a sudden wind. "They'll stop crying soon, for they are young."

"It's easy to see you never loved them," he accused her bitterly.

"You know that's not true," she replied hotly. "I love them all the same, all my children, all the same, and I never should have left our three had you been kind. I did not want to leave them. It was you who forced it on me with your talk of the stables for poor Charlie."

"I did not mean it," he exclaimed. "Surely you must have known it was only fustian." He paused and added, "I miss the lad."

"You miss him?" she echoed incredulously. "You?"

"Yes, I do," he glared at her. "You know I love the boy— It's only—"

"How might I know that when you have ever treated

him as a stranger, jeering at him, beating him for no good reason, and in his hearing called our home a cuckoo's nest, shaming him, and shaming me in any way you could. You'd not listen when I told you"

"Blanche," he burst out, "I know I've been cruel and heartless. I don't know why I made you suffer so, but I might tell you, your sufferings have been no more than mine. It was like a madness come upon me, but it's over—gone. If you'd come back with me, I'd take you to court and—" he paused, seeing her doubtful stare. "You don't believe me, but I swear to you, it's the truth."

"The truth?" she repeated dryly.

"The truth!" he exclaimed. "You must believe me."

She looked at him steadily, "Once I begged you'd hear a truth from me, but you'd not believe me either."

"I—I tell you that I do believe you, Blanche. On my soul I do."

She sighed. "Five years ago, I'd have given my life to hear those words from you, my lord. Isn't it strange that they mean nothing to me now."

Lunging toward her, he caught her in his arms and kissed her roughly, "And does this mean nothing either?"

She waited, unmoving, unresponding until he had released her. "Oh, Rupert," she said, "is this the only me you know?"

"I—I do not understand you."

She nodded, "I think that might be true."

He took a hasty step forward, then stopped. "I'll not argue more."

"It would be a waste of time and breath," she agreed. "Indeed, you'd best go now."

"Is that what you want?"

"I do."

"Blanche," he said desperately. "Can't you believe that I am truly sorry."

"Yes," she said.

"Then—why?"

"I have other things to do."

"Other things—" he burst out. "Who is he?"

She sighed, "Fare you well, my lord."

Chapter Ten

It was raining hard. Gusts of wind-driven drops spattered against the small panes of glass in the windows near Blanche's bed, awakening her. She opened her eyes immediately. Though it was only her third day in London, she did not experience her usual sense of displacement. The exhilaration she had been feeling ever since her arrival in the city was even more heightened. Reaching for the new journal she had been keeping especially for this particular sojourn, she changed its scarlet ribbon to the next blank page and wrote at the top, "Thursday, 15 November, 1666." Underneath, in heavily underscored capital letters she she inscribed the words: "TODAY, TO THE KING'S COMPANY, KING'S THEATER, RUSSELL STREET & DRURY LANE, FOR THE FIRST REHEARSAL OF *ADELIZA OR: A QUEEN'S ROMANCE.*" With a little grimace, she added, "BY BASIL CARLISLE."

"I would," she continued writing, "feign reveal to the world that I am Basil Carlisle, but Mr. Peel has assured me that his friend Sir Thomas Killigrew's arguments against it are most sound and, indeed, upon introducing me to him yesterday, I could not but conclude, though reluctantly, that they had some merit. Indeed, they did please me too, for he said, "The play's too good to be classed as an oddity, my dear. If it is known to have been written and rehearsed by a woman, a lady of quality, the audience will view it, not for its merit, but for its author's name and sex for, as you know, there's been no female that has ever written for our theaters or has commanded actors upon the London stage."

"He was so kind that I had perforce to agree and so invented one Basil Carlisle, a bedridden invalid in Shropshire, my distant cousin, who, out of respect for my judgement and my minor skill with words, has elected me his representative with full jurisdiction over the work in regards as to such changes as will be necessary. I am told that these will be given me during the course of our three weeks of rehearsal. Actors, I am told, often stick at learning lines that do not lie easily on their tongues, though Sir Thomas assures me there will be little cavil at my play. As for the rehearsing, I find myself relieved to let Sir Thomas preside, for I have not seen enough plays to warrant my exercising myself in this regard." She stopped writing, then started again. "I did think this day would never happen. . . ." She paused, then slammed her journal shut.

"I can write later," she muttered, "I want to be there." She started to pull the bell for Rose, whom she had borrowed from her mother, then stopped. It would be better to dress herself, for Rose, being a perfectionist, would take far too long in arranging her hair, and like as not there would be another of her gentle lectures about looking her best in London. She did not care how she looked, she was not trying to make herself beautiful for any of the courtiers who patronized the playhouse.

She frowned, thinking of Rupert and, of course, the children, still a gnawing pain in her heart, but which, for her own good, she dared not consider; but oh, how she yearned for them, for all they were in kindly hands. Other young matrons, she knew, were only too happy to leave their babies in the country while they dallied with their lovers at court, but she had done more than leave them with their nurses, she would never see them more, for certainly after her dismissal of her husband five months earlier, he would never have her back. She did not want to go back! The very idea was madness! Subject herself to that tyranny again? Never.

"Then what will you do with your remaining years?" her second self demanded.

"There's Charlie and my plays and—" She shook head. She would not think beyond this play!

She dressed hastily. Certainly she was not as adept with her hair as Rose, but she looked tolerably well, she thought. She hoped Esther would be ready. Since her grandfather Carlisle did not want to make the long trip to London until the roads were better and since her mother would not leave him, she was most fortunate in having Esther with her again. She had missed her greatly and Esther had confessed that she had been miserable without her.

She had spent the last few years traveling from house to house, spending a month with a cousin, half a year with an old friend, and so on. "But it was all so dull, my love. Either my hosts talked of their losses in the war or of their dissatisfaction with the old regime and their disapproval of the new. Other than that, there was endless gossip about people I didn't know and after hearing them tongue shredded to the bone, didn't want to know. Then, to receive your letter! I vow, I danced for joy."

She found Esther sitting on a stool in the parlor, her gloved hands folded in her lap and her hooded cloak already tied about her neck, "Why you're ready ahead of me!" she exclaimed in delighted surprise.

"How might I not be, love," Esther demanded. "I've been waiting for this moment these thirteen years, past."

"Thirteen years?" Blanche echoed. "How could that be?"

"But you were always gifted," Esther said earnestly. "Those poems and stories you wrote while we were in France. Her eyes grew pensive, "And your poor novel. Seeds, my dear, seeds from which this glorious tree has grown."

"Not glorious yet. It still needs nurturing before it bears fruit, dear Esther," Blanche said. "Have you supped, yet?"

"I've had a pint of ale and some cold chicken. There's a plate I had them leave for you."

"Oh, I couldn't—I couldn't swallow it." Blanche told her, suddenly whirling about and looking, Esther thought fondly, twelve again, with her eyes shining the way they used to when she had just composed a poem, "Oh, Esther, I can't believe it. Actors, real actors—famous actors reading lines that I have written. Come, let's hurry. Oh, I am glad we have our own coach. I don't think we could ever hire one in all this rain. Come." She stretched out her hand, but before Esther could even rise, she had run down the stairs. Esther, following more slowly, was pleased to hear her executing what sounded like a little dance in the hall below.

"If the horses could only go faster," Blanche sighed, looking out at sooty streets, crowded with drays, sedan chairs, running footmen, coaches, pedlars, pedestrians, as well as an occasional sheep or pig. "It's always so much more congested when it rains!"

"True," Esther agreed, "but rain will wash the offal from the gutters and quell those fires that may still be smouldering."

"Still—after two months?" Blanche asked.

"My cousins tell me that there are cellars that are burning yet." Esther rolled her eyes. "Such a horror and poor Saint Paul's—a gutted shell! I wept when I first beheld its fallen roof."

Blanche nodded a little self-consciously. The news of the fire had reached her but a week after Mr. Peel had told her that Sir Thomas Killigrew would stage her play. Though the theaters and other places of amusement were still dark by reason of the plague, he had hopes of a September reopening; then had come the dread tidings. She still blushed at her grandfather's look when she had blurted out, "Oh, dear, my play." She had foreborn to express her relief when Mr. Peel had told her that the theaters, having escaped the holocaust, were opening not six weeks later!

It was not until they had arrived at the city limits that she became aware of just how much the city had suffered. She had hardly recognized the skyline, so many of the steeples she had been used to seeing had vanished, and so many, many buildings and houses too.

Yet, in spite of the devastation, the city, in common with its theaters, was just as busy as it had ever been—with shopkeepers selling their wares in such makeshift hovels as they could erect and the streets already echoing to the sounds of reconstruction.

"They'll not have wood again," Esther said, as if in answer to her thoughts. "It will be brick and better so."

"We're turning," Blanche said. "I think we're hard by Drury Lane. That great building just ahead—that's the King's."

It was amazing to Blanche that the King's House had not suffered the same fate as other similar structures, for it was made of wood and plaster, and a single spark could have ignited it; she could only thank Saint Jude, patron of thespians, that the hot, dry winds that had fanned the September blaze had not found their way down Drury Lane. Indeed, it was the more amazing for there were so many little crooked streets running into each other, all bordered by houses built at least a hundred years before and looking to her newly tutored eye as if they could be firetraps.

She had half-expected to see Sir Thomas waiting for them at the stage entrance, but a disheveled and grumbling custodian growled that he had not arrived. It took some little persuading for him to believe that Blanche was there to speak for the author.

"You be sure you ain't anglin' for Mr. Kynaston or Mr. Mohun," he dared to say, only to be quelled by Esther's formidable glance and admirable command of icy speech.

Blanche was inclined to giggle at his confusion, once they were inside, but Esther was indignant. "I keep forgetting it's such a wicked place. I could wish you did not have to come here at all."

"I hope you've not turned Puritan, Esther. The theater's only wicked if you make it so."

Esther did not answer. She did not want to spoil Blanche's pleasure, but she was beginning to have qualms as to the wisdom of the venture. She had become too used to Blanche's beauty to remember what an effect it would have upon the court bucks who thronged the playhouse. Once it was known that she lived apart from her husband, she could be subjected to their gallantries whether she willed it or not. In the last six years, the court, aping the king, had acquired a reputation for licentiousness and depravity unequaled at any other time in England's history, groaned the clergy, and most of these divines insisted that the theater was the very crucible of its vice. However, Esther pursed her lips, Blanche had herself and Mr. Peel for protection, and without a scheming Glenmore to foil her as he had before, she would see that her charge was very well protected.

Yet, what if the king were to favor Blanche's play with an appearance. There was no accounting for his preferences, Sir Thomas had told them. Sometimes he came, sometimes he didn't, though it was known that he had more of a liking for comedy than tragedy, even to the point where he had cheerfully countenanced the changed ending of *Romeo and Juliet* with the lovers on a bed instead of in a tomb. Esther laughed, then sobered. She hoped his prejudice might hold true in the case of *Adeliza*, for if the ending were happy, the main parts of the work were sad; and even if the king's presence was an inducement for a longer run if he liked the piece, and how could he not, she did not relish the idea of his meeting Blanche. She rather believed Blanche was equally reluctant, for the young woman had told Esther, she would not attend any of the court balls or other functions to which she might have had a card. She had said coldly, "I am not here for dancing or for sport, but as a working author."

Esther thought there was a tiny strain of fear in Blanche's attitude. She wondered if, after all these years, she were still attracted to the king, whose brief dalliance had had such bitter consequences. Each time she recalled her recent meeting with his bonny little son and pondered on all that Audrey had told her of Blanche's miserable marriage with a man she had loved all her life, she shuddered and wondered what the future held. She had seen a brooding look in the girl's eyes, and she could not imagine that Rupert was gone for good, no matter what Audrey contended. If there had been no children . . . but there were and . . .

"Esther, Esther!" Blanche exclaimed. "Why will you not listen to me?"

She started. "What my dear, what did you say?"

"I said you're getting wet. The rain's pouring through the cupola right onto your head!"

Esther moved back quickly, "Oh, I was thinking."

"You certainly were, and hard," Blanche laughed. "I hope you didn't think yourself into a chill. It's monstrous damp in here. I'm glad I wore my warmest cloak."

"Yes, it is." Esther circled the auditorium with her eyes. It was dim as well as damp, and the wavering light issuing from a few candles burning in brackets along the wall threw the tiers of boxes into shadow, dulled the gilding on the high proscenium arch, and turned the stage itself into a vast, black cavern. It was, she thought, uncomfortably reminiscent of an engraving depicting the mouth of hell she had once seen in an old Bible. Judging from what she had heard about theaters in general, she decided her analogy was apt but daunting. "I do hope Sir Thomas will be here soon," she said nervously.

"He should—" Blanche began and paused at the sound of footsteps echoing through the outer corridor. Two laughing male voices reached them.

" 'Swounds, what weather. First they'd burn us, now they'll drown us," one said.

"Not so loud, Harry, my head," the other groaned.

"Too much French brandy at old Nan's."

"French brandy! Belike it's the old hag's piss I drank. I swear it's still boiling in my bowels."

"That's not her piss but Elly's pox, I think—" They came into the auditorium and stopped short, seeing Esther and Blanche.

"Lud's bones, what have we here?" A fair young man wearing his own long blonde locks, eyed them boldly.

Blanche said coolly, "I am Lady Yule, and this is my friend Madame de Coligny."

"Lady Yule is it?" he bowed low and, groaning, clasped his head. "I vow, I nearly overbalanced myself on that." He straightened. "Your servant, Lady Yule, Madame de Coligny. I am Edward Kynaston. My friend's Sir Harry Beauchamp."

Beauchamp, a darkly handsome youth with a roguish eye, bowed. "If you ladies are here for the performance, you've a deal of waiting ahead of you."

Blanche said, still coolly, "We're here for another purpose. We are waiting for Sir Thomas Killigrew."

"Blast Killigrew, he has too damned much luck with the ladies." Sir Harry boldly ogled Blanche.

"Lady Yule," Esther fixed him with a withering stare, "is the representative for Mr. Basil Carlisle, whose play, I believe, begins rehearsals this morning."

"Ah," Kynaston's tired face suddenly tautened, and the lines of dissipation were magically smoothed away.

He looked a full ten years younger. "You represent the Carlisle who wrote *Adeliza*, my lady?"

"Yes," Blanche's coolness quickly vanished, for she heard admiration in his voice.

"Ah," he clasped his hands, "what a love of a role, and six years ago, it would have been mine." He sighed deeply. "It should have been, you know, it was written for me. What could I have not done with that queen! I should have surpassed my Epicene!"

"Come, you make a better gallant than a maid," Harry Beauchamp laughed, then leered, "or should I say you make a better maid than many a better gallant."

Kynaston put a slender finger to his lips, "Hush, you'll shock the ladies. But of a truth, I should have played Adeliza. Hear this! Striking an attitude, he recited:

> "Good father, thou knowest I, thy daughter, Adeliza, bear the reverence, love thee, honor thee as well.
> But as you know, that portion of my heart not thine, is fast entwineth with my William. . . .
> Yet, you and mine uncle would have me break this, my sworn vow, and marry with England's Henry, a man venerable and with children, grown beyond my years. . . .
> As thou me cherish, I pray thou wilt not force me to this match."

Blanche had listened with amazement, for not only had his voice lost its masculine timbre but his face had become that of a grieving beauty. She had not expected she could be so moved by lines that she had written. Torn between pride and shyness, she was trying to think of what to say when she heard a burst of applause from the side of the house; and a slight, young girl came running forward, and, standing a few feet distant from them, clapped again.

"Adod, my pretty, I'll have you for my tiring woman yet!" she exclaimed in accents making her as London born. She had a head of springing chestnut curls and a saucy, heart-shaped face dominated by huge blue eyes full of a wisdom beyond her years, which in Blanche's estimation, could not have numbered more than sixteen.

Kynaston, dropping his feminine attitude, put an arm around the girl's slim waist, "I'd have you for my retiring woman, Nell, my love, if you'd tell me where the line ends."

She grinned up at him, "Just short of your long court sword, my Neddy." Slipping out of his grasp, she looked around her, "Lud, where's everyone? Killy will dock them shillings!"

"No, no, we're early," Beauchamp assured her and then winked. "And you're passing early, love—or have you been abed at all this night? He made a grab for her.

"Early, but not easy, and my sleeping habits concern but me alone." She made a face at him. "I've been reading this *Adeliza*—God save me from good women!"

"And God save good men from you and keep you here with us, my child." Kynaston caught her again, but she broke from him quickly and skipped over to Blanche, looking at her curiously." You're never of the boards!" she exclaimed.

Blanche shook her head, "No, I represent the author of this play."

"The author, eh?" her mobile features were momentarily a mask of pity. "Ah, that poor, sick lad. What ails him? It's probably all that fresh Shropshire air."

"What would you know about all that fresh Shropshire air, Nelly?" Beauchamp looked at her in some surprise.

"Too much, love. I'd three months of the same when mama and I were in Oxford this past summer. Odd's blood, I'd rather chanced the plague. It was too damned fresh there for us Gwyns."

"Ginns?"

"Gin for mama, Gwyn for me," she stuck her tongue out at him. "I'm not for strong waters."

"Better orange juice, eh?" drawled a tall, slender young woman who strolled over to them, negligently dragging a furred cloak behind her. She had a beautiful but very weary face. There were dark circles under her eyes and there was a droop to her mouth. However, giving Nell a wicked side-glance, she raised her voice to call, "Oranges—oranges—get your sweet, ripe oranges—"

"Bravo," little Nell applauded loudly, causing the other to wince and raise a trembling hand to her head. "That was an excellent performance, Mrs. Marshall, love. Better than any you've done in the house. Say the word, my Nan, and I'll have Orange Moll find you a place."

Mrs. Marshall only laughed and looking at Kynaston said pointedly, "Methinks, I heard a cricket cry." Sinking down on a bench, she added, "Odd's blood, I'm in no mood for a rehearsal. I am quite, quite undone."

"By whom, my fair one?" he inquired solicitously.

"Never ask by whom," Nell giggled, "Like Killy, they give her coin and she gives out tickets before each performance."

Mrs. Marshall did not even glance at her, "Oh, my head, my head," she groaned.

"Let me massage you, sweet," Kynaston offered, sitting down near her. "You'll find I have healing hands."

"Healing or seeking?" she demanded dryly, but smiled as he began to knead her neck.

Other actors trailed in after Mrs. Marshall, and the lot of them formed a small circle across the room, where they talked in low voices, often laughing immoderately.

"A scurvy crew, my dear," Esther muttered distastefully.

Blanche did not answer. She was feeling more disappointed than she cared to admit. A line from an old ballad ran through her mind, "For she's gone with the raggle-taggle Gypsies, O!"

They were much like Gypsies, the actors, she thought. In spite of their appearance, the men, uncommonly handsome and the women, lovely, there was something unwholesome about their restive bodies, their restless eyes, and their bawdy speech. Standing at the very threshold of her involvement with them, she would not have minded closing that particular door. Furthermore, she wondered if her play would be well served. She could imagine them in a light comedy, but feared that they might present a very weightless tragedy. Of course, Kynaston's reading of Adeliza's speech had been quite moving, but he would be playing the part of William de Albini. She could not imagine that handsome but debauched young man in the role of a noble twelfth century knight. Mohun, who would enact Henry I, however, did look satisfactory as to type, and both she and Esther had appreciated an approach which had none of the leering familiarity of Beauchamp, Kynaston, and some of the other men. As for Nell Gwyn, obviously a comedienne, she wondered what there could be for her to do since there were only four female roles: Adeliza, Matilda, her formidable stepdaughter, Constance, a lady-in-waiting, and Ursula, an aged nurse. She was too young for either Matilda or Ursula, too common for Constance. Mrs. Knepp, whom she had not yet seen, would enact Matilda, and as for Adeliza, her role fell to Mrs. Marshall. Blanche choked down a small groan. The lady was certainly beautiful and looked distinguished enough but would she, giggling now as Kynaston's massaging fingers strayed from neck to breast, understand the virtue for which the queen was so celebrated.

Dreading her instant agreement, Blanche did not mention any of these fears to Esther, and scarcely a half-hour later, she was glad she had held her peace. In that time, Sir Thomas Killigrew, a cheerful, dark-haired man, had arrived, and with him pretty Mrs.

Knepps. From the moment he stepped into the room, a change had been apparent among the company. In obedience to his commands, they settled down on various benches, and producing the parts he had handed them the previous day, they began to read and even to speak them from memory. Listening, Blanche was amazed at their quick grasp of the characters, but even more amazed at Kiligrew's sharp, even insulting criticism, which they took in their stride. By the time the rehearsal had ended, some three hours later, she was feeling much more encouraged.

Consequently, she was surprised when the manager, looking most apologetic, took her aside to say, "They're mighty rough, I fear, but in three weeks, I think you'll not be disappointed, Lady Yule."

"I'm not disappointed now," she assured him. "Indeed, I am astonished at their comprehension."

"I beg you'll not let them know that," he smiled. "There's nothing spoils an actor's performance as much as early accolades."

"Oh, I shall say nothing," she promised, feeling very gauche.

"No, do not say nothing neither, for you don't want to discourage them. However, I think you'll soon know when you must speak or be silent. The more I listen to your play, the more I'm convinced that you're a young woman of singular acumen."

"Singular acumen! Did you hear that, Esther?" Blanche demanded gleefully, as they settled themselves in their coach.

"That's praise you deserve, my love," Esther smiled. "Yet, I do not like to see you in such an atmosphere and with such people. I wish Mr. Peel had been of a mind to come with us this morning."

"I wish so too, but I am sure he did not. He's probably far happier trying to find those books he said escaped the fire." She shook her head. "Imagine, whole warehouses of them gone up in flames. He says it's a disaster akin to the burning of the library at Alexandria."

"All the same, he should have been with you," Esther insisted.

"He'll come with us to the performance. That's enough."

Esther looked at her anxiously, "Rehearsal in the morning and the performance at three. Are you sure you're up to it, my love? There'll be other days and other plays, you know."

"I must go to this one," Blanche said. "It's by Killigrew, himself, *The Parson's Marriage*. Her eyes glinted. "I'm quite dying to see it. It will be my first time at a London play. And we'll have a chance to see the actors at work as well."

"The actors." Esther clicked her tongue, "I vow I never heard such an ill-spoken crew."

"They were," Blanche admitted. "At first I was quite put off myself but," she laughed, "I begin to believe their bark's worse than their bite."

"Um," Esther muttered doubtfully. She decided not to say anything to spoil Blanche's pleasure. Time enough to warn her that the actors were not as harmless as she imagined and that more than once she had caught Kynaston and his crony Beauchamp looking at Blanche so lasciviously that Esther had longed to black their eyes. More than that, she wished that there were a way to visit her wrath on Lord Rupert Godwin for, if he had been a proper husband, Blanche would not have been thrust into their questionable company.

Esther disapproved. Blanche could feel it, even though she could not, would not, turn to look at her or Mr. Peel. Sitting in the front of the box Kiligrew had provided for the three of them, Blanche marveled over the change in the theater. The gilding over the proscenium expressed it best, she decided. Dull and shabby three hours earlier, it gleamed like a massive nugget in the light of hundreds of candles set along the wall and shining from an immense center chandelier. The auditorium was a mass of color. The ascending tiers of boxes were filled with courtiers in the great curled periwigs, which she, personally thought very awkward but which were more and more the fashion. She, who had been used to the burgeoning splendor of Louis XIV's court, was still amazed at the brightness of the brocades and at the lavish use of gold and silver lace at throats and cuffs. She loved the ornamental buttons that lined their long, silken vests, a new fashion lately imported from France, Esther had told her. Another new fashion was the bright red heels adorning leather boots and shoes. In contrast, the women, herself included, were almost drab in their full, loose, billowing gowns, however artfully draped they were to expose satin kirtles. At least her gown, a new one provided by her mother, was in her favorite blue. She smoothed it, loving the feel of the silk. It had been a long time since she had worn so fine a gown, a long time since she had been part of such a glittering company too. Let Esther disapprove, as the author she was not going to let anything spoil her excitement. She felt a little like a sailor, shipwrecked upon a desert shore, who suddenly sees a rescuing ship. The theater was her ship, she thought defiantly, and she would not hesitate to mingle with its passengers.

Resuming her scrutiny of the auditorium, she saw that the citizens in the pit, clerks from the various government offices, she had heard, were also clad in their best and were only slightly less magnificent than the nobles. With them were their wives, darting envious glances at the boxes and probably memorizing the cut of the gowns so that they could copy them. Then there were various ladies circumspectly described by Mr. Peel as "fair frails." Garbed in vivid, tawdry finery, they strolled slowly up and down the aisles, their questing eyes peeping through the slits of ruffled vizard masks. Occasionally, they accosted one of the numerous gallants engaged in saluting ladies in the boxes.

Moving among the throngs in the aisles were little girls of twelve and thirteen with trays of oranges harnessed to their shoulders. They were overseen by raddled old drabs, who appeared as wishful of selling their charges as their wares. She thought they must be calling as Nan Marshall had that morning, "Oranges—sweet oranges—who'll buy my oranges—" but though their mouths were open, she could not hear the words. There were too many other sounds: from the musicians warming up beneath the stage, from the audience's incessant chattering, from the men who were gathered below her box and commenting on her beauty. She sighed and wished she could tell them they were wasting their time because she was an *author*.

The curtain rose late, and if the house were a revelation, how much more so the actors. Since it was a contemporary play, their costumes were of the moment and rivaled anything she had seen in the house. Mr. Peel had told her that the nobility often deeded their fine clothes to their favorite players, and looking at them, she could well believe it—save that they were worn more gracefully. But it was their faces which amazed her, they, who had resembled so many drab, dissipated, tired, sullen ravens at rehearsal, now could outshine any bird of paradise. Yet, it was still difficult to hear them; the noble audience had come, it seemed, not to listen but to talk; and talk it did with hardly any cessation right through the first act, causing the poor performers to bawl rather than declaim. Furthermore, some of the so-called gallants, she noted indignantly, strolled right onto the stage and fingered the bosoms of actresses, who went on valiantly performing in spite of this invasion. Listening, or rather trying to listen, she was torn between anger and indignation, for the play had lost all coherence and could hardly pass as entertainment. Thinking of her own work, her disappointment was almost more than she could bear, and when the curtain finally fell on the first act, she was blinking tears away. Yet, much to her surprise, the audience applauded quite as loudly as if it had caught every word, and the actors were called back again and again to bow in answer to enthusiastic cheering.

Seeing her distress, Mr. Peel leaned forward. "It will go better later, dear," he assured her. "They need but to calm down. Besides, they're well acquainted with this play. It's a revival done three years ago. You'll always find them more attentive to anything that's new."

"Yes?" she said faintly, feeling that he was trying to comfort her, and well he might, she thought with some little ire, since he had encouraged her. She was about to make a tart comment on his failure to warn her as to the pitfalls in store for playwrights, when suddenly the curtains behind her were pulled open and her name rapturously pronounced.

"Darling Blanche, fancy you being in town and I not informed of it until this moment, you sly puss. And Sir Harry here has told me that you speak for a cousin, whom I do not even know. Dearest, how on earth did I miss out on Basil?"

Blanche looked up into the face of a plump, red-haired woman, heavily bejeweled and with patches on cheeks, chin, and at the corners of both eyes. She was clad in a gown of rich, green silk embroidered in gold, and a strong scent of musk emanated from her. Standing behind her was Sir Harry Beauchamp in a huge, black periwig and silver brocade suitings, looking mischievously amused. Her eyes came back to the woman. She said "V—Venetia."

"The very same," her cousin said archly. "And I don't think you even knew me, did you? I expect I have filled out some since I married Holcomb—such cooks as that man employs. You knew I'd married Lord Holcomb, did you not, my dear? Cousin Audrey must have told you."

"Yes, she did," Blanche acknowledged. It was true that she had not recognized her. Six years ago, she had been slim and almost serpentine in her movements.

Now she was plump and bouncy, but if Blanche did not know her at first glance, a second, longer look assured her that the change in Venetia was only surface deep. True, she smiled more, but still her smiles stopped short of eyes as hard and green as they had ever been.

Staring into them, Blanche seemed to see, as in a crystal, the wan visage of her dying nurse. She had not seen her cousin since that terrible night, nor had she ever wanted to see her again, but she could not turn from her now, not with Sir Harry at her side. It would have been too awkward. With as much cordiality as she could muster, she said, "You must remember Madame de Coligny and Mr. Peel."

"Of course," Venetia said effusively. "My dear Madame de Coligny, my dear Mr. Peel. And do you know Sir Harry, but you must, it was Harry told me about your attending the rehearsal this morning. Such a rare privilege, my dear. We may all sit on the stage if we choose and invade the dressing rooms, but none of us is ever allowed at Sir Tom's rehearsals. He's quite adamant on that score, Harry being the exception because he occasionally deigns to act. I've often wondered if Killigrew beats the actors, but Harry says he's never seen it happen, though perhaps it should. No matter, I am talking far too much and not saying what I wanted to ask you. Cousin *Basil* Carlisle, how might he be connected with us?"

"He's my father's cousin, actually," Blanche answered glibly, "A son of great-uncle William."

"Oh—and in Shropshire? I didn't know there was a Carlisle branch in Shropshire, but of course being only related to dear Audrey, I can't be expected to have memorized your whole tree. And he's written a play, fancy that! Is it good? Dear Harry says it has merit." She glanced at Sir Harry. " 'Very perceptive, admirable insight into a woman's heart.' Weren't those your words, my dear?"

"Exactly," he smiled over her shoulder into Blanche's eyes.

"How did your cousin happen to choose you as his representative, my love? Oh yes, I seem to recall that you had some literary leanings too."

Blanche forced a smile as she answered, "Oh, some very minor ones, Venetia. Nothing compared to Basil's, but he does trust my judgement."

"Very good," Venetia nodded. "Certainly I am glad it's brought you back to town. I thought you were lost to us forever, buried in the country," Venetia shivered, "and in the wilds of Yorkshire and incarcerated in that vast, stony pile Rupert used to mention when we were in Germany. You were away a very long time, weren't you, my love? I thought we'd quite lost you to domesticity, what with all your babies. Fancy, Harry, she's a mother four times over and looking still like eighteen. I cannot think you've aged a minute since I saw you last, dear Blanche. And do you have any of your darling's with you? I should love to meet them."

"No," Blanche said. "They're all in the country. My eldest is visiting at Carlisle."

"Oh, divine—"

Esther, aware of Blanche's paling face, said pointedly, "I think the play's about to begin, Lady Holcomb."

"Is it?" Venetia cast a disinterested glance at the stage. "Such a paltry business. Killigrew's a better manager than a playwright." She turned back to Blanche. "And where, my love, is Rupert?"

Reading an avid and malicious expression in her cousin's eyes, Blanche said merely, "He's not with me at this time."

"I thought he might not be," Venetia replied. "I did not think he'd return to London so soon after his experiences in that ghastly fire."

"He was very brave in that fire," Sir Harry commented, "the way he worked to evacuate houses and the like."

"Indeed he was," Venetia agreed. "Quite desperately daring. He could have been killed a dozen times, I hear, but he was not even singed."

"I've heard the king's rewarded him quite handsomely," Sir Harry observed.

"Yes, that's true," Venetia nodded. "You must be very, very proud."

"I am," she said faintly. "Very." She looked at the stage. "If—if you'll excuse me, Venetia, Sir Thomas is just below us in the aisle, and he'll think it very rude if I don't listen to his play."

Venetia laughed lightly, "Bless you, my dear innocent, no one ever listens, but I expect he will appreciate your courtesy. Lovely to have seen you, my dearest Blanche. Now we're reacquainted we must go about together. Holcomb's in his dotage and oftentime hangs very heavily on my hands. I shall welcome the diversion of your visit here."

Blanche managed a smile, but it fell on her cousin's retreating back as Venetia edged quickly from the box. The playwright caught Sir Harry's glance and did not care for the look she read in his eye. As for Venetia, did she know of the separation? She had an uncomfortable conviction that she must, else why had she sought her out but to exult? And Rupert, why had he come to London last September? Odd how her heart had seemed to beat more heavily when Venetia had first mentioned the fire and had grown calmer when she had known him to be safe. No, not odd, she reasoned dismally, no use to tell herself she no longer loved him. If only she might have trusted him as well. She stifled a small sob and turned a somber gaze upon the stage. Mr. Peel had been right, the audience had quieted, she could hear the speeches now, but she had lost the will to heed them.

The sky was leaden, and the road beneath stretched between trees denuded of all but a few yellowed leaves. Their bare branches were silhouetted against fields still gray with morning frost. There was an old woman, the wife of one of his crofters, gathering twigs for firewood, and at her hailing, Rupert, mounted on his new, gray Stallion, stopped, albeit impatiently.

"Yes, Eliza?"

She squinted up at him with some dismay. "I smell rain upon the winds, my lord. It's no morning for a journey. I pray you'll not go far."

"Not far," he assured her with a smile and spurred his horse. She was right. It was no morning to be riding off to London. But he touched his chest and felt the crackle of the paper, then he smiled at the lowering clouds, for in his mind, he saw the letter's message imprinted on them, as clearly as though he yet held it in his hand; and no wonder, for he had perused it at least a hundred times, and now again he repeated it:

My dear Lord Yule:

I take it upon myself to write to you without Blanche's knowledge; indeed I must needs tremble at my temerity, but feel that what I know must not remain unsaid.

Lady Carlisle has told me of the reasons for this rift between you, and though I cannot condone your actions, they appear to me as arising out of hurt, not spite. My lord, I can assure that what Blanche has told you regarding C. is no more than the truth. I was with her then and know how Glenmore gloated. It was his intent to turn the situation to his benefit, though how I know not, since he died so soon. This I swear upon my mother's soul and upon my own as well.

My lord, I do not like this society into which my Blanche is thrust. She is little able to cope with those who pursue her, and though Mr. Peel and I do our best to guard her, I am always fearful that we might fail, for I find them most devious and determined.

I take a great deal upon myself in writing you, but I know Blanche suffers, speaking often of her children, and I believe from what I have heard that you are unhappy too. I beg you'll return before much longer and effect a reconciliation. I will do my best to aid you and pray you will keep my confidence.

Your servant.
Esther de Coligny.

A drop splashed on his nose, and then another. Looking up, he saw a great fork of lightning split the sky to be followed by an ominous roll of thunder. Gaily he cried, "Come do your worst, you'll not stop me," and happily rode onwards.

"One o'clock of a cold and frosty morning," bawled the watch in the street below. Blanche, standing at a window, gratefully breathing in some of that same frosty air, heard his call without the surprise she would have felt even a week ago.

She was in a small, snug house near Chelsea—one which had miraculously escaped the flames. It belonged to a couple who had been hastily introduced to her by Venetia upon their entry. She had not really heard their names or titles. She rather thought he was a baron, but it did not really matter. They were not there to seek their society but rather to watch the gaming, though Venetia was doing more than merely watching. In company of pretty Mrs. Myddleton and the man Venetia described as her current lover, they were playing hazard, a game in which you could win a fortune as Captain Tom Paton had recently proved, garnering a staggering fifteen hundred pounds. You could also lose, as Venetia herself had been proving at three separate establishments these last three nights.

Watching her, Blanche, who had steadily refused to play, was amused. Venetia had certainly changed her spots, she thought. Marriage to a rich and doting old man might not have been what she wanted, but she had admitted that actually it had proved ideal, for she had her lovers and unlimited funds for the pursuit of expensive pleasures.

If her way of life had rounded her figure, it had also sweetened her temper, and Blanche, wary at first but gradually yielding to her cajoling ways, found her a lively companion, certainly more lively than Esther's cousins, who did nothing but complain about the excesses of the king and court, pity his poor little Portuguese queen, and predict that he was ruining the country with his dissipations. It was odd in her, she knew, but she still hated to hear him criticized, and after evenings of this carping, she was more than ready for the diversions Venetia could provide.

Esther had been much against her seeing her cousin; indeed, they had had quite a quarrel. She still recalled it with some indignation. Really, Esther had no right to treat her as if she were still fourteen, she a married woman who was past twenty-five, and especially when she was moving in the very best society. In the last week, she had met the duke of Richmond and the chevalier de Grammont, who being married to Elizabeth Hamilton, was by way of being a distant connection of Esther's. She had also encountered Queen Catherine herself, with several maids of honor. She flushed at that particular memory. It was very difficult to imagine the dumpy little Portuguese being married to Charles; not only was she ill shapen and badly dressed, but her teeth were black, and in five years she had yet to produce an heir or even a living child. Blanche hastily put that thought from her mind. In spite of Audrey's letters on the subject, she was still not inclined to force the issue of her son. She was glad, too, that she had not seen Charles, save in the royal box at the play. He had looked older and more weary, she had noticed, and he had only stayed for half an act.

She wondered if he would come to see her play. The idea was unsettling, particularly now. She did not want to depress herself by thinking about the rehearsals. After progressing very well for the last week and a half, they had turned very sluggish, and the actors were sadly out of sorts, inclined to blame their troubles on the absent author. They all joined in damning his work as much as they had once praised it. Though Sir Thomas had warned her that rehearsals often went that way, she was still worried, and the constant reiteration of her lines had left her without any objectivity. Though she hated to admit it, even to herself, she was becoming thoroughly bored with the whole project and was doubtful if she would ever want to write another play.

"Ah, the fair Perdita—"

Starting slightly, she turned to find Sir Harry at her side, "Why Perdita?" she inquired.

"Because you look lost," he said. "Why not join us at the tables?"

"I prefer to watch."

"But you're not watching," he complained. "I wish you'd come and inspire me. I've a feeling, you'd bring me luck."

"You've my cousin for that," she said.

"All too often for my liking," he sighed. "I seek variety."

"You might find her at another table," Blanche suggested.

"I might find—ah, variety, you mean. You've quite a little sense of humor. I've noticed it before, and other senses besides, most surprising in a beauty."

"Why?" she demanded somewhat edgily.

"Because those with beauty are often loathe to exercise their brains."

"Perhaps with some encouragement they might," she retorted tartly.

"I am willing to encourage you, my Lady Yule," he put his hand on her arm. Then, as she lightly disengaged it, he continued, "Lord, you're cold. What must one do to win you?"

"You must do your gambling over there," she pointed to the tables. "I'm no game to win or lose."

He laughed, "I should call you fair game, fair and rare."

"You wax poetical, Sir Harry."

"How may I not, with such a muse nearby."

"I vow, you'll turn my poor head," she curtseyed. "I pray you will excuse me."

"But why?" he demanded.

"Why not?" she shrugged and left him.

He watched her angrily. A handsome man, he was used to having his way with practically any woman he chose to court, but he and Ned Kynaston too, had laid seige to Lady Yule for over a fortnight, and neither had made any progress with her. He could not understand it.

"I vow, dear Harry, you're looking very black." He found Venetia confronting him. "I saw you talking to my little cousin. Do you find her to your fancy?"

"I find her something of an enigma," he growled.

"Because she's chaste, I think. But the chaste can be chased, dear Harry. As a hunter, you should know that."

"This little fox seems determined to outfox me."

"You must use different weapons then."

He gave her an intent look. "Have you any suggestions."

"I might try and think of some," she said.

"Tell me, Venetia, would you be encouraging me in this particular sport?"

Little sparks appeared in her green eyes. "Perhaps."

"Why would you be so accommodating?"

"Call it—a favor to a friend."

"That's very friendly, love."

She gave him a small smile and looked around for Blanche. She saw her at a gaming table and quite unaware that her presence was distracting to the players. How had she remained so lovely after all these years, and five children dropped from her loins as well, the little bitch! It was amazing how very much she resented her, the more so, she expected, because she still had a soft corner of her heart for Rupert, for all he had made her very weary with his lamenting.

He had spoken of his cruelty to his wife, spoken of it often enough to make her ears ache, but he had not defined it. She had not cared to ask; it was enough just to sit with him and comfort him. He had been grateful for her sympathy and would be more grateful yet if she could prove his perfect little wife imperfect. Her mouth twisted in a wry grin—that particular endeavor was proving more difficult than she had believed. Blanche was obviously lonely and confused, just ripe for a flirtation. Venetia had had hope of involving her in one when she had persuaded her cousin to accompany her to the gambling hells. But damn her, she had acted like a heavenly visitor—an observor but never a participator. Yet, those who would not respond to a little push might need a hefty shove, and with Harry as the shover she might have her revenge and Rupert too. She wished he were in the city, but even if he were not, bad news always carried faster than the good.

Chapter Eleven

"Odd, that hours which have seemed to move so slowly have turned to days that have flown so fast," Blanche wrote in her journal. "I think that is a good lie as well as apt," she continued. "Better than any in my play, I fear. I wish I were a thousand miles from here. What ever made me think I wanted to write plays. Esther tells me not to brood about it, but how can I help it. She is brooding too, though she pretends not to be and gave me all sorts of false smiles while we were watching rehearsal this morning. I was not fooled for an instant. It was all terrible. I know my only consolation will be that I am Basil-in-the-country, otherwise I am sure I should be pelted with rotten vegetables and bad eggs, as was that poor Mr. Browne the other afternoon. He swears he'll never write again, and nor will I. It is too painful an exercise. The opprobrium that has been my 'cousin's' lot these last few days! Today, however, was the worst of all—the final rehearsal and the performance only hours away and they moved about the stage as though their feet had turned to lead. And they all looked at me out of eyes gone dull as swamp holes. At least yesterday they knew their lines, but this morning one would have though they had never seen a part for all the stuttering and stammering that went on. Of course, I need not worry about this last, for who will hear my lines? Sir Thomas has told me that the audience is only attentive at *good* plays. No one I know, not even Killigrew, for all his sweet assurances, thinks this is a good play. No one can understand why he decided to stage it, least of all himself! Oh, misery! I could almost wish that they would change the bill. When this afternoon's torture's at an end, I shall burn this journal and myself."

Reading what she had written, she drew a line through "and myself." "Esther would say that I am being self-indulgent. Sure, I have a right to be. At least, I am glad that it's Basil will bear the blame. Else I should have ruined the stage for women. I think women will have a chance to write one day. I do not think my work's any worse than a man's—it might be even better. I will never say—" she stopped. She was writing far too much. She, who had hardly ever written in her other journals at all, save to mention the weather and the births of her babies, was filling page after page, and much of it was pure nonsense. It was keeping her busy, that was all. She arose and, replacing her journal, moved back and forth across the room. She was already dressed, a new gown made especially for the occasion. It was silken velvet in her favorite blue and edged with sable at her neck and cuffs. It was warm in her heated room, with the fire crackling on the hearth, but it would be fine in the cold theater. She wished she had not thought of that place, not yet. It was at least an hour before she need go. She wished it were later and the play over. Afterwards, she was going to a ball, a masked ball that Venetia had persuaded her to attend.

Esther, of course, had objected. "I do not like to see you with your cousin. I cannot trust her."

"You've had no cause not to trust her. I've been with her all this last week and nothing untoward has happened," Blanche said.

"Something will," Esther had answered, "and soon, unless I miss my guess."

"The past is past," she had insisted, though thinking about it now, she was willing to concede that the past was not quite that past. She was still not quite comfortable with her cousin, but she did not want to stay at home with Esther and Mr. Peel, nor did she want to join them at some cousin or friend's house. Whether the play went will or ill, she wanted to be out on the town that night. If it went badly, she knew she would brood and make her hosts feel uncomfortable, and if, by some marvelous chance, it went as she had once hoped it might, she would be too exhilarated to remain with these quiet, elderly people whose main enjoyment beyond talking was the harpsichord and where, between solos, she would fall to thinking about Charlie in the country or Rupert and her babies at Yule. That was part of the reason she had gone about with Venetia. It took her mind from the painful past and kept her from dwelling on the uncertain future.

"Blanche, my dear," Esther tapped lightly on her door.

"It's n—never t—time," she quavered, opening it.

Esther kissed her, "Come," she said gently, "and never fear, it will go well. I am sure of it and so is Mr. Peel."

Blanche gave her a tortured look, wondering if all playwrights felt as if they were going not to an opening but to an execution? A wry smile twitched at her lips. "They are much the same," she decided as she hurried out the door.

The house was uncommonly silent in this fourth, this final act. Looking up at the rows of boxes, then peering down into the pit, Blanche decided dismally that they must all be sleeping. True, the audience had clapped loudly at each curtain, but that was probably to encourage the actors. Many of them were very popular with the courtiers. She heard a strange sound from the box near her, a rasping noise. Out of the corner of her eye, she saw a heavyset man in puce with cheeks so highly flushed that they almost matched his suit. Slumped in his chair, his wig askew, he was snoring! Yet, the woman beside him was weeping as she stared at the stage where King Henry was dying.

Mohun, so uncertain in the morning, was speaking his final words weakly, yet with a pathos and a power which filled the auditorium, while Anne Marshall as Adeliza projected both noble grief and secret yearning as her eyes moved from her royal husband to the man to whom she had been pledged before her summons to the throne. The little Gwyn, amazingly subdued as Constance, knelt at Henry's bed, while Kynaston, though he had garbed his medieval knight in gold brocade with periwig to match, was conveying her honorable lover to perfection. Furthermore, though there was a prompter crouched in his accustomed box, not one word had come forth from his lips to shatter the continuity of the scenes. It was, Blanche thought gratefully, as if some fairy had waved a magic wand.

The play was ending—Adeliza and her William were happily united. The curtain closed and there was silence, a total silence in the house. In an agony, Blanche wondered if they were waiting for the epilogue Sir Thomas had wanted her to write. She had refused. Should she have consented. She . . . The curtains were apart again, and there were the actors bowing, and there were cheers and wild applause. Yet, that might be only for the actors—wait! Killigrew was on stage, he raised his hands for silence, he mentioned the author's name, Basil Carlisle, the new, young playwright, and the cheers were even louder than before!

Esther kissed her and astonishingly so did Mr. Peel. "You should have been there on the stage," he said gruffly.

"Yes, my love." Esther, wiping tears away, agreed.

"I—I am glad I am not," Blanche said. It was enough, she thought, enough that she should know, but she always had, hadn't she? She really could not think coherently; she felt exhultant, exhausted, triumphant, drained. She could not sit still either. Jumping to her feet, she said, "I must thank the actors, in my cousin's name, and Sir Thomas too."

"Yes, of course," Esther agreed and impaled her with a stare. "Afterwards, you should go home and rest, my love. You look passing tired."

"Darling Blanche, such an asset to the family!" Venetia, with Sir Harry close behind her, burst in upon them. Your cousin should be very pleased. What a pity he's not here to partake of all the praise. You must see he has a full account. And if you don't mind, I mean to own him too."

"I don't mind at all," Blanche smiled.

"Will you come home, after you've seen the actors?" Esther prodded. "I think you should, my dear."

"Sure she'll not," Venetia laughed. "We're going to supper and a masquerade at Lady Drake's tonight."

"I've already accepted, Esther. You know I have." Blanche said.

"You ought not to remain abroad too long," Esther warned. "Your day's been too full already."

"She will be home in good time, Madame de Coligny." Venetia said impatiently. "And now, if we might go, my dear, the crowds are dense and becoming denser in the back."

There was something in Venetia's eyes that Esther did not like, a hard glitter that did not match her smile. Yet, she could hardly argue anymore. Reluctantly, she kissed Blanche a second time. "Do hurry home, my child," she urged.

"I shall," Blanche told her, a little impatiently.

"What do you want with that old dragon shadowing your every step," Venetia laughed as they came into the pit.

"Yes, God save us from the faithful servitor that knew us while we were yet in swaddling clothes and thinks we still should be," Sir Harry said.

"She's neither dragon nor servitor. She's my friend," Blanche defended. "One finds far too few of those."

"Not as few as you might think, my dear." He slipped his arm around her waist. As she tried to free herself, he tightened it. "Come," he admonished, "I only want to see you through these crowds."

Actually, she was glad of his presence, for all of the court seemed intent on occupying the dressing rooms. She saw many faces that she knew; Rochester, Richmond, Mrs. Myddleton, the Countess of Castlemaine, and there was Kynaston looking warm and harried, and Mohun, who accepted her compliments grandly and told her where to find Anne Marshall. Backing out, she collided with someone behind her.

"I—I beg your pardon—" she said nervously and stepped hastily aside, then came to a full stop, looking up at the king.

His slumberous, dark eyes fastened on her face and widened, "But I believe I know you—do I not?" he said.

"Yes, you—Your Majesty," she stammered.

"Little—Galatea, as I breathe." Smiling, he took her arm and drew toward a crowded alcove, hastily vacated at his approach. "I hoped I might find you here."

"You hoped," she whispered incredulously.

"I thought I glimpsed you in your box. I wasn't sure that it was you."

"Oh." She felt bereft of breath.

"I've wondered about you very often. I never heard from you again."

"My husband—Glenmore died. I went home afterwards—to Carlisle."

"Carlisle—any relation to Basil Carlisle."

"My cousin," she said.

"Ah, then you must be Lady Yule. Sir Thomas mentioned you to me."

"Yes, that's true." She managed a smile.

"And will you stay in London, or shall you leave once more?"

"I will need to—to see my cousin," she murmured.

"Might we not bring him here?" he demanded. "I welcome all such talents to my court."

She blushed. "My cousin's crippled. He—he never leaves his room." Unable to meet his probing eyes, she looked down and saw his slender hands—which were Charlie's hands as well. His hands, the shape of his eyes, and the darkness of his hair and skin. If he could see him, would he be proud of his son?"

"Yule," Charles murmured. "There was a Lord Yule, a young man from Yorkshire who helped fight the September fires, whom we did reward. Your husband, perchance, my Galatea?"

"Yes," she breathed, looking up at him again.

He smiled a trifle ruefully, "Should I—er—praise him and call him a fine young man?" he inquired almost caustically. "Or should I rather say I am glad he's not here and should be pleased to have you grace my court alone? I've two choices and I think I much prefer the second. Would you perhaps agree?"

She was trembling and tremulous. She could not answer yet. She had not anticipated this. Should she tell him of his son. Undoubtedly, he would bring him to court. It was the boy's chance and could be hers as well. Charles remembered and was disposed to be generous, perhaps much more. She scanned his weary, disillusioned face, finding marks of dissipation she did not remember from before. In only six years he seemed to have aged a dozen. Meeting his cynical and expectant stare, she knew there was only one answer he expected. Yet, she was not ready to give it.

"I—I—" she stammered.

"Come, say nothing yet, my dear. Sleep on it and let me know. Will you?"

"I will, Your Majesty."

"Not Majesty," he corrected, as he had once before. "Charles." Placing a finger beneath her chin, he tilted up her face and smiling said, "You know, my Galatea, I think I'd forgotten just how beautiful you are. And why did I call you Galatea?"

"Because you—you thought me a statue at the first." She blushed again.

He laughed, "I think you are no statue, now," he said. Taking her hand, he kissed it gently. "You must not run away again, you know." Bowing, he left her.

Transfixed, she watched him as he strolled down the corridor and then moved purposefully into a dressing room. A second later, she heard the excited laughter of the little Gwyn.

At Lady Drake's, the masqueraders were dancing from room to room, dancing, shrieking, and laughing, with a brace of fiddlers following them. "Come, Come, Blanche, what ails you sitting all alone? Come join us," Venetia, hanging onto the arm of Sir Harry, called to Blanche. But she would not heed her.

Seated in a corner, she was still thinking of Charles and marveling over what had happened. It was almost as though their meeting had been ordained and, of course, it was only for one purpose—for Charlie. She could call it God's will and bow to his command. Yet, she was not sure. Since she was in London, she had heard much of the duke of Monmouth, the bastard son of Lucy Walter, Charles's first mistress. Esther's cousins had been quick to condemn her, insisting that she was no better than she should be. Had she not been prisoned in the Tower and with the boy beside her? Yet, there were others who praised her extravagantly. As for her boy, there was no doubt but that he was handsome and that his father loved him dearly, but still he was spoiled and bitter, his character warped, perhaps by his blood but more likely by his chancy birth. She did not want that doom for Charlie. She did not want him branded with the name of bastard, royal or not. Yet, given his own choice, would he refuse a dukedom? Better to sue for the return of Glenmore's title from the cousin who had it now. Yet, he was known as Rupert's son. It would be difficult unless she confessed the truth and if she did, and if he were to see his boy, there was every chance he might insist . . . She ran her fingers through her hair distractedly.

"I do not know what I can do!" she said out loud.

"Might we be of help, my dear?" Venetia laughed.

She looked up, startled to find her cousin and Sir Harry standing in front of her. "Oh, I—"

"My dear Blanche," Venetia cut across her excuses, "you look sorely distracted and have seemed so ever since we arrived. I fear this day's been too much for you."

"It has been long," Blanche admitted. "I—I have a headache."

"Perhaps you'd best go home," Sir Harry suggested.

"Oh, if I might," she breathed. "But you don't want to leave now, do you?"

"Come, my dear, certainly, we'd not keep you here against your will." Venetia assured her quickly. "We'll take you now.

"Yes, come. I am agreeable," he said.

"That would be kind," she smiled, "but I don't want to spoil your pleasure."

Venetia laughed, "But you'd not be spoiling mine, my dear. I too am tired, nor am I in the mood for a masquerade. I'd as lief go, myself."

It had been a strange day, she thought, as she gratefully sank back into a corner of Sir Harry's coach and pulled the fur robe about her. The play and the king, each a triumph in its way. She shook her head, not wanting to think of either now. She looked out of the window. The sky was filled with stars, and every so often she saw the mōon-brightened shell of some burned-out house. Then she thought of Rupert, and Charles's words came back to her. He had offered her a choice between himself and Rupert, a choice that was no choice since there was no Rupert anymore. . . .

The coach was slowing, and she started from her reverie. "Are we there, already?"

"Not to your lodgings, my dear. Sir Harry's been kind enough to take me home first. It's on the way, you see. Shall you be at the playhouse tomorrow, too?"

"Yes, I expect I shall," Blanche said.

"Then—I'll see you there. Perhaps I will bring Holcomb. Good night, my sweet. "Venetia kissed her hastily. Her lips were cold and she was trembling.

"Have you caught a chill?" Blanche asked concernedly.

"No," Venetia said. "Why should you think so?"

"You're shivering."

"It's a cold night."

The stairs were brought, and she watched Sir Harry take her cousin toward the door. It seemed to her that she heard Venetia's laughter, she laughed a great deal more than she had been wont when they were younger, Blanche thought idly.

Sir Harry returned quickly. "Are you warm enough?" he inquired solicitously, as the footmen shut them into the coach.

"Yes," she said. "This robe is very warm."

"It's fox," he told her. "I killed most of them myself. Do you enjoy the hunt, Lady Yule?"

"I've not hunted much," she replied. "I don't like killing things."

"Ah, but it's a rare sport," he laughed. "I've pursued it in many places—and it doesn't always end in killing. Sometimes it's far more pleasant to capture my quarry while it still lives." He put his arm around her shoulders.

She moved away from him, saying coldly, "I would find that even less to my liking."

"But you are not a hunter," he said softly. "I am." He pulled her into his arms.

"Sir Harry, please," she protested. "I've not given you leave to take such liberties."

"I'm not a soldier, so I never ask for leave," he gently kissed her ear.

In a panic, she tried to thrust him back. "Let me go—" she cried.

"All in good time—all in my time," he said.

"A mask, a mask, where's your mask, my pretty gallant? . . ." A leering woman sidled up to Rupert, as he strode among the revelers at Lady Drake's. He had gone grimly from room to room looking for Blanche and Venetia. It was hard to distinguish faces, for most of the candles had dwindled to tiny flames, seething and spluttering in their widening pools of wax, while those guests who were still dancing reeled about him in a writhing mass, clasping each other drunkenly. Many others lay half-stupified upon the floor and in their hostess's golden bed. On it, he had seen a masker with a mass of tumbled, reddish hair and near her a slender blond, energetically kissing the man who was trying to mount her and who had screamed furiously when Rupert, seizing her hair, had peered into her face. Finally in desperation, he yelled, "Blanche—Venetia—" and heard his cry fall like a stone into that pit of sound. Raising his voice, he called again, "Blanche—Venetia!"

"Netia—who wan's Netia, you wan' Netia—" an unsteady hand was fingering his shoulder. A tall, young man in a wine-stained suit of gold, his wig half-off, peered at Rupert owlishly, "You wan' Netia—Netia Holcomb—"

"I am looking for Lady Venetia and my wife, Lady Yule." Rupert said urgently. "Have you seen them?"

"Not here—saw them go—with m' friend Harry—lucky Harry Beauchamp an' the little Yule."

"Where?" Rupert demanded furiously. "Where did they go?"

"Home—heard Netia say she was goin' home—an hour since—queer that—damned early for her to be goin' home—not cockcrow yet—but she went home—damned early for her—"

He shook him, "An hour, you said? But my wife's not home yet."

"Tha's no concern of mine," the man said with tipsy hauteur. "No call to shake me—No call to shake Ned Kynaston. You know who I am?"

Rupert released him and strode out. The night air was very cold, but he was used to cold; he had been on the mired roads ten days, and then, to finally arrive and find her gone to Lady Drake—a woman who held open house to actors, gamblers, and whores!

"I swear she did not know it," Esther had told him desperately. "It was her cousin Venetia who took her—"

"Venetia, why is she seeing Venetia who hates her!" he had demanded furiously.

"Because," Esther had glared at him, "she's been locked away in the country so long, there's none other that she knows."

Venetia!

"What, she's not home yet?" Venetia, swathed in a green velvet robe, thrust a hand through her sleep-rumpled hair, looking at Rupert blankly, "I cannot understand it. I left them a full hour since—" her green eyes narrowed. "Unless—but I cannot believe it. Sir Harry knows she is my cousin."

"What are you suggesting?" he demanded.

She shook her head, "I never should have let him take her home. I should have gone with him. Oh, God, it will be my fault if—if what I fear is true." Moving to Rupert, she clutched his arm, saying fearfully, "You must go after them at once."

"Go where?"

"Sir Harry's house—let me give you his direction. Oh, I shall pray you're not too late."

He gave her a suspicious glance, "Why'd you leave her with him if you—you suspected that—"

"Come," she said hurriedly, "you must not stop to

question me, nor have I any excuses. It was my own folly, that was all. I was tired and I thought I could trust him."

"What's the direction?" he rasped.

"It's not hard to find. It's in Leadenhall Street, the second house from Saint Katherine Cree, a tall, half-timbered place."

He left without another word.

It was not until she heard the door close behind him that she dared to laugh and had to stuff a pillow over her mouth to keep her howls, her shrieks of merriment, from waking Holcomb. She had never expected matters to work out so neatly—with Rupert arriving from nowhere! She had been inclined to heap blame on Blanche, to hint at liaison perhaps, but anxiety and concern were by far the better ploys. She would be absolved of any complicity unless, of course, Sir Harry betrayed her, but perhaps he'd not have the time.

The advances that had been impeded by the jolting of the coach had, on Sir Harry's forcing Blanche into his house, turned into a desperate struggle.

Coldly angry, at first, she was terrified now, for in common with the late earl, her efforts to fend him off only excited him more. In the beginning, she had managed to scratch his face and she had bitten his lip savagely when he had tried to kiss her. He had struck her for that, so hard that her cheek still ached. Then, pushing her to the floor, he had ripped away her garments leaving her naked to the waist. Alternating between shame and fear, she had tried desperately to roll away from him, but he had thrown himself on top of her, sucking and kneading her breasts until she had cried out in agony. It would have been easier to lie passive and let him have his way, but the thought was horrible to her, and so she continued to fight; but he was hurting her dreadfully, and she was growing steadily weaker. Soon, very soon, she would be ravished and dishonored.

"Best have me, love, for I mean to have you and soon," he panted.

"Never—" she gasped and was silent as he pressed his mouth on hers.

Then, dimly, she heard a pounding at the door and second later, angry voices in the hall. Sir Harry raised his head and listened. She tried to roll away, but he caught her quickly, whispering. "No matter, my dear love. My servants with deal with any intruders—" His mouth was on her breast again.

"Let me go—let me go," she screamed, struggling to rise. "Help me—someone please—"

Then to her utter amazement, the door was pulled back and Rupert, sword in hand and with a pair of protesting servants at his heels rushed in, his face white with anger.

Sir Harry, starting up, looked at him incredulously, "What in hell do you want and by what right—"

"Rupert!" Clutching her torn gown about her, Blanche stumbled to her feet. "Oh, God, take me home—I pray you—take me home."

He did not heed her. Advancing on Sir Harry, he said furiously, "On your guard, you bastard."

"Odd's blood, you'd not be the outraged husband?" Sir Harry, laughing, seized his sword from the floor. "You'd be advised to take your—property and not to deal with me. I always kill my man. And husbands are my specialty."

"Rupert, please, I pray, you don't," she screamed.

Springing forward, Rupert lunged at Sir Harry, who, for all that he was drunk, proved to have a fluid grace of movement and a lightning attack. Indeed, to Blanche's horror, he seemed by far the most expert swordsman. Marvelously supple of wrist and agile of foot, he was all feints and glissades, easily parrying Rupert's dogged, anger-driven rushes. At length, his blade, snaking under Rupert's guard, buried itself deep in Yule's right shoulder. He staggered back to the sound of Blanche's agonized scream, but he did not lose his grip upon his sword.

"You see," Sir Harry smiled, "it's not always the worthy and the wronged must needs win the bout."

Rupert made no answer. Ignoring the blood welling from his wound and pouring down his arm, he lunged again, and Sir Harry, momentarily caught off guard, failed to parry the thrust that pierced his heart. With an incredulous look at Rupert, he essayed a laugh, and in that moment dropped and died.

Determinedly, Rupert beckoned to Blanche, "Come," he ordered faintly, and clutching her hand, he stumbled a few quick steps before falling unconscious at her feet.

For a week the doctors despaired of Rupert. Their remedies, the poultices of raw oysters and of scalded cats, had failed to quell the fever in his wound, but on the eighth day it had diminished, and the swelling had gone down.

"I am sure he will recover," the doctor had said in answer to Blanche's fearful questioning. He had frowned, "but if I am not to have another patient on my hands, you must leave off nursing him and rest."

"Yes, my love, you must rest," Esther had pleaded.

"No," she had told them both gently, and, deaf to all further pleading, she had remained there the long afternoon.

It was close on five, and he was sleeping. She went to the window. It had begun to snow. She stood watching the flakes softly drifting down, but she was not actually seeing them. She felt very tired, very happy, very sad, all at once. She loved him and he loved her. All through his delirium he had called her name and had talked confusedly about Glenmore, a badger, and the king. He had asked for the children too, but never Charlie. If only he would have mentioned the child, but he hadn't. What could she do? It seemed to her that the coldness of the snow was in her heart as well.

"Blanche—" Rupert whispered.

"Oh, you're awake!" She hastened to the bed. "What can I get for you?"

"Nothing—" His eyes, huge in his wasted face, stared into hers. "Have I been here long?"

"Not long—just past a week. You're on the mend, my dearest. The doctor said so this morning."

His hand closed over her fingers. "He didn't harm you?" he asked anxiously.

"No, you prevented that." She could not restrain a sob. "But at what a cost. You nearly died."

"It was not enough to—to cancel out the debt I owe to you," he groaned.

"Hush," she said. "You must rest, please."

"Listen to me. Oh, Blanche, how can you listen—how can you even look at me? I've been so cruel, everything that's happened's my fault. I should've been here to stand by you, to take joy in your success—"

"Rupert," she urged, "you mustn't talk—wait until you're better."

"No, now. I feel so unworthy of you. I—I'm almost afraid to ask you—but I must." Much to her confusion, his eyes filled with tears. She wanted to kiss them away, but she could not. Much as she loved him, Charlie still stood between them, a persistent little shadow, fatherless Charlie, who might, at a word from her, be a duke. "Blanche," Rupert's voice was only a thread of sound. "Will you forgive me?"

"I—I've told you all this week, I do. I thought you heard me once or twice."

"I did, but I feared I might have dreamed it. I had so many dreams."

"No, you didn't dream it," she said.

"But will you come back to me?" He paused and then he added, "Will you come back and—and bring with you our eldest son."

The coldness and the shadows fled. Bending over him, she kissed him very gently on the lips, and then, smiling at him, she said tremulously, "Oh, yes, Rupert, I should like that above all things."